# WATCH YOU BURN

ALSO BY AMANDA SEARCY

*The Truth Beneath the Lies*

AMANDA SEARCY

DELACORTE PRESS

Text copyright © 2018 by Amanda Searcy
Jacket art copyright © 2018 by Steve Gardner

All rights reserved. Published in the United States by Delacorte Press, an imprint of Random House Children's Books, a division of Penguin Random House LLC, New York.

Delacorte Press is a registered trademark and the colophon is a trademark of Penguin Random House LLC.

Visit us on the Web! GetUnderlined.com

Educators and librarians, for a variety of teaching tools, visit us at RHTeachersLibrarians.com

*Library of Congress Cataloging-in-Publication Data*
Names: Searcy, Amanda, author.
Title: Watch you burn / Amanda Searcy.
Description: First edition. | New York : Delacorte Press, [2018] | Summary: Jenny, seventeen, moves to small-town New Mexico with her father after police nearly discover she is an arsonist but her urge to start fires persists, and she knows she is being watched.
Identifiers: LCCN 2018012591 | ISBN 978-1-5247-0093-5 (hardback) | ISBN 978-1-5247-0096-6 (trade paperback) | ISBN 978-1-5247-0095-9 (ebook)
Subjects: | CYAC: Arson—Fiction. | Fathers and daughters—Fiction. | Moving, Household—Fiction. | Hotels, motels, etc.—Fiction. | New Mexico—Fiction.
Classification: LCC PZ7.1.S3369 Wat 2018 | DDC [Fic]—dc23

The text of this book is set in 11.8-point Adobe Caslon Pro.
Interior design by Jaclyn Whalen

Printed in the United States of America
10 9 8 7 6 5 4 3 2 1
First Edition

*To all the new friends I've made along this journey*

# 1

Twigs pop and crackle under my feet, like I'm walking on a field of old brittle bones. I kneel and scoop up a handful of dry leaves. They turn to dust as I rub them between my fingers.

One match—one tiny spark—and they'd go up. Fire whooshing through the brush, blackening the trunks of trees, licking up to the tops.

I shiver and stand. My legs are still stiff from the plane and the drive from the airport. I've brought nothing but my coat with me on this walk by the river. A bitter wind blows, shaking the cottonwood trees. Against the darkening sky they look like mourners, faces twisted in agony, arms reaching toward the heavens.

A snapping sound. I look behind me. A figure stands in the shadows twenty feet away. Hands stuffed in pockets, hood up. I can't tell if it's a man or a woman. They don't call hello or nod at me in greeting.

No movement at all. Just staring.

I'm not near the road. I picked my way through the weeds

and leafless trees to get to this spot. This spot away from people. Away from where anyone would see me.

I turn my back to the figure and start to walk. My heart
races, but I keep my movements calm as I listen for the pop
of footsteps. I don't hear any. I hazard a look behind me again
and see nothing but trees.

Maybe it was someone who needed to take a leak and was
just as surprised to see me as I was to see them. Maybe it was
my imagination.

When I come out of the trees and onto the dirt access
road, I pluck another dry leaf from the ground and crumble it.
I let the pieces float away in the wind.

Everything out here is a fire starter.

My right hand slaps at the top of my left arm, protecting
it. Tears form in my eyes.

Twenty-four hours ago, I was standing in the snow in
Ohio suburbia. A few hours on the plane and the ride from
the Albuquerque airport, and now I'm here.

A dog jangles up to me, mouth open and panting in a
smile. I reach down and pat him on the head. His owner pulls
him away, apologizing. She gives me and my glassy eyes a long
look. She's going to ask if I'm okay.

No. I'm not.


The lights are on in the motel's office. I told Dad that I didn't
want any dinner. He doesn't know that I went out. He thinks
I've been tucked away in my room unpacking.

I dash across the parking lot to the melon-colored door

with the shiny brass number 2. It's unlocked. I didn't ̮
to risk Dad hearing me fumble with the key. Not that I
doing anything wrong. I just went for a walk. My pockets are
empty.

I close the door gently and flop down on the bed. Despite
the room's fancy amenities, it's still a motel room. The Los
Ranchitos Inn in Las Piedras, New Mexico. A thousand
people have occupied this space before. They've slept and
watched TV. Argued and had sex. Drunk beer and shuffled
their kids out to the pool.

That was fifty years ago. It's been an empty, falling-down
shell since then. Where I'm lying now was shelter for someone with no home, a place for bugs, and a nest for whatever
kinds of rodents live in the desert.

But not anymore. This room is perfect. It has thick, plush
carpet; yellow walls with crown molding; a lavender-oil-
spritzed down duvet with a million pillows. That's what the
people will come for. The people with money.

This isn't Route 66, but they'll still want the old-timey
road trip experience—to drive their cars right up to their
rooms, but then stay at a five-star hotel. Or, at least, that's
what the brochure promises.

The bathroom is amazing. Marble, granite, Jacuzzi tub,
glassed-in shower. It's bigger than my entire bedroom in
Ohio.

Outside, the place looks like a scene from a dystopian
movie. Slabs of fallen concrete litter the parking lot; the other
rooms are missing ceilings and contain decades of debris,
broken bottles, and the remnants of old campsites. The pool

was filled in years ago so no one would break their neck stumbling around in the dark.

Dad's room—number 1—is on the other side of the office. Our rooms are the models, spaces full of hope, dreams, and possibilities. Enough luxury to bring in the investors. The project is a go. Five months from now, every room in this rundown eyesore will look like mine. The outside will be freshly stuccoed, the parking lot repaved, and the original neon sign illuminated for that extra cheese factor.

They'll charge two hundred dollars a night to stay in this desert town. In a motel in the middle of nowhere, half a mile from the interstate, along a drying river.

I stare at the pristine white ceiling from my giant lavender-scented bed. I should unpack. Release my old life into my new one.

Most of my old life, that is.

I unzip my carry-on and pull out a framed photo. Smiling faces gaze at me.

Some old things need to stay packed away forever.

FaceTime rings. My chest tightens. I don't want to answer. They're calling to make sure I got here okay. To look me up and down. To see if I'm a brand-new girl now that I'm in New Mexico.

I let it ring a couple more times while I take deep breaths and arrange my face into a calm, happy mask.

"Hi, Hailey," I sing when I answer and see the bouncing, smiling face of my seven-year-old half sister appear on the screen. My stepfather, Brian, hovers in the background.

Hailey wants to hear all about my "adventure." That's what Mom told her I was doing—going on an adventure. I walk my phone around the room, giving her a tour. I make up a story about a famous movie star having stayed here. I don't give her one tiny bit of doubt that this isn't the coolest place on earth.

For my grand finale, I pull out the hat she made me and stick it on my head. It's pink and crudely knitted, with two giant black felt eyes glued to it. Hailey is obsessed with butterflies and how some of them have markings on their wings to make predators think that the butterfly is much larger and scarier. The hat is meant to help me feel brave on my adventure.

She claps her hands and laughs. Mom appears behind her. Hailey and I wave goodbye, and her father ushers her out of the room. He shuts the door, but he's still there, standing behind Mom. Her fake smile is replaced by an anxious expression as soon as Hailey's gone. I know she's wringing her hands in her lap.

"How's your father?" she asks.

"Everything is great, Mom." She doesn't look convinced. "The motel is nice. I got the welcome packet from Riverline Prep, and my uniforms were waiting for me." Mom arranged everything. She wasn't going to leave it up to Dad. She barely trusted him to pick me up from the airport.

Her voice drops to a whisper. "You can come home. Anytime. Just call, and I'll get you a plane ticket."

My eyes flit to Brian and then back to her. "Have you seen where I'm living?" I throw a hand out behind me. "It's like I'm a princess." I inwardly cringe. That was a step too far. Brian's eye's narrow.

I yawn dramatically. "I should get ready for bed. It was a long trip, and I'm really tired."

Mom nods. "Okay. We'll talk again soon. Call me if you need anything."

My eyes land again on Brian. His face has fallen. He looks older, as if the last few months have taken ten years off his life.

I smile at Mom. "Night-night." I hang up and place the phone facedown on my bed.

I dig through my suitcases until I find some pajamas. I put them on and crawl into bed, hoping sleep will overtake me instantly.

It doesn't.

My heart is still beating too fast. In my mind, I see Hailey's face over and over again. I see flames surrounding her. Hear her screaming my name.

And the trees.

They're so close to where I lie. The area's isolated. There's no one who could get hurt.

I rub at the puckered, melted skin that runs in a line from my shoulder to elbow. It itches. It's an itch that my nails can't scratch, no matter how deeply I drive them into my skin. An itch that starts in my arm, runs down my chest, and plants itself in my heart.

I force my hand back down to my side and take a deep breath. I can make it through this. I can be a new girl in New Mexico.

On the nightstand next to my phone is a bottle of magic pills, full of promises of drifting off into sweet blackness. I swore to myself I wouldn't take one tonight. They're for emergencies only. For when I really can't stop the movie that's projected over and over again on the back wall of my mind.

I take one anyway.

Then, like every night, I mentally check the exits—door, window, bathroom—and feel some relief. I settle into my too-soft bed and turn my back to the window and all that's outside it.

# 2

*Ugh.* My head feels like it's full of cotton. This is why I hate those sleeping pills. Even after I wake up, it takes hours for them to clear out of my system. Until then, it'll feel like I'm walking through six feet of water.

I uncurl myself from the ball I was sleeping in. I've never had anything other than a twin bed, but this king-size bed, with its six pillows and thousand-thread-count sheets, wants to swallow me whole. I can spread out my arms and legs and still not find the edges. Any monster living beneath it could crawl in next to me and I would never even know it was there.

Dusky light filters in through the curtains. It must be seven or so. School hasn't started yet, and there's no reason to get up this early, but even in my semidrugged state, sleep won't come again. My mind spins through the sludge in my head. The trees are outside. Exactly where they were last night. Still dry and crunchy, still isolated.

*Focus on something else.* I crawl out of my massive bed, sink into the carpet, and walk to the bathroom, where I've laid down one of the person-sized towels to protect my feet from the cold marble.

I splash water over my face to wake up my darkly circled eyes. It doesn't work.

Coffee. I need coffee.

I throw my ultradown coat on—overkill for this Southern winter—and slide on my sneakers. The door opens with a *swoosh*.

The morning has a bite to it, but there are no clouds in the brightening sky; there's no snow on the ground, no hint of moisture anywhere. The traffic on the interstate has picked up. The wind blows the noise in my direction. Otherwise, it's quiet and still.

I take the three steps to the office that will function as our temporary living room and kitchen.

"Dad?" I call as I open the door. I jerk back with a start. A woman stands in front of me wearing a navy blue T-shirt that reaches her midthigh—and nothing else. She holds up the coffeepot, frozen. The door shuts behind me.

"Um, hi. Jenny, right?" Her cheeks flush red. Her blond hair looks like it was smooth and blown out yesterday, but it's now mussed in the back, as if she had a night of little sleep. My eyes flit down to her T-shirt. It has "Breland Construction" written across the front in green block letters. Dad's company.

"Do you want some coffee?" she asks. I nod. She glances up at the mugs on the shelf above her head. If she reaches for one, the shirt is going to ride up, exposing whatever she has or hasn't got on under it. She chuckles nervously.

The door slurps open with great force behind me. We both jump.

Dad takes in the scene. He doesn't have the decency to look sheepish. "Morning, sweet pea," he says, and kisses me on the top of the head, the same way he did when I was four—the last time I lived with him.

"Good. You've met Monica." He takes the coffeepot from the woman. She gives a little wave and then tugs on the bottom of her shirt.

She nods at the door. "I'm gonna ..." She takes off into the cold.

"Monica's the architect," Dad says, and points to the blueprints on the table.

"That's nice." I don't know what I'm supposed to say. He's unfazed, as if it's a normal thing to have your teenage daughter walk in on your half-naked "architect" first thing in the morning.

I grab a mug, fill it to the top with coffee, and then open the minifridge, which, paired with a microwave, makes up our "kitchen." Inside is a bottle of white wine, a block of yellow cheese, and a bunch of grapes—half missing. Great. This just keeps getting better.

"Is there any milk?" I call over my shoulder. Dad has flopped down on the couch—the "living room"—and is messing with his phone.

"Huh?" he mutters.

Dad and I don't know each other. Other than a few awkward holidays and the week he spent with me when I was in the hospital, we've been complete strangers for the last thirteen years.

I hold my breath and take a long sip of the black, bitter coffee. My face twists of its own accord as I swallow.

I glance around the office and take a deep breath. My room looks like the brochure, but nothing else does.

When Dad told Mom it was going to be perfectly safe to live in a run-down old motel in the bad part of town, he also said that there was a full kitchen stocked with healthy food, where we would be eating father-daughter dinners.

He failed to mention an "architect."

A truck rumbles up outside. Dad stuffs his phone into his pocket and stands.

The door opens. On the other side is a muscular guy—not too much older than me—huddled in a puffy blue ski jacket.

"Jenny, this is Cam Vargas," Dad says.

"Hey," Cam grunts, and leans into the heat coming from the office.

"Cam's learning the business. He's going to be my assistant. If you have any problems, he'll take care of them." Cam's gel-slicked black hair doesn't move as he nods. His face is neutral, but his eyes look like this is the last place in the world he wants to be. "He's got one of the company trucks, too, so he can drive you if you want to go anywhere."

Cam smiles with too much teeth. He's sucking up to Dad. I bet driving me around is not what he thought his "assistant" job would entail.

"Okay, thanks," I say, and try to sound genuine. I don't want to be a problem to Cam—to anyone here.

Dad and Cam start to turn around and leave me alone to ponder my newfound life in this motel. My stomach growls, but I'm not touching Dad's sad attempt at romance in the fridge. I cringe before calling out, "We need some groceries. There isn't much in the kitchen."

Dad finally has the sense to look embarrassed. He pulls his wallet out of his pocket and hands me a stack of bills.

Cam's eyes narrow. He looks at the money and then at me. I crumple the bills into my hand and hold the sides of my coat together. Even though I'm completely covered, I suddenly feel as bare as Monica.

I point toward my room. "I need to get dressed."

Cam moves out of the way to let me pass, but then he takes a step like he's going to follow me.

"Uh, I'll meet you back here in, like, a couple of hours?" I slip into my room and hold the door shut behind me. A minute later, when I peek out the curtain, Cam is sitting in his truck, motionless, eyes straight forward, like a puffy-blue-coated guard.

Once I'm dressed, I peek out again. Cam's still there. When I see Dad later, I'm going to have to tell him that he's hired a creep for an assistant.

My stomach growls in complaint, but I'm not asking Cam to take me for something. I'm sure going shopping later will be enough of his company for one day.

When I look out again, Cam's eyes are closed. Is he sleeping? On the job?

I slowly open my door. He doesn't move. His mouth is open, as if he's snoring inside the truck.

It's worth the risk to get away from here for a while. I dash out of my room and into the condemned section of the motel along the inside of the construction fence.

I'm not supposed to be here. No one is. The engineers have declared these rooms unsound and pasted red notices saying so on every wall.

But it's my exit—a secret passage that I discovered yesterday. A hole has been busted in the back wall of one of the rooms. It's big enough for me to step through. An opening has been cut into the fence on the other side, but you have to push on it to see that it's there. That's how I got out to go on my walk unchaperoned.

I fight back the weeds and push through the chain links. I emerge in an old parking lot, with my back to the trees. This whole section of town is being redeveloped. Across the street is a crumbling strip mall with a drugstore and lots of empty spaces with newspapered windows and For Lease signs.

The rest of my new "neighborhood" consists of more abandoned storefronts and empty fields surrounded by fences and signs that say "Vargas Properties. No Trespassing." Cramped duplexes and small stuccoed houses fill in the blocks around them. Everything is gray and depressed, as if under an overcast sky, even though the sun is shining.

I glance over my shoulder as I cross the street. Cam hasn't followed me.

Henderson's Drugstore is a local knockoff of Walgreens. It even has that same cheap-perfume-and-cardboard smell.

In the back, there's a real emergency exit with "Alarm Will Sound" printed across the push bar. I like that. The exit and the alarm.

I wander up and down the aisles until I find a box of granola bars that will have to do for breakfast.

The clerk at the front checkout greets me with a friendly smile. "That must be an interesting place to live."

"Excuse me?"

She points toward the Los Ranchitos. "I saw you pull up yesterday."

"Oh. My dad's doing the construction."

She rings up my granola bars, and I automatically swipe my debit card before I remember Dad gave me cash. Money's not something I have to worry about. My debit card is tied to an account Mom has filled with more than I could ever spend on things like snacks.

"Be careful in this part of town. Stay far away from the colony," the clerk says as she hands me my bag.

"The what?"

"You know, Russell's Utopia."

I shake my head.

She points vaguely toward the trees and sighs. "It's the reason no one comes around here. In the 1920s, there was an artists' colony along the river. They called it Russell's Utopia. I don't know who Russell was, but his colony obviously wasn't very utopic. It's been abandoned for a long time. The squatters from the motel have moved in there now. Before, I'd see the regulars wander by, but now that they're hidden in the woods . . . it's attracting a different kind of person."

I take my bag. "I'll be careful," I say, and inwardly roll my eyes. It's not like Mom didn't already tell me to be careful a hundred thousand times on the way to the airport in Ohio.

I rip into a granola bar before I'm out the door. Cold air hits my face. I don't want to look, but I can't help it. To the right of the Los Ranchitos, I see it: The colony. The remnants of fallen wooden houses disappear into the weeds. Newer plywood and sheet-metal shanties and tents crowd together in the trees.

There are people there. People in the dry brush. The granola bar sticks in my throat.

My scar starts to itch. I snap my head away from the trees. *No. I'm stronger than this,* I remind myself. *This is my fresh start. I'm out of Ohio. No one knows me. I can be anyone I want to be here.*

I check the time on my phone. Cam's going to be expecting me for our trip to the store.

Sliding through the hole in the fence and into the condemned section is easy. Getting back to my room without being seen isn't.

I poke my head around the corner. Dad is guiding a bulldozer through the gate. There's a smile on his face. This project is a huge opportunity for him. *The* opportunity. Even Mom, who always mentions him through gritted teeth, was impressed. It's the only reason she let me come here—that, and Brian's subtle but firm insistence that it would be "good for me" to get to know my father better. Brian's a great actor. He almost had me believing him.

Dad thinks I'm in my room right now. I need him to keep thinking that. No one can know that I've found a secret way out.

Cam's still in his truck. I won't know if he's awake until I get closer.

When Dad's back is to me, I tiptoe out to the parking lot. I keep my focus on Cam as I step lightly over the chucks of cement and debris in my path. He won't hear a thing.

I've been practicing.

# 3

Cam's eyes stay closed. I stop in front of my door and slowly turn the knob until it pops open. I toss my Henderson's bag inside and slam the door closed.

Cam snaps to attention.

"I'm ready," I say, and climb into the truck.

He blinks hard. His face is slightly red. He knows that I know he was sleeping. But I don't say anything. I'll save that little secret in case I need it later.

"So you want to work in construction?" I ask as I buckle my seat belt.

Cam's eyes slide over to me. "Mike Vargas is my father," he says, as if that's the answer to every question.

"Ah." At least I know how he got the job. Dad probably didn't have a choice but to hire his boss's son. Great. The sleepy creep stays.

After several minutes of painful silence, we pull up to the grocery store. "You can wait here. I won't take long," I say.

Cam shakes his head and gets out.

"Or you can come with me," I mumble to myself.

Inside, I grab a cart and head down the produce aisle. Cam trundles along behind me. I feel like I'm being followed by store security. He watches every move I make. Every apple I pick up to check for bruises. Every box of cereal I put in the cart.

I don't know why he's doing this. No one here knows my secret, but it's as if he's afraid I might stuff a frozen lasagna under my coat and make a run for it.

I turn down an aisle of miscellaneous things that don't fit into other categories. My eyes drift up to a top shelf. My scar twinges.

I throw my arms out to the side. "You know what? I forgot we needed milk. Will you go get some?"

Cam doesn't move.

"The faster we get everything, the sooner we can go."

I see the debate playing out in his head. He wants to leave the store, but for some strange, creepy reason, he doesn't want to leave *me*.

He finally nods and trudges down the aisle toward the dairy section. As soon as he's out of sight, I reach up to the top shelf.

My fingers tingle as I wrap them around the matches. I examine the print on the box and glance over my shoulder. I'm supposed to be good, but good is a spectrum. This isn't *that* bad. Besides, I'm not going to use them. I'll just put them in a drawer. A tiny compromise to make the itch calm down.

I pretend to scratch my neck and drop the matches down my shirt. My coat's half zipped up. No one will see a thing.

Cam comes back with a carton of milk. His eyes wash over

my face. I feel it burning hot, like my scar. The box of matches sends little sparks of excitement through me as it touches my skin.

"That's everything," I say. "Let's go."

Cam raises an eyebrow. I know he's wondering about the smile I can't wipe off my face.


Later that night, I look at the matches in the dresser drawer for the hundredth time and dig my nails farther into my skin. It's been a long day. Once I got back from the store with Cam, it was a long, *boring* day. I stayed in my room. I didn't sneak out and go for a walk. I did everything the new me is supposed to do.

The rake of my nails across my scar smears a line of blood on my arm.

The sleeping pills are on my nightstand.

I don't take one.


It's just past midnight. I have on black jeans. Black soft-soled shoes. Black hoodie—hood up. Hailey's hat is on underneath it, holding back all my hair. I slip out of my room and away from the bulb that hangs over the sidewalk. Once I'm in the dark, I'm invisible.

It's cold. Steam puffs out in front of me. I take short shallow breaths so that there's less to exhale. Nothing to give me away.

I creep into the condemned section; out the crack in the

wall; through the fence. My shoes make a soft *whoosh* sound, but nothing more. I bought them when I was still in Ohio. I tested them out on Becky Sloan in an empty hallway at school. She didn't turn around until she felt my breath on her neck. When she screamed and dropped her books, I acted apologetic, but my insides trembled with delight.

I go around the back of the Los Ranchitos—away from anyone who could be stumbling to the artists' colony.

Into the trees and down to the river.

In the moonlight, sandbars covered in dried-up weeds create an abstract pattern over the water. The other bank is more cottonwood forest. It's thicker and wilder on that side; no houses, no colony—just agricultural fields. In the distance, a narrow bridge connects the two sides.

It takes twenty minutes to get to the bridge. It's one lane in each direction. Hanging off the side a few feet below the road is a pedestrian walkway. It's in the shadows and pitch-black. I don't know who or what could be waiting in that darkness.

I almost reconsider. I almost turn around and go back to the motel. But my scar itches and burns and screams. I've needed this release since I left Ohio. Just this one time and it will be out of my system. Then I will be the new girl I'm sup-posed to be—Jenny who lives in the Los Ranchitos instead of Jenny with soft-soled shoes and a secret.

I run on my toes across the walkway. There's no one in the darkness to come after me.

It takes a while to find *the* spot. One with lots of leaves and underbrush, but also with a clear path for me to make my exit.

I pull the matches out of my pocket and flick one against

the strip on the box. My heart races with ecstasy. Puffs of steam from my rapid breathing cloud my vision. I drop the match.

It's not enough. I need more. I strike another.

It's still as mesmerizing as it was when I was seven. I let this match burn down to the tips of my fingers before I drop it. Then I do it again and again. And again.

My circle of fire glows against the night sky. It takes longer than I hoped to start gnawing away at the first tree, but when it does, everything picks up. Another tree starts to blacken; more brush lights up. Sparks crackle and pop and fling themselves into the air.

I feel what I've been waiting to feel, what I haven't felt since I watched the abandoned house go up in Ohio: Relief. Release. Control.

But I'm not a monster. I don't hurt anyone.

I'm as high as I'm going to get and watching too long increases my chances of getting caught. I use my clear path to leave, feeling a little more empty with every step I take.

When I see the flashing lights driving along the other side of the river, I run back to the bridge and crouch on the pedestrian walkway until the fire trucks zoom past.

My heart returns to its normal pace. My scar purrs with contentment.

I sneak back through the fence and the wall and cross the parking lot to my room. As I reach for the doorknob, something catches my eye; something that wasn't there before.

A cigarette on the sidewalk. Still burning.

# 4

I couldn't sleep. My euphoria dissolved on the sidewalk next to the burning end of that cigarette. I was filled instead with jumpy fear over whoever had been outside.

I lay in my too-big bed under my too-warm covers all night, clawing at my scar and waiting for a police car to pull up. Waiting for a knock on my door.

It never came. Either the person outside my room didn't see me, or they didn't turn me in. Whichever it is, I'm done. No more fires.

In the morning, I don't bother to put on my coat before stumbling to the office. Monica, fully dressed, is sitting at the table drinking her coffee and flipping through the newspaper. She looks up at me and smiles. Her eyes flit to my bare arm. Her face falls.

"Good morning," she says, trying to recover from the misstep. Dad must have told her about what happened to me.

I grab a box of cereal and dump some into a bowl. I open the fridge. The milk's gone. "Where's the—"

I'm interrupted by Dad opening the office door. He does it

slowly, which is odd for him. Since I've been here, he's thrown it off the hinges every time.

He takes in my drawn, tired face; the fresh scratches across my scar; the fear in my eyes.

Monica flaps her newspaper. "It looks like someone was camping illegally in the bosque. There was a forest fire."

Dad cringes. Monica just broke the cardinal rule. We don't talk about fire. He steps forward and wraps his arms around me.

"It's okay, sweet pea. I won't let anything happen to you. You don't need to be afraid."

Tears fill my eyes. See? This is why I have to be good. For Dad. For Mom and Hailey. For the people who love me. The ones who would be devastated if they knew my secret.

"I should go get dressed."

When I open the office door, I see a flash of gray. It moves so fast among the camouflaging debris that I'm not sure what it is. It runs into the condemned section.

I'm tempted to follow it, but I can't when Dad and Monica are on the other side of the office door.

In my room, I peel off my pajamas and step into the shower. The massaging jets beat forcefully across my back, but they don't do much to release my tension. The cigarette on the sidewalk freaked me out, but it doesn't mean someone saw me heading for the woods. I'll just have to be more careful from now on—not that I'm going to do it again.

• • •

After my shower, I'm feeling a little better and ready to reclaim my abandoned dry cereal in the office. I open my door. The swoosh sends the gray blur—a kitten—running again. Its tail is tipped with white that bounces like a beacon into one of the condemned rooms.

I've always wanted a kitten. Mom promised me one when I was in the hospital, but after I was released, she started dating Brian, and he's allergic. No kitten for me.

I glance over my shoulder. The construction crew is busy working on the other side of the parking lot. I don't see Cam. Dad and Monica are huddled over plans laid out on a folding table.

No one is paying attention.

I dash into the condemned section where I'm not supposed to be and press myself against the inner wall of a room, out of sight of the crew.

The kitten is on the floor in front of me, lapping up milk as it's poured into a bowl.

Poured into a bowl by a girl.

# 5

The girl has her back to me. She murmurs to the kitten and reaches out to stroke it. I hold my breath so I won't startle them, but it doesn't work. The kitten's head shoots up. The girl turns and jumps, sending the kitten off to hide in the debris outside.

"It was hungry. I won't take anything else. I swear." She holds out the milk to me. Her eyes are wide and afraid, like the kitten's. The look stabs me in the heart. Why is she here? A girl on the cold, dirty floor on a cold winter morning?

And more importantly, was she here last night?

I'm too far away to tell if she smells like cigarette smoke, so to disguise that my heart is racing and my palms are sweating, I force my face to smile.

"Hi. My name's Jenny. Jenny Breland." I motion toward the trucks painted with my last name.

The girl drops the milk carton to her side. She examines me. Her long, skinny legs are tucked underneath her so that she's sitting on her knees. Dirt smudges her jeans. She's wearing a red jacket that's too thin. Her hair is short—about chin length. It was probably once dark, but it's been bleached blond.

"Ro," she says. "People call me Ro." She sits up straighter. The fear is gone, replaced with a hardened shell.

The clatter of construction equipment rings off the walls. Most of the ceiling is open, and the dusty winter sky shines above us.

"This part of the building isn't safe." I point to one of the red signs.

Ro scoffs. "Yeah, I can read."

"Oh. Sorry." I feel my cheeks heat up. This isn't going well. If she was outside my room last night, I need to make her my friend. I need to make sure she doesn't tell.

Ro sinks farther down on the floor in front of the bowl of milk. She glances at the doorway. The kitten's head peeks around it. When it sees me looking, it dashes off.

"How'd you get in here?" I ask.

"I followed the kitten. There's a hole in the fence right outside." She points to my no-longer-secret gap in the wall.

A gust of wind sends a howl through the ruins. "We shouldn't be here."

Ro peers around me, looking for the kitten.

"We could get it some treats and some cat food and see if it will come out," I suggest.

Ro's eyes dance over my face, like she's sizing me up. She doesn't say anything. I can't quite peg her. Her clothes are old and too thin, but she seems clean. Her hair is brushed. I don't think she's homeless, but I also don't know why she'd be hanging around the motel in the early morning.

"Do you live around here?" I ask.

She waves absently behind her. "Over there in that neighborhood. But I just moved here."

"Me too."

"I know. I saw you with all your suitcases."

So she has been hanging around. Palpable silence fills the space between us. I try to keep my breathing from speeding up.

I suck in a lungful of cold air. There's one way to find out if she could have seen me last night.

"You wouldn't happen to have a cigarette, would you?" I fake laugh. "I swore I would quit when I moved, but you know how that goes."

Ro looks me up and down. My performance wasn't convincing. We both know it.

She shakes her head. "No. Sorry. I don't smoke."

I think I believe her. My whole body relaxes.

"So, um, okay." I point over my shoulder at nothing. The bulldozer rumbles right outside. I cringe. Now I'm stuck here until it moves.

"You can go that way." Ro tips her chin at the gap in the wall.

I step past her, but then turn around. "You really shouldn't stay here."

She rolls her eyes. I feel a twinge of regret. Having friends in Ohio was hard. There was always a cloud hanging over us—a cloud of smoke. Parents would make excuses for not inviting me to sleepovers. I pretended it didn't bother me, but it hurt.

In my new life, I want to make friends. Friends who know nothing about my past. Ro's the first person my age I've met here—maybe the only one nearby.

"I'll see you later?" I ask with too much hope in my voice.

She shrugs. Our conversation is done. I slide through the hole in the wall.


When I walk into Henderson's, the clerk from yesterday smiles. I find kitten chow, treats, and a fluorescent pink mouse toy; then I toss another box of granola bars into my basket. I'm going to keep them in my room, since breakfast doesn't seem to be working out for me.

The clerk starts to ring up my stuff, but then she pauses and looks at me. I try to smile, but my stomach clenches. There's a display of colorful plastic lighters on the counter. It wasn't there yesterday.

"We just adopted a kitten," the clerk says. She's about the same age as my mom, but deep lines carve into her face, like she's had a hard life. She smiles wistfully. "We finally live in a place where we can have one."

I keep my hands flat on the counter and away from the lighters. The construction equipment growls outside. The clerk glances in its direction. "I hope they're right about that place. Everyone who comes in here says it's a bad idea. I think they don't want outsiders coming to town. But if it brings more jobs . . ." She shrugs.

Even with my head turned away, I still feel the lighters on the counter.

I swipe my debit card. The clerk hands me my bag. "Have a nice day."

I take it and bolt outside.

My eyes are glued to the sidewalk. I count the cracks as they pass under my feet. I'm not looking up at the trees. I'm not thinking about how easy it would be to go back into Henderson's and buy a lighter—or two.

I head for the front gate. I'm not doing anything wrong; I shouldn't make it seem like I am by sneaking back in.

When I lift my head, a man in a red scarf stands in front of me. He's thin, with long, greasy hair that falls in clumpy strands around his face. He holds a handmade cardboard sign that says "Breland Construction Kills."

I jerk back when I see it. The man starts to laugh. Then his laughter turns into a coughing fit. He puts a hand on the fence to support himself.

The gate slides open. Dad comes charging out. He takes my arm and pulls me onto the property. "Go to your room," he says. "I'll take care of this."

I stop halfway across the parking lot and turn around. Dad's movements are smooth and deliberate, but the tension in his muscles betrays his fury as he faces the man. I cringe and will Dad to keep the gate between them. I don't want anyone to get hurt.

"Breland Construction kills!" the man yells. Dad leans in and says something I can't hear. The man backs off. He salutes and steps away from the gate.

Then he sees me watching. "Did you sleep well, pretty girl?"

Dad spins around. I should run to my room and slam the

door, lock out everything outside. But my feet are frozen to the asphalt. Dad turns and steps forward until his nose is against the metal of the gate. It's the only thing holding him back from tearing this man limb from limb.

"Get out of here, Suds," Dad growls. This is obviously not the first time this man has been at the gate causing trouble.

The man waves to me; then, with another laugh and coughing fit, he turns and walks down the sidewalk, limping slightly on his right leg.

# 6

It's not late, but it's middle-of-the-night dark outside. Dad tosses our paper plates after dinner and wishes me a good night. We both pretended not to hear Monica sneaking into his room while we were eating and chatting about the next phase of the motel.

I step outside. The construction lights scatter bright dots around the parking lot and buildings—except for the condemned section, which is blacked out.

I'm not tired, and I can't stand the thought of sitting in my room watching mindless TV until I am.

I go into my room and dig through my suitcase until I find the flashlight that was another part of my adventure kit from Hailey, but contributed by Mom, who doesn't trust Dad to be able to keep the electricity on.

Outside, I pick my way to the dark section of the complex. I'm being good—just going exploring. No matches, no lighters. I have nothing that creates fire anymore. I'm done.

No matter what my scar thinks.

I jump when I see Ro on the floor of the condemned room.

She has a little flashlight of her own. It's pointed away from her, which gives her the look of a ghost hiding in the shadows. Above her head, she holds a piece of the kitten chow I had left out earlier. The kitten leaps for it, misses, and tries again. The white tip of its tail glows in the dim light.

"I'm teaching him a trick," Ro says without looking up at me. She gives in and lets the kitten have the food. It gobbles it up and climbs onto her lap for more.

"Do you want to pet him?"

I slide forward and kneel in front of them. My light catches the kitten's eyes, and they glow green, but it doesn't run away. I put my hand out, and the kitten sniffs it with disinterest before crunching down on another mouthful of kibble. My fingers brush its soft grayness. Its body rumbles with a purr.

Ro laughs. "I think he likes you."

"How do you know it's a boy?" I ask.

Ro shrugs. "He has a boy face."

I lean in to examine the kitten's face. He meows.

"Do your parents know that you're hanging around a crumbling motel in the dark?" I try to laugh and keep my tone light, but it's a serious question. Does she hang around every night?

Ro looks away. "No parents. Just my aunt. She doesn't care where I am."

"Oh," I say, and wait for more details, but she doesn't give any. She holds up another piece of food for the kitten.

The deep, throaty scream of a siren sounds and stops my heart. I jump. The kitten startles and runs into the shadows.

"What?" Ro asks.

I leap to the doorway and run out to the parking lot. A fire truck races past.

My body stiffens. My scar burns. My head spins.

I walk toward it.

I'm stopped by the gate. I put my hands against it and grip down hard. The icy metal cuts into my fingers.

The flashing lights congregate at the end of the street on the edge of the trees. Smoke stings my eyes. It takes a second for my brain to click that what I'm smelling isn't woodsmoke. To my right, in a deep shadow, is the burning end of a cigarette. The smoker shuffles over to me, but my hands won't release the gate. My feet won't run away. It is the same man I saw earlier. The one Dad called Suds.

"It's dry out there," he says. "A single spark . . ." He snaps his fingers. Then he laughs, drops the burning cigarette on the ground, clears his throat with a hack and spit, and limps away.

# 7

Why did I have to go to the gate last night? What was I thinking? I can't be seen chasing fire trucks when there's an arson investigation going on in Ohio. If I give people too many pieces, they'll start to put them together. Like that man—Suds.

*A single spark,* he said.

It must have been him. He dropped the burning cigarette on the ground outside my door the night I went out into the woods.

He knows.

It was bad that he saw me. Very bad. But it could have been worse. Even if he spilled everything about me, who would believe him? Maybe that's why he hasn't said anything to the police. But he keeps coming back. I'll have to be extra careful until I know for sure what he wants.

I get dressed, pull on my coat, and slip out the door into the ruins.

Ro isn't in the condemned room. She probably thinks I'm weird after my sudden departure last night. There wasn't a fire. It must have been a medical emergency. But I couldn't pull myself away from the flashing lights illuminating the night. They were hypnotic.

I wanted to make more come.

My coat snags on the spiky metal of my escape route through the fence. I lose my balance trying to free myself and pitch headfirst into the weeds. When I stand up and brush myself off, I think I hear laughter. I snap my head around.

"Hello?" I call. "Ro?" No one answers. If someone's there, they're hiding. The thought gives me a chill and sends my heart racing. Is it Suds again? I walk fast out to the road without looking back.

The sky is overcast today. Not with heavy clouds filled with snow, but wispy ones. Another lazy attempt at winter.

As I approach the dirt access road that runs along the trees, I see the colony to the right.

I turn left and stay on the road, keeping the trees in my peripheral vision. Everything is brown. Real winter may be unpleasant because of the darkness and the piles of dirty snow, but this is like everything rolled over and died.

A police SUV is parked up ahead. The officer inside is poking at her computer. When she senses me approach, her head snaps up. I freeze. My hands scramble for my coat pockets. They're empty. *I'm not doing anything wrong.*

The officer wrinkles her brow in concern. I pull my hands out of my pockets and smile at her.

I don't hear the second person until he's standing behind me.

"At least it's still cold. But if we don't get some rain soon, the spring fire season's gonna be a bitch." I spin around to face him. He turns red. "Sorry."

He's my age or maybe a little younger. His blond hair is parted and combed down. His blue eyes pierce through the dull surroundings. He has a black trash bag in his hand.

"Community service," he says, holding up the bag.

I must flinch, because his eyes go wide.

"It's not like that. I'm not in trouble. It's for my internship with the police department." He points at the SUV. "I have to do a ton of community service hours to complete the program. Today is trash-pick-up day."

The officer knocks on the inside of her window.

"Maybe I'll see you out here again," he says with a genuine smile. I force a smile onto my face. *I hope not.*

He gets into the SUV. The officer's window rolls down.

"Be careful out here by yourself," she says.

They pull away, and I start to pick my way through the brush toward the bridge. I'm out for a walk. I'm not scouting places with dense, crunchy growth and safe exits. I don't do that anymore.

My skin suddenly prickles.

I stop and listen to the sounds of the forest around me. A twig snaps, and a chill moves up my spine. Someone is there. Watching from behind a tree. I feel his eyes on the back of my neck.

It isn't Suds. He couldn't sneak up on me, not with his cough and limp. This is someone else. Someone whose movements are slow and calculated.

I spin around fast.

I see *someone*. Face hidden, body mostly concealed by brush. Only a flash of blue gives him away.

"Where'd you go last night?" Ro asks when I stick my head through the hole in the fence.

I can't come up with a lie right now, not after what happened in the trees. I have to settle for a half-truth. "To the gate." My voice shakes. I shiver like I'm freezing. I want to go to my room and lock the door, but Ro stands in my path.

"What are you doing here?" I ask, hoping I don't sound irritated. She's still the closest thing I have to a potential friend.

"I was looking for the kitten," she says. Then she narrows her eyes and examines me. "What's wrong with your arm?"

I release my grip on my scar. "Nothing."

She creeps toward me. "Let me see."

"No." I pull back, but Ro stands at her full height in front of me. She's taller than I am, and all limbs. She sucks in her cheeks and tilts her head. It's a look I haven't seen since I was seven and everyone was still curious—before Mom and my soon-to-be stepfather announced to the whole town that I was not a museum specimen and I would not be on display.

After a couple of months, other news happened and I drifted back into normal life. But when anyone saw my scar, they would look away and make a comment about the weather.

I strip off my coat and pull my arm out from the bottom of my sweater. The cold brushes my half-bare stomach.

37

Ro steps forward and leans in to look at my scar. "Does it hurt?"

I shake my head. I can't tell her about the itch.

I push my arm back into the sleeve of my sweater and pull on my coat. Ro stares at me. I sigh. "I was in a fire when I was seven."

She blinks but doesn't respond. What I've told her isn't enough. She wants details.

"It was a sleepover at a friend's house. I was the only one who made it out."

She looks down. "Sorry."

I shrug. "It was ten years ago." Which means nothing. I can still see every detail as if it happened ten minutes ago, but she doesn't need to know that.

A gust of wind whistles through the ruins. It stings my ears. Ro thinks she hides her reaction, but I see her shiver in her too-thin clothes.

A truck rumbles up outside. It could be Cam's. He could be sitting in it in his blue coat.

His coat that's the same shade of blue I saw in the trees.

"Do you want to come to my room?" I don't want Cam finding me alone.

Ro's face lights up for the briefest of seconds. Then it's as if she catches herself and forces a blank expression again. "Okay."

I stick my head out the doorway. It wasn't Cam's truck. His is gone. The construction crew isn't paying attention. I wave Ro over.

She doesn't hesitate to go in when I open the door to my room. I pull the duvet up on the bed and toss the decorative fluffy pillows back on it. Now that my stuff is spread out, the room looks less like a luxury hotel room and more like a teenager's bedroom. A rich teenager.

"Wow," Ro says. She touches all the surfaces, lifts my things, listens to her laugh echo in the bathroom.

She pauses in front of the open wardrobe. "You go to the bee school?"

When I look confused, she pulls out one of my Riverline uniforms: a yellow-and-black plaid skirt and a bright yellow sweater with an insignia patch on the chest.

Beyond hanging them in the wardrobe when Dad gave them to me, I haven't looked at them. But she's right. I'm going to look like a giant preppy bumblebee.

Ro laughs. "When the bell rings, it looks like all the bees leaving the hive."

"You've been there?"

Ro picks up a bottle of perfume, gives herself a squirt, and puts it down again. "There's a dollar store near there." She lifts the framed photo of Mom and Hailey.

"That's my mom and my little sister. Half sister."

She sets the photo down. "If you have a mom and a sister, why'd you come here?"

Her question makes me want to confess—partially confess, that is. I want to tell her about my fear that Hailey will die in a fire. About Ohio. About the arson investigation. About Brian. Instead, I shrug. "I just wanted to come live with my dad."

"Huh" is Ro's response.

She shimmies out of her red jacket. Underneath, she's wearing only a T-shirt. She must be freezing. If she lives in the neighborhood behind the motel, she can't have much money. Maybe what she's wearing is all she has.

"Are you hungry?" I ask with too much enthusiasm. Ro pulls into herself. I pushed too far. She knows I feel sorry for her.

She grabs her jacket. "I have stuff to do." She opens the door, takes a quick look at the construction crew, and leaves without turning back.

I'm being paranoid. The rhythmic crunch I hear outside isn't footsteps. I'm just shaky from being watched in the trees. From Suds knowing too much about me.

*A single spark.*

The sound stops outside my window, feet from where I lie.

The naked bulb hanging over the sidewalk projects the outline of a man onto my curtains. He shuffles forward to place the sides of both palms on the window.

I freeze, but he must hear the pounding of my heart. He leans into his hands to shield his face from the light. His nose presses against the glass.

My phone is on the nightstand. I should call Dad or the police. The fence is supposed to keep everyone out. No one should be here.

Unless they found the hole.

I wrap my fingers around my phone. Do I risk it? It could be Suds, or it could be the person in the trees. He could have been watching me the night I snuck out. He could know what I get up to in the dark.

The figure brings his hand to the dark space where his mouth is. A waft of cigarette smoke finds its way through a vent or a hidden crack in the wall.

It's got to be Suds again. Tomorrow I'll find a cigarette stub on the sidewalk.

If I call the police, he could tell them every single detail of what I did.

*They wouldn't believe him,* I remind myself. Besides, I'm good. I don't leave any evidence. Even if the cops got suspicious, there's nothing to tie me to the fire in the cottonwoods.

I swipe my phone on. I'm calling the cops and ending this right now.

Maybe Suds sees the light coming from inside my room. He steps back from the window and moves beyond the reach of the bulb over the sidewalk.

I stand up, creep over to the curtains, and slowly lift them. I can't see anyone out there.

Maybe the whole thing was my imagination.

I put the phone back on the nightstand. I can't call the cops to an empty parking lot.

I crawl into my bed and try to go back to sleep, but my heart won't calm down. Every noise, real or imagined, sends my eyes back to the window. I know Suds was there. I didn't make that up.

Did I?

Sweat forms on the back of my neck. My hands grip the duvet and wrap it around me like a life jacket—like it's the only thing keeping me afloat.

I can't take it anymore.

I grab the sleeping pills off the nightstand and pop one into my mouth, swallowing it dry.

Then I wait for sweet sleep to overtake me.

# 8

The alarm on my phone goes off. I slap at the nightstand for it, but it isn't there. I must have knocked it onto the floor sometime during the night.

My head is fuzzy from the pill *and* it's the first day of school. Great.

I stumble out of bed and into the bathroom. A scary sight greets me in the mirror. I look like hell. Bloodshot eyes peer out of my puffy red face. My scar has new, fresh scratches raked through it. The nails on my right hand are ragged.

I need coffee *now*, or I'll never make it to school.

Outside, I look down at the sidewalk, but it takes my mind two clicks to catch up to what I'm seeing.

Nothing.

The sidewalk is clean. No cigarette butt. I scan the parking lot and trace a path to the condemned rooms.

Was it all in my head? Is my scar not enough? Is my mind now conjuring up smoking, hooded figures to further torture me?

Dad and Monica both look up when I walk into the office.

I turn my back to them and focus on the counter. Cam's blue-coated figure looms by the window.

"Cam will take you to school when you're ready, Jenny," Monica says.

He points over his shoulder. "I have to run an errand, but I'll be back by then." He steps out, and the door closes behind him.

I don't want to ride with Cam. I need some time to think. Think without having my every movement examined.

"Can't you take me to school? It's my first day," I ask Dad. "Or I can find a bus. Or walk."

Dad looks like he's about to give in. Then Monica pipes up again. "We've got that early meeting, remember?"

"Sorry, Jenny. We'll do something else for the first day of school. Maybe we can go get ice cream after dinner. Okay?"

I've lost this one. I'm riding with Cam.


When the truck pulls up, I'm standing in the parking lot outside my room, looking like a giant bumblebee in my Riverline Prep uniform and holding a messenger bag full of school supplies I collected from Henderson's.

Cam isn't alone.

A guy sits in the passenger seat. He's wearing a hoodie—hood up. I step back onto the sidewalk.

The passenger-side door opens. The guy steps out. When the sun hits his face, I see a lock of black hair flopping down over his forehead. His high cheekbones draw attention to his brown eyes. He smiles. His front teeth are crooked—but just enough to add extra charm to his smile.

He looks completely nonthreatening.

But that's what dangerous people want you to think.

I should know.

Cam's window rolls down. "Are you coming?"

Monica is watching us from the office window. I don't know what I'm supposed to do. The guy in the hoodie glances around like he's nervous. "We should go," he says. I don't move. He reads the look on my face. "I'm Ben. Cam's cousin? This is my uncle's project."

The boss's nephew. This just keeps getting better. I have to get in the truck.

I move forward. Ben steps to the side to let me pass. I'll be sitting in the middle seat. Between them.

Emergency exits: none.

I slide into the truck.

As soon as Ben shuts the door, Cam throws the truck into reverse, and we peel out from the parking lot, throwing up little rocks. Ben sinks down into his seat, head dipped low under his hood. I keep my arms in my lap, gripping my bag so that I don't touch either one of them.

As we're pulling past the gate, a shiny black BMW is pulling in. Ben sucks in a breath and turns to look out the window. Cam gives the car a curt wave.

Once we're on the street, Ben relaxes and flips off his hood. Cam yawns and reaches for his travel mug of coffee. His hand accidentally brushes my knee. My whole body tenses.

Ben gives Cam a half smile. "You've got to start sleeping. You can't keep staying up all night forever."

Cam ignores him. I pull my arms in even closer to me. *Cam stays up all night?*

Ben gives me a whole smile. It lights up his face. "How's it going? I bet it's really different here than in Ohio."

"Yeah. No snow."

Ben laughs.

We drive into the closest thing that Las Piedras has to a downtown—a strange collection of mismatched buildings and mismatched people. Workers slog in from outer parking lots. Men wrapped in scraps of blankets are gathered in front of the still-closed library.

A hundred bumblebees descend on a repurposed, two-story historic building in the middle of a chunky cement office block. Because of Riverline Prep's "super college preparatory curriculum," we start earlier in the morning and end later in the afternoon than public school.

"I do not miss the uniform," Ben says.

"You went here?" I ask. I wouldn't have thought he was much older than me—not as old as Cam.

"For a while," he says, and continues gazing out the window. He looks back at me. "Cam graduated from here."

Cam's hands tighten on the steering wheel.

I really, really want to get out of this truck.

We pull up to the curb. Ben slides out.

"Thanks," I say to Cam—but only to keep up the charade of politeness. He blinks hard and opens his eyes overly wide, like he's fighting to stay conscious. I point back in the direction of the Los Ranchitos. "I can walk home now that I've seen the way."

"I'm supposed to pick you up," he says to the air in front of him.

"Dad will be okay with me walking home."

"I'll be here after school," he says forcefully.

His tone knocks me back. How am I going to get out of this? I can't keep riding around with him.

I get out of the truck and stand next to Ben. Across the street, a girl in a uniform stops midstep. Ben waves to her. She raises her hand tentatively and gives a small wave back.

"Have a nice day," Ben says, smile wide. Eyes twinkling.

"Thanks."

The truck drives away, and I'm faced with Riverline Prep. My new school. My new fancy private school.

My scar starts to itch. I hold my hand over it, take a deep breath, and let go as I approach the security guard at the front door.

"Um, hi. I'm new here. This is my first day." I reach into my bag, ready to produce my Ohio driver's license. The guard glances up, eyes my bee uniform, and goes back to reading his paper without saying anything. "Thanks?" How secure is this school if they let in anyone wearing preppy yellow-and-black plaid, no questions asked?

Mom picked this school because of its academic program. Brian liked the idea of a security guard. I don't think Dad got any say in the matter.

I step inside and walk down the main hallway, which is lined with doorways edged in carved wooden decorations. The front office has carpet and paintings on the walls, but otherwise, the building is scuffed linoleum and rooms of desks and whiteboards like any other school.

Mom already registered me and had my schedule and locker number waiting at the Los Ranchitos. The school has only a couple hundred students, and it's not hard to find my first class. I go in and stand in the back corner. It's the start of the second semester. Everyone will already have their desks, their cliques, and their favorite lunch spots. I know better than to get in the middle of that.

I wait until the class is full. I get some disinterested glances, but in general, I'm ignored. When the teacher comes in, she jumps, like I've materialized out of thin air.

She has wild, curly hair that she makes no attempt to contain. Her peasant skirt and a long blouse are cinched at the waist with a silver concho belt. She walks over to me.

"You must be our new Jenny. I'm Teresa, your homeroom teacher and general guide to school life." She laughs and sticks out her hand. I shake it. I've never called a teacher by their first name before. I didn't even know that was a thing.

She points toward an empty desk, and I sit down. The boy in front of me turns around and smiles. The girl sitting next to him has sleek blond hair, dark eyeliner, and pink lipstick. She's wearing the same uniform as the rest of us, but she, instead of looking like a frumpy bumblebee, looks like the uniform was made for her. It hugs all her curves.

The blonde sees the boy smile. She eyes me up and down. Her bright pink top lip rises in disgust. I have to force my hand to stay on the desk and not reach for my scar.

Teresa claps at the front of the room. I steel myself to stand up and give the speech I've memorized about where I'm from and why I'm here, but the order doesn't come. Teresa never glances back at me. I blend into the sea of yellow and black. I've become interchangeable with anyone else.

Emergency exit: the classroom door.

"Welcome back!" Teresa says. Her enthusiasm isn't contagious. "I hope you had a great holiday and are ready to work again." No one answers, but Teresa isn't daunted. "It's second semester of junior year. You know what that means." A couple of moans echo through the classroom. I sit up straighter. I have no idea what that means.

Teresa produces a box of clipboards from under her desk. "Service-learning time!"

I vaguely remember Mom mentioning something about the school requiring a service project for all juniors, but at the time the words were meaningless. I had much bigger things for my mind to chew around and around.

"These are the projects." Teresa taps the clipboards. "But"—she pulled them back, as if someone had reached for one—"they won't be posted until the last bell this afternoon. That way everyone will have an equal chance to sign up." She Cheshire Cat grins. "We have a new project this year. One that's close to my heart. I think you're going to like it."

• • •

None of my other classes are like Teresa's. All the other teachers are Mr. and Ms. My math teacher is about 120 years old and insists on writing on an old-fashioned chalkboard that he smacks with a yardstick to get the class's attention.

When the last bell rings, I've almost forgotten about the service projects. A line has formed in the hallway. All my teachers walk up and down the corridor, keeping order. I stuff my bag into my locker and jump into the line. If there's this much fuss about the sign-up, there must be some bad projects.

Teresa makes a big production out of hanging each clipboard on the wall. I can't see what the projects are from my spot, but I can see that there are only a few slots under each one.

The line starts to move. None of the students in front of me have to stop and read. They must have known in advance about the good ones.

When it's my turn, I feel the line pressing behind me. I don't have time to examine all the clipboards. The one in front of my face has a single slot left. In bold writing on the top it says *Community Garden.*

I don't have a pen. Everyone else has one ready to go. If I leave to go back to my locker, I'll lose my spot. The line stretches out of sight. By the time I get back to the clipboards, what's left will be whatever no one else wants.

My feet dance back and forth. Teresa looks concerned.

"Here." A pen appears over my shoulder. It's being held out by a girl who's about my height, but with mousey brown hair half covering her face, and enormous round, unflattering glasses. Her uniform hangs on her like a sack. She's the girl Ben waved to this morning.

I take the pen, scribble my name on the community garden sheet, and hand it back to her. I smile, but she's too focused on the clipboards to notice.

Several people back in line, the girl from my homeroom— the pink-lipped blonde—glares at me as I walk by.

# 9

Cam's truck isn't parked outside the school. Before I get my hopes up that he didn't show, I walk around the block to check. He's not here.

I pull out my phone and find a bus that's part of the meager public transportation system here.

The bus drops me off in front of Henderson's. I'm surprised to see Ro walking through the parking lot toward me.

When she sees me, she breaks into a smile and waves. "Hi, Jenny." I wave back.

"Where's that dude who drives you around?" she asks.

"He didn't show after school." Venom leaks out in my tone. Mostly I'm relieved that I didn't have to ride with him, but a little part of me is pissed off. He's taking Dad's money without working for it.

Ro puts a finger to her chin in a thinking gesture. "Hmm . . . I bet I know where he is."

"You do?"

"Come with me," she demands, and marches toward the Los Ranchitos.

I follow her but then stop. Suds has found an old fold-up lawn chair. He's planted in the middle of the sidewalk in front of the motel, with numerous cardboard signs propped up around him. They all say horrible things about Dad's company.

A car goes by and honks at him. He gives it the finger and yells, "Fuck you!"

Ro keeps going.

"Wait." I try to hold her back. "I don't want him to see us."

Too late. He struggles to his feet and waves. "Hello, pretty ladies."

"Hello, pervert," Ro calls back.

"Ro," I mutter under my breath. I grab her arm and pull.

"Don't leave, pretty ladies." Suds takes a step toward us and looks straight at me. "Do you like your fancy room? I bet your bed's real comfy." He laughs.

I freeze in place. Maybe he really was outside my room last night. He just didn't leave a cigarette butt this time.

Or maybe that's wishful thinking.

Ro looks like she's gearing up for another comeback. I pull her arm hard. We have to get out of here, away from Suds.

I dash back across the street toward the strip mall. Ro follows without complaint. "Maybe we can wait in the drugstore or something?"

"Do you want to come to my house?" Ro asks.

I see her shiver under her thin jacket. She should be inside. "Okay," I say, and follow her into the neighborhood behind the strip mall.

The block is lined on both sides with boxy, flat-roofed,

stuccoed houses. Some of the front yards are filled with rocks, but most are knee-high weeds.

Ro leads me down the street. We stop in front of a house where the stucco is peeling off, leaving big gray patches. It looks like a surreal representation of thunderclouds in a sun-setting sky.

She walks up to the front door and pushes on the handle. The door doesn't move. "That bitch," she mumbles.

"What's wrong?" I ask.

"My aunt locked me out again. She does that when she's mad. I don't know what I did to her this time."

"You don't have a key?"

Ro shakes her head. "After I spent a night out in the cold, I learned to leave my bedroom window open. She hasn't figured it out yet. But I have to be superquiet. Come on, I'll show you." She takes a step into the weed-covered yard.

"I don't think we should." If her aunt is that mad, Ro shouldn't be showing up with a random friend. But she's not listening. She's halfway to the side of the house. "Come on," she says again.

I glance over my shoulder. The street is quiet. The curtains are drawn at the house across the way.

Ro stops in front of a side window. Below it is a black rolling trash can. Ro pushes on the window. "See," she says, "unlocked." She puts a foot on the trash can in preparation to hoist herself up.

"Ro, I'm not crawling through your window. Let's go back to the motel."

She peers inside the house and then turns and looks at me like I'm being unreasonable.

All my frustrations of the day come pouring out. "How can your aunt get away with this? I'm pretty sure that making you spend the night outside in the cold is child abuse."

Ro shrugs. "Where else am I supposed to go? A group home? Some nice foster family somewhere?" Her voice is full of irritation, like she's challenging me. Ro's never told me much about herself. I knew she didn't have a lot, but I didn't realize it was this bad.

I look down. "I don't know. Please, let's go back to the motel."

I don't want to be here. I can't imagine what kind of monster Ro's aunt must be. I'd rather take my chances with Suds. I walk back to the sidewalk and brush off my uniform.

"Fine," Ro says behind me. I head back to the main road. "Do you want to know where Cam is?" she calls.

I do. I'm going to keep a very close eye on him until I figure out for sure who's outside my room and watching me in the trees.

Ro leads me to the access road along the cottonwoods, but right before we get there, she makes a sharp turn. Hidden from sight is a small open area—maybe a parking lot for joggers and bird-watchers.

Cam's truck is there. He's inside. Asleep.

I knock on the window. He wakes with a start. "Your job was to pick me up!" I yell through the glass.

"Shit. What time is it?" Cam fumbles for his phone.

Ro giggles. "That guy is camped out in front of the motel. Aren't you supposed to get rid of him?"

My head snaps over to Ro. She shrugs. "I was visiting the kitten, and I heard your dad say that he"—she points to Cam—"was supposed to take care of the guy."

Cam's eyes widen. He picks his keys up off the seat and rubs them nervously between his fingers. "I, ah . . ."

I glare, but he doesn't say anything else.

Ro kicks at a rock. Her arms are clasped around her. She's pretending she isn't cold, whereas I want to unzip my thick coat to let some cool air in.

I smirk. "Hey, Ro," I call over my shoulder. "I need some stuff for school. Do you want to go to the mall?"

Cam huffs.

Ro figures out what I'm doing. "Hey, Jenny. Did you know that guy was in front of the motel before and after school? I saw him both times."

"Get in," Cam says.

Ro giggles. It's infectious. I find myself smiling too.

She slides in next to Cam, not caring that she bumps into his side. He doesn't ask me about her or seem to care that I have manifested a friend out of nowhere.


At the mall, Cam doesn't get out of the truck.

"Aren't you coming?" I ask.

He glares at me. "No."

Ro and I get out. "Well, that's disappointing," I say. Ro looks at me quizzically. "At the grocery store he followed me around everywhere. I was going to spend a lot of time picking out a new bra."

Ro giggles. "It would have been funny to see him all red in the lingerie section."

The mall isn't much of a mall. It has a couple of anchor department stores with a few smaller shops in between and a food court that only serves hot dogs.

Ro examines every piece of clothing in the first store we enter. She holds up a black dress, looks at it with dreamy eyes, sighs, and puts it back.

I can't help but glance at what she's wearing. If her pilling sweater and worn jeans came from the mall, it was a long time ago. Her red coat isn't much more than a jacket. She must be cold all the time.

I point to the dress. "You should try that on."

She shakes her head.

"I'll try it on," I say. A plan is forming in my head. We aren't the same size. She's taller than me, but if I get things a little too big, they might fit her.

Besides, this shopping trip is courtesy of Mom and her I-feel-guilty-that-my-daughter-is-halfway-across-the-country money. There's plenty more where that came from.

I go into the dressing room and shed my coat. "I'm dying in this. It gets so much colder in Ohio. I'm going to need a new one." I toss it out to Ro, like I want her to hold it. She folds it over her arms and hugs it to her chest.

I try on the black dress. When I come out of the dressing room in it, I pretend not to notice that Ro is wearing my coat.

We have fun. Ro hands me thing after thing to try on. I

make duck faces and contort my body into model-like poses to show them off. I've never paid too much attention to clothes, but Ro seems to love them. The smile never leaves her face.

When we're walking back to the parking lot, I realize that I haven't thought about my scar once since I've been with Ro.

Cam is asleep in the truck.

"What's going on with him?" Ro asks.

I knock on the window and hold up my shopping bags. "We're done."

Ro is still wearing my coat. It's a little short in the arms for her, but once she put it on, she never took it off. I also bought several of the things she admired most. Maybe she'll have a birthday or something soon, so I can find a reason to give them to her.


When we get to the motel, it's dark. Suds is gone. The crew is packing up. Dad stands outside the office talking to a guy in a gray suit. He's a slight man, wiry and fit. Strands of silver weave through this dark hair. He has a sharp nose, high cheekbones, and deep brown eyes. He's handsome.

Cam stops midyawn and inhales in surprise.

When we get out of the truck, Dad and the man walk over. Cam stands up straight.

"Jenny, this is Mike Vargas. He's the developer." Dad chuckles. "My boss."

I shake hands with Mr. Vargas.

"This is my friend Ro," I say to them. Dad gives her a

courtesy smile and doesn't seem to notice that Ro's wearing my coat.

Mr. Vargas isn't paying attention to us anymore. He's standing next to his son. Never in a million years would I have guessed they were related. There's maybe some resemblance around the forehead and eyes, but that's where it stops. Cam is stocky and moves slowly. His face doesn't show much. His father vibrates with energy. There's no hiding the disappointment on his pursed lips.

"Where have you been? I had to kick that guy off the property."

Cam shifts his weight from foot to foot. He's trying to come up with something, but he's taking too long. At this point, even if he were to tell the truth, no one would believe him.

I should let him go down in flames for sleeping in his truck—and for maybe watching me in the trees. But the look on Mr. Vargas's face is serious. Cam has been transformed into a little boy in front of me. I feel a prick of sympathy for him. I step forward.

"It's my fault, Mr. Vargas. When Cam picked me up, I asked him to take me to the mall. I needed to get some things." I hold up my shopping bags, but Mr. Vargas doesn't look convinced. "For school."

Cam puffs up and nods, as if he has made a great sacrifice for my education. That little bit of sympathy I had for him evaporates. Next time he's on his own.

Mr. Vargas gives us a toothy fake smile. "Fine," he says. He turns to Dad. "Let's come up with a game plan for tomorrow." They start to walk away. Mr. Vargas turns and waves for Cam, who hasn't moved, to follow.

When they're out of earshot, Ro starts to laugh. "You own him now, you know that, right?"

"What?"

"Cam. You saved his ass. He'll have to do whatever you say now."

"I don't want anything from him."

"Uh-huh." Ro raises an eyebrow.

I look away from her. She barely knows me. Am I leaking something? Something that would imply that I've been collecting things to hold over Cam? That I *need* to have things on Cam?

I make sure my face is completely blank before I look back at her. "Do you want to stay for dinner?"

Ro considers it.

"It'll just be something microwaved," I add.

She links her arm through mine. "Okay," she says, "friend."

# 10

My name has been crossed off the community garden clipboard. In its place is the name Kara Johnston. Ten bucks says
that's the pink-lipped blonde. There's always one. In Ohio,
I didn't have to deal with this sort of crap since I had always lived there. That, and everyone knew about the fire at
the sleepover. They couldn't pick on me without looking like
huge assholes. But now I'm the unknown new girl. There will
be an elaborate hazing before I'm accepted. Or I'm not.

I feel a little pulse of joy. The pink-lipped blonde has completely underestimated me.

I scan all the other clipboards, looking for my name. I see
it, alone, on the last one. It reads "Free Clinic." Great.

I think about ripping it off the wall and marching it over
to Teresa. But I won't do that. I don't want to draw attention
to myself by getting a reputation for being the tattletale. I
really do want to make friends here, and I never will if I start
off that way.

I walk into homeroom and give a sparkling smile to the
blonde. She looks confused. Good.

• • •

At lunch, I pick a table—one off to the side—and wait to see whose territory I've invaded today. Emergency exits: two doors, with tables and bodies blocking my paths to them.

The cafeteria continues to fill up, but no one comes to claim my spot. Then the blonde and her entourage sweep in. She smirks at me and whispers something to her friends. All the girls look at me and start to laugh.

I turn back to my lunch and roll my eyes. I was expecting this. I'm the new girl from far away, starting in the middle of the year. I've seen it happen before. I might have even done it a time or two.

"Ignore her." I jump at the voice behind me.

I turn and see the girl who loaned me the pen. "Can I sit here?" she asks, but she doesn't wait for my reply before sitting down.

I nibble my PB and J while the girl pops open a container full of vegetables and grains. She looks longingly at my sandwich.

She picks up her fork, but doesn't start to eat. Then she glances around, like she's about to tell me a secret. "I'm sorry, Jenny," she whispers.

I try to speak, but my mouth is full of peanut butter. I gulp my soda to wash it down. She takes my silence as some sort of shaming. She looks down and picks at a broccoli spear.

"I don't know what you're talking about," I whisper back.

"The learning project. I'm sorry I took your spot."

"Wait. You're Kara Johnston?" I say at full volume. Panic

briefly passes over her face. Then she nods and looks away. I lower my voice again. "Then who's that?" I point at the blonde.

"That's Emma."

I focus on Kara. Under her big glasses and messy hair, her skin is flawless. Her eyes are a beautiful shade of green. She looks like someone going to a lot of trouble to hide her natural beauty.

She chews a carrot and swallows. "When my parents heard that I didn't get the garden spot, they called Teresa." For a third time, she glances around the room, but no one, not even Emma, is paying attention to us. Kara's making me nervous. It's not exactly like her name or service project is classified information.

She leans in so close that I want to automatically jerk back, but I will myself to stay still. "I'm not allowed to leave campus unless it's to go straight home. The garden is out back so . . . ," she trails off.

"Oh. Wow. I'm sorry." And I am. There's obviously something bad going on in her home life. I'm not sure Dad would notice if I didn't come home at all, much less restrict me to only going to school.

"Don't worry about the project," I say, and she relaxes. "If you hadn't given me that pen, you would have gotten the garden spot anyway. I'm sure working at the free clinic will be great." I don't believe that for a second, but it sounds better than whatever Kara is dealing with.

We chat more normally for the rest of lunch. She fills me in on our classmates—who's nice and who I should avoid.

Later, whenever I see her in the hall, we smile. But I notice that even though she knows everyone, she's always by herself. It seems self-inflicted. People smile at her in the hallways and look like they want to make conversation, but she keeps moving. The only person she stops to talk to is me.

One thing seems clear: Kara's got a story.

After school, Cam's truck is waiting for me, but he's not sitting in it. I walk over to peer inside, expecting to see him stretched out asleep, but he isn't. The truck is empty and clean, except for a shiny object in the cup holder. I put my hands up against the glass to block the glare so I can see better.

It's a chunky silver cigarette lighter, the kind you see in old movies. It has "CAV" etched in swirling letters on the side.

My heart rate shoots up to a thousand beats per minute. I instinctively jump back into the street to get away from it. A car honks at me.

Is he a smoker? I've never smelled it on him.

A disturbing thought hits me: Maybe he only smokes late at night. Maybe I wasn't imagining anything, and it *was* him outside my window. I remember the flash of blue in the trees. The same shade as the coat he is wearing today. Was it him?

I start to walk in the direction of the bus. I'm not riding with him.

There's an alleyway on the other side of the truck. I hear muffled male voices. I slide up to the corner and peek around it. Cam, huddled in his coat, is facing Ben—hood up.

I can't hear what they're saying, but it sounds like they're arguing. Cam throws his hands out, like he's imploring Ben to do something. Ben stands stoically, listening but not reacting.

Cam rubs at his eyes. Ben steps forward and does the last thing I would ever expect: he gives Cam a hug.

It's not a quick pat-on-the-back hug, but a real one. His hands make deep dents in Cam's puffy coat.

When Ben releases, he looks up and sees me.

"Hi, Jenny," he calls out.

Cam turns. I dive back around the corner, but I'm too late. Dammit. Now that he knows I'm here, I won't be able to slip away to the bus stop.

Seconds later, Cam comes plodding around the corner. Ben doesn't follow him. Cam's face is red, and his eyes are moist.

I open my mouth like I want to ask something, but I close it again. My heart is beating so fast I can't think straight. What would I ask? If he's okay? What he's so upset about? Why he's secretly following me around?

He storms past me and unlocks the truck door. "Get in."

I press my back into the cold brick wall. Cam steps forward, like he's going to grab my arm, but his hand drops. He looks like his exhausted, barely conscious self again. "Monica said I need to take you straight home. I'm on some sort of probation. I can't mess up again."

That little bit of sympathy flows into me unbidden again, but I don't want to get in the truck with him.

"Please," he says. There's little emotion behind it, but my ears hear a raw pleading for help. Dammit. I step forward and get into the truck.

Cam starts the ignition. My eyes zero in on the way the light glints off the shiny silver side of the lighter. I imagine how it would feel in the palm of my hand. To flick it on and see the flame appear like magic. A controlled, beautiful, deadly magic.

I snap back to the truck. To Cam.

"Do you smoke?"

His eyes flit over to me, and he sneers in disgust. "No."

"Then why do you have that?" I point to the lighter.

He picks it up. "It was a gift." The sneer is still there.

We stop at a light. Cam's face relaxes, and his eyes start to droop. He absentmindedly flips the top of the lighter open and then closed.

Open, closed. Open, closed. *Click, click. Click, click.*

I stare at it. When the light turns green, his thumb is millimeters from pressing the button and making a flame dance to life. My head spins. The whoosh of the traffic around us changes to the crackle and roar of fire. My scar screams.

*But I've been doing so well.*

"Stop!" I yell. Cam jumps. "Stop the truck. Now." I reach for the door handle while the truck is still rolling. I don't have control over my actions. I just have to get *out*. I jump onto the curb. The car that was behind us screeches into the other lane to pass.

"Jenny, what the hell?"

I hold my hand out, struggling to maintain my composure. "Just drive away and leave me alone."

"But—"

"Just go!" I feel tears in my eyes. "I'll tell Dad and Monica I had to stay late at school."

Cam's jaw clenches, and his face burns an angry red.

I stumble down the sidewalk. My scar itches, my fingers twitch, my head aches.

The truck slowly follows me. "Go!" I yell at it.

The passenger-side window rolls down, and Cam leans toward it. "Jenny . . ."

I glare a thousand daggers at him. A car honks. Cam glances in the rearview mirror and then back at me, like he can't decide who he would rather tangle with.

The other driver slams his palm onto the horn.

"This is not worth the money," Cam mumbles. The truck pulls forward, leaving me alone by the side of the road.

It's a long way to the motel, and I have to cross under the interstate. The underpass is dark and cold and filled with graffiti, pigeon poop, and the remnants of people's sleeping spaces.

There's a slight movement in the shadows. I feel eyes on me. Someone is there. Hiding. I make a run for Henderson's, which shines like a beacon of warmth and safety in the winter sun.

The doors swish open. I'm out of breath, but my heart starts to quiet down.

Until I see the display of plastic lighters on the counter.

I grab a basket and shove stuff into it. Toothpaste, shampoo, deodorant. I take it up to the counter and set it down. The usual clerk smiles. "Good afternoon," she says, and starts ringing up my stuff. I try to smile back as I slip a cigarette lighter into the basket.

My heart thuds. I've lost all control.

I swipe my debit card, grab my bag, and leave without my receipt.

My scar itches with a ferocity that I've never felt before. I can't go to the motel. There are too many people there. Someone would get hurt.

I force myself to stroll down the sidewalk. I'm just a girl heading for the cottonwoods to clear her head and commune with nature.

I hesitate for a second at the edge of the trees, but I can't hold back this time.

Once I cross into the underbrush, I run, pushing through weeds and leaping over tangles of fallen branches until I get to the river—the farthest point from the motel. The farthest point from people.

I step back into the trees. As I drag my feet, it creates a pile of leaves and dry, crunchy plants. My breath catches in my chest. I claw at my scar.

I crouch down and reach into the Henderson's bag. My hand closes around the lighter. My scar vibrates with delight.

I pull my hand from the bag.

A branch snaps. Footsteps.

I jump away from the pile of leaves and stumble to the fallen tree. I drop the bag at my feet and shove my hand into my coat pocket.

A figure comes through the brush toward me. I turn my head from side to side. There's nowhere to go. The river is behind me, and I'm surrounded by the trees and thick under-brush. He's coming straight for me. There's no sneaking away.

I bite my lip and brace myself. I'm alone and completely vulnerable right now.

"Hello." The figure waves. He steps out into the open. "I thought I saw someone come through here."

My knees almost give out on me. The guy I saw before—the one picking up trash for his police internship—stands in front of me. His blue eyes shine.

I glance around, waiting for the officer he was riding with to appear. "Am I not allowed to be here?" I try to smile, but my breath coming in short little gasps betrays how I'm really feeling.

"You're fine. You can be here until dark. As long as you're not up to no good." He winks.

I display my empty hands in front of me. "Not up to any-thing. Just watching the birds."

"I'm Allen," he says.

"Jenny." I point at his empty hands. "Is it trash day again?"

He scratches the back of his neck. "Uh . . . no."

He has a police radio on his hip. It crackles to life. He slaps his hand on it and turns the volume down.

"They give interns radios?"

"Uh . . . no." He turns red. "I borrowed this one. I thought if I saw anything criminal happening out here, I could call it in. It would be faster than using my phone." The way he avoids my eyes makes me think that that's a half-truth.

"It's not like I really need to be in this internship program. I already know all the stuff they're teaching us. I knew all the ten codes before I was nine. They should use me for something real."

The lighter in my pocket throbs at my side. He has no idea how close he came to seeing something real, something *criminal.*

I pick up my Henderson's bag. "I have to get home. My dad is waiting for me. He's probably already worried." I pass Allen, but then I turn around.

"You said I could be here until dark. What happens after dark?"

He shrugs and gives me a grin. "I don't know. The forest is closed."

I get back to the motel, and as I stick my key in the door, I hear noise on the other side. My hand freezes. Someone is in my room.

I slowly turn the key. If it's Cam, I'll scream, and every construction worker here will come running. He'll be caught red-handed.

The door pops open, and I'm greeted with a blast of steam. The shower is running. The ultradown coat and Ro's jeans are shucked off on the floor.

My lungs remember how to work and take in a big breath of the moist air.

"Ro?" I call. The shower turns off. A few seconds later, she comes out of the bathroom wrapped in one of the person-sized fluffy towels. She holds my shampoo bottle under her nose.

"This is nice. It smells like strawberries."

Relief floods through me. "How did you get in here?"

She points over her shoulder. "You left the bathroom window open." Her eyes widen. "Are you mad? My aunt knows about my bedroom window. It was locked and barred last night. I didn't have anywhere to go, and I didn't want to break into some stranger's house." She gathers her things up off the floor.

I turn my back to her and blink hard. Our situations are very different, but I know what it feels like to be unwelcome in your own home. I turn around and smile. "No, I'm not mad. Come over anytime."

She heads back to the bathroom, clutching her dirty jeans. "Wait," I say, and open the wardrobe. "Wear these." I hand her the clothes I bought a size too big at the mall. She hesitates, but then she reaches out and takes them.

When she comes out clean and dressed, she flops down on my bed.

I pull out my box of granola bars, take one, and then toss one at Ro before she can protest. I point at my laptop. "Do you want to watch a movie?" I know she doesn't want to go back out into the cold.

She smiles broadly. "Okay." She picks a movie, tears open her granola bar, and lies down on the bed. Soon she's fast asleep.

I look at her still, peaceful figure. My scar calms down. It's happy that I'm helping her. I think we're starting to become real friends now. And maybe I'm making her life a little better, too.

# 11

Kara crunches down on a broccoli tree.

She has a container of bland-looking healthy food in front of her, but she doesn't chuck it and buy something from the cafeteria like a normal person.

She looks over at my lunch *again*. I rip off a piece of my PB and J.

"Please. Take it. I can't stand it anymore."

She grabs it and takes a big bite. "So good," she mumbles with peanut butter mouth. She swallows. "Sugar, fat, refined carbs." She takes another bite.

I laugh, but then realize that her parents are so strict that they won't even let her choose what she eats. I don't know what that's like. Brian sent me a thousand miles away once he found out what I'd done. And Dad's so preoccupied with Monica and the Los Ranchitos that I could get away with murder—or setting fires.

"Let me see it again," she says, and points to my bag. I pull out the motel brochure—the one of what the Los Ranchitos is supposed to look like in a few short months. Kara oohs and aahs over it—especially the infinity pool that will go in the back.

"Do you want to come over?" I ask.

She shakes her head. "My parents . . ." She trails off.

The first time we had lunch together, Kara mentioned that her parents work in Albuquerque and don't get home until late, so it's not like they would ever know.

I try one more time. "Are you sure you don't want to drive by? It's not too far. You don't even have to get out. You can pull your car up in front of my room, and I'll open the door."

She looks around like her parents might be standing over her shoulder. "Okay," she whispers.

"Really?"

She flinches.

I lean in and whisper, "I won't tell anyone."


After school, we laugh as we walk out the main doors to get Kara's car. She seems freer, like this little rebellion has made her happier than she's been in a long time.

I stop. Cam's truck is parked along the street facing us. Why is he here? I took the bus this morning, and I haven't seen him since I flipped out in the truck yesterday. You would think me diving into traffic would be enough to convince him not to come back.

He's not alone. Ro sits next to him, throwing her arms around as she talks. Ben is seated on the other side of her, gazing out the window. What are they here for? To be human shields? Witnesses so I'll behave?

Kara steps out behind me into the winter sunlight and gasps. Her body goes rigid. Ben smiles and waves to us.

"What?" I ask.

"I have to go," she says.

"Wait. I'll tell them you're giving me a ride home. You can still come to the motel."

"No." Kara shakes her head furiously. "I have to go." She turns quickly and jogs to her car.

She drops her keys twice as she tries to unlock the door. I look around again. Whatever spell her parents have cast over her can't be broken by me. I wonder if there's a reason her parents are so strict.

I'm here because I got caught. Maybe Kara got caught too. But caught doing what?

Ro spots me and waves. I walk over to the truck, examining both Ben and Cam for some hint of what scared Kara.

Ben opens the door. Ro points at Cam. "Mr. Sleepyhead is taking us for coffee. He's buying."

Cam puts his phone in one of the cup holders. The lighter is still in the other.

I hesitate.

"Why aren't you getting in?" Ro asks. All three of them stare at me.

"Uh ..." I don't have an answer—not one I can tell her, anyway.

Ben scooches over as far as he can, pressing Ro into Cam's puffy coat. I get in and balance on the edge of the seat with my knees against the glove box.

My shoulder knocks into Ben's.

"Sorry," he says. In the tight space, we can't avoid touching. Heat radiates off him. He smiles apologetically.

The image of him hugging Cam in the alley flashes into my mind. For a brief, strange second, I feel disappointed that Ben doesn't put his arm around my shoulders and hold me next to him. I turn to look out the window.

We drive for a couple of blocks to a place called the Java Shop. It's on the ground floor of a three-story stuccoed building. Ben hops out and jogs inside. We follow at Cam's slower pace.

The coffee shop is a surprise. The outside looks like every other old crumbly building in this town, but the inside is brand-new. The walls are painted in muted orange and green. Lavender trim lines the windows. Tall, un-nicked wooden café tables fill up the center space. There's another door on one side. Two emergency exits, plus stairs that lead down from the upper floors.

When we walk up to the counter, I expect to be met by a perky girl with a ponytail or a hipster wearing an ironic visor, but instead, a woman who looks like she could be in her fifties greets us. Her face is marked with deep lines, but it's lit up with a smile.

Ro launches into her complicated—and expensive—drink order. She glances over her shoulder at Cam, who's got his wallet out to pay, and smirks.

The woman is obviously not accustomed to using the register. She holds her finger up high, like the register is going to bite her before every tap.

Ro leans forward to look. "And whipped cream."

The woman shakes her head in frustration. Ben steps out

from the back, tying on an apron. The relief the woman feels at seeing him is palpable.

Ben finishes punching Ro's order into the register, and then he looks up at me. "What can I get you?"

"You work here?" I ask, and immediately feel stupid.

Ben laughs and points to his apron. "Yep." His eyes meet mine. I feel flustered—and I can't remember how to order coffee.

Cam sighs behind me. I snap out of it. "Vanilla latte."

I join Ro at a table by the window. Cam lingers at the front. When Ben and the woman have their backs turned making our drinks, Cam quickly stuffs a bill into the tip jar.

Our names are called. As Ro bounces up to her massive concoction on the counter, I glance over at the tip jar. A hundred-dollar bill is pressed up against the side.

"What is that?" I whisper to Ro, and point at the jar.

Ro whistles through her teeth. "A lot of money."

"Cam slipped it in there when no one was looking. Where's he getting that kind of money? And why would he put it into a tip jar for his cousin?"

Ro turns her head and examines Cam sitting with his plain black coffee. He clasps it between both hands and blows over the top.

She laughs. "Do you think your dad would give me a job?"

I smile weakly at her. I can't believe Dad is paying Cam much. Maybe it's from Mr. Vargas? But after the show he put on when we got back from the mall, I doubt he's handing Cam hundred-dollar bills—especially not ones to put into tip jars.

"What?" Cam asks as we approach the table.

"Nothing," I say quickly, and give Ro a warning glance.

Cam gazes up at me through the steam. His eyes are round and wide, like a confused child's. That's what he looks like right now. A child. My mind can't wrap around it. Is he following me? Has he been outside my window at night?

Ro bounces back to the counter for a straw.

I look away from Cam. "Why isn't Ben working for my dad like you?" I glance at the tip jar. "The money would be better."

Cam doesn't take my bait. "They don't talk. Ben and my father."

"Why?" It's the wrong question to ask. Cam's whole body clenches. I see the tension in his neck and jaw. He suddenly looks like someone worthy of being afraid of. I check that the side exit is clear.

Ro hops back to the table. She has whipped cream on her face. I focus on the counter and sip my latte. Ben is patiently walking the woman through the register. He looks like a younger version of Mike Vargas. They both project the same restless energy. But Ben has a crease in his forehead and an aura about him that doesn't shine. It's duller, like it's been roughed up with sandpaper.

Ben sees me watching him. He smiles.

My cheeks go red. Ro notices and giggles before licking the last of the whipped cream out of her cup.

· · ·

At lunch the next day, Kara is distant. Her face is pale. She looks like she didn't sleep.

"Are you okay?" I ask.

She blinks hard, like she's trying to hold back tears. "I think I'm getting a cold." She fake clears her throat.

"So . . . you know Ben? I've seen him wave to you a couple times." I try to sound light, like I'm making conversation—not like I'm trying to pump her for information, which I am.

Kara's head snaps up at his name. Her eyes are wide.

"It's none of my business," I mumble.

"It was a long time ago," Kara whispers. "I was like another person then."

"Oh . . . did something happen?"

She shakes her head. "I'm glad he's doing better."

And that's it. She stuffs a forkful of quinoa into her mouth and looks down at her lap as she chews.

I start to sigh, but then catch myself before Kara hears. I have learned exactly nothing.

I guess we both have secrets.


After school, Cam doesn't show. When the bus pulls up to Henderson's, flashing lights line the street in front of the Los Ranchitos. I jog over to them. Two police cars and an ambulance are blocking the right lane. Suds sits on the curb with a team of paramedics surrounding him.

I dash behind them through the open gate and into the office. I freeze in the doorway. Dad, Mike Vargas, and another man in an expensive suit are huddled around the table. Dad has an ice pack on his hand.

Mike Vargas snaps his head around. "Where's Cam?"

I shrug. I can't speak. My eyes are focused on the ice pack. Dad looks up at me and then turns away. "Jenny, go to your room, please," he says too calmly.

"Dad?" My voice cracks. Did Suds say something about me? Did he tell Dad?

"Jenny, it'll be okay. Just go to your room."

Mr. Vargas holds the door open for me. I glance over at him. He gives me a tight-lipped smile. Something bad has happened.

As I walk through the door, Cam's truck pulls up. Mr. Vargas thunders out behind me. Cam's eyes are huge. Fear leaks from his every pore.

"Where the hell were you?" Mr. Vargas yells. Cam gets out of the truck. I cringe. He won't be able to use picking me up as an excuse for his afternoon nap.

I need to get out of the line of fire, so I creep along the sidewalk to my door and open it, but I don't go all the way in.

Cam says nothing. Mike Vargas leans into him. His face is atomic red. "That asshole"—he points to Suds on the ground under the flashing lights—"came onto the property *because there was no one here to stop him.* There was a confrontation. Now he wants to sue." Mike Vargas lunges forward and plants a finger into Cam's chest. "My project is in jeopardy because of you."

I slide into my room feeling relieved. This wasn't my fault. It was Cam's.

The screech of metal against metal comes from the bathroom, followed by a shuffling sound. Ro thunks down into the bathtub. Her face is lit up with excitement when she comes around the corner. "Dude, your dad punched that guy. It was so sweet!"

"What?" Anxiety fills my stomach.

"The pervert was standing right outside, trying to look into your window. Your dad walked up and slugged him in the face." Ro beams with pride, as if it were her honor that has been defended.

"Wait. Suds was outside my window?" *I knew it was him.*

Ro nods with glee. "Suds started screaming that he was going to call the cops and sue and shut everything down. Then Cam's dad showed up with the guy in the suit. They talked to the cops while the pervert was writhing on the ground like he was dying." She laughs. "The cops were not sympathetic. I bet they wanted to punch him too."

I pull the curtains aside and look out the window. Those are Suds's smeary handprints; his cigarette butt. For a split second, I'm afraid of what could happen next. I imagine the police tracing everything back to Ohio. My whole life going up in flames.

But then a wave of relief washes over me.

It doesn't matter what Suds saw the night of the fire. There's no proof, and he's a loudmouth Peeping Tom. I'm a young, pretty girl in a bumblebee school uniform. The police will laugh in his face if he turns on me.

Or, at least, that's what I have to believe.

I watch as the ambulance takes him away. One of the cop

cars remains with the officer inside filling out paperwork. Cam is sitting in his truck—wide-awake—waiting for his father and the other man, who must be a lawyer, to come out of the office.

A shiny white news van pulls in through the open gate. "No," I whisper.

Cam cringes and sinks down into his seat. The door of the van opens, and a woman with giant sprayed hair, bright red lipstick, and a pantsuit that squeezes her cleavage to within an inch of its life jumps out.

Ro nestles up beside me at the window. The reporter makes eye contact with us. She smirks like she's beaten us to winning a prize. Her cameraman, already rolling, is hot on her heels. They walk to the office door and knock.

I hear the scuffing of chairs on the floor and raised voices through the wall. A moment later, the man in the slick suit comes out. He arranges himself like he's done this a hundred times. His back blocks the office door and keeps Dad and Mike Vargas inside.

The reporter points a mic in his face. His hands are clasped in front of him. His body language is calm. I can't make out what they're saying. The camera pans toward us in the window. I rip the curtains shut.

"Hey!" Ro says.

"This isn't a game," I snap, a little too harshly. I take a deep breath and recover. "If the project gets shut down, I'll have to go back to Ohio."

"So?" Ro asks. "Don't you have a nice mom and a sister and a house and stuff there?"

My stomach ties in a knot. Of course Ohio would look wonderful to Ro.

She leans in and lowers her voice. "Is it your stepfather?"

"No. Brian is Dudley Do-Right. He loves Hailey more than anything."

"So what's the problem?" Ro asks. I shake my head. I can't tell her. I can't tell her about the arson investigation in Ohio, the one that Brian covered up to save me. The one he's being investigated for now. If I go back to Ohio, he might turn me in.

I feel nauseated. My scar itches. I want to rip my arm off.

"I've just started school. I have a friend there," I say. "I have two friends here." Ro smiles broadly. "I just don't want to leave."

"Is your school friend the girl with the big glasses? The one who acted like a vampire when she stepped into the sun?"

I laugh. That's exactly what Kara looked like. I'm surprised Ro noticed. "Yeah, that's Kara. She has strict parents. They have her scared to do anything."

Outside, the news van door slams and the engine starts. Ro peeks out the window. "I don't want you to leave either."

When the local news comes on, Ro and I huddle together on the edge of the bed. I have the sound down low so that there's no chance of it being heard in the office.

We're the lead story.

"More trouble for the controversial Los Ranchitos redevelopment site. Let's go live to Las Piedras and our reporter, Lulu Alvarez."

The reporter pops up on the screen, holding her ear and nodding. The news van is now parked outside the gate. The light from the camera illuminates her made-up face. "That's right," she says. "We've learned that a man was attacked here today."

The scene cuts to a tape of Suds being unloaded at the hospital by the paramedics. "It's my freedom of speech, man. I want the people to know that this project is killing. This was a home for so many, and now they're out there dying in the cold."

The screen jumps back to the reporter. "That's local activist Jonathan Roybal, who was assaulted here today while exercising his constitutional rights. We asked for comment from Vargas Properties and Breland Construction, but they weren't very forthcoming."

The lawyer appears on the screen. He smiles. In the context, it makes him look like a shark, ready to snap at his prey. "Mr. Roybal was trespassing on property he has been asked to leave multiple times. My client removed him, as is his right."

He keeps talking, but it's muted, and the reporter comes back on looking doubtful. "Mr. Roybal was treated at the hospital and released. But it's clear that this plagued project is now in further jeopardy."

I flip the TV off. "How is it clear?" I yell. "They got it all wrong. Everyone's going to think my dad is a monster."

"They didn't mention that Suds is a perv, either," Ro chimes in.

I pace back and forth and rub my scar. I know Ro notices, but I can't stop. "I don't want to go home."

Ro stands up, wraps her arms around me, and gives me a hug. It doesn't feel as awkward as I thought it would.

"You won't have to go back to Ohio," she says.

No, I won't. I'll figure it out. Some way to stay.

I reluctantly put my arms around her too.

# 12

Breakfast is a quiet affair. It's just Dad and me. I glance one too many times at his red, swollen knuckles. He doesn't know that he could have put me in danger by handing Suds over to the police. He thought he was protecting me.

He moves his hand to his lap. "I'm sorry you have to see this, Jenny."

"It'll be okay, right? It was just a misunderstanding. That lawyer will clear it up." My voice is not confident. I'm pleading for information, for reassurance.

But Dad gives me none. He lifts a spoonful of cereal to his lips. Most of the milk drips back into the bowl. "Right," he says.

His eyes are as red as his knuckles. All the skin on his face sags. He didn't sleep last night.

I know what kept him up. I was awake thinking about it too. About what happened when I was five. When I couldn't see Dad for a long time; when Mom's explanation about where he was never quite made sense.

I step out of the office. Cam is using a shovel to dig holes on the perimeter of the property. It's possible the holes have a purpose—like to plant trees or shrubs—or it's possible that he's being punished. Either way, he looks miserable.

I rub my nose. The air still has a thin haze of smoke in it. My scar buzzes, but my stomach churns.

I didn't want to do it again. I fought hard against the urge and spent an hour staring at the lighter in the dresser drawer. With what happened between Dad and Suds and the thought of going back to Ohio, I needed . . . something. Something to make the itch stop. Something to keep me from exploding. To keep my mind sharp so I can figure out a way to stay.

I went to the other side of the river. No people. No one got hurt. No one saw.

The toolshed sits in the corner of the parking lot. Inside it, all the hand tools—printed with "Property of Breland Construction" in green ink—hang in neat rows on the walls. When I appear before Cam in my bee uniform, he moves faster than I've ever seen him move to put the shovel away and lock the shed behind him.

"Is your dad still mad?" I ask in the truck.

Cam glances at me with what he must think is his normal blank, non-emotive look, but the skin around his mouth tightens. I think what I'm seeing is shame—or embarrassment. Maybe there *is* a heart beating in that chest of his.

Looking at him now, I can't believe that I thought he was outside my window. Cam is just so . . . Cam. He's a hulking, unhappy, sleepy guy. But he's not dangerous. Maybe the lighter really was a gift.

I glance down at the cup holders and suck in a breath. The one that held the lighter is now empty. I sweep my eyes around the truck. I don't see it anywhere.

Good. No more temptation.

Something's been bothering me: no one is talking about the fires. The abandoned house in Ohio was front-page news. People talked about it everywhere I went.

It was hard at first. I had to keep my eyes down to keep my secret. But then I started to like listening to them speculate and theorize. I had answers no one else did. It gave me a power I hadn't felt before.

But here, it's like nothing. A couple of paragraphs in the local section.

"There was a big fire last night," I announce to see Cam's reaction.

Cam turns his head all the way to look at me. I cringe, because it means his eyes aren't on the road. "It happens," he says.

"Do you think someone did it on purpose?"

He sighs like this conversation is especially taxing and motions to the windshield. "No clouds in the sky." His eyes narrow and drill into me. "It wasn't *lightning*."

I shrink back against the door. He couldn't possibly know about Ohio. Or know that lightning was what Brian used in his report. But the coincidence gives me the chills.

I should be happy that no one is talking about the fires.

Not that it matters. I'm done—for real this time.

• • •

I lean against a bank of lockers and wait for Kara. She doesn't show up until right before the last bell. Her eyes are red, and her hair is barely brushed.

"Hi," she says, and half smiles. I move out of the way so that she can get into her locker. When she opens the door, a piece of paper slides out onto the floor.

It's facedown, so I can't see what it is when Kara picks it up. When she does, she turns a ghostly shade of white. Even though her body is perfectly still, I can see her breathing speed up.

"What? What is it?"

She crumples the paper and shoves it into her locker. "Nothing." She slams the door. When she faces me again, she looks the way I do in the mirror when my scar is itching and I know there are matches around—like she wants to run and fight at the same time.

"If you need to talk about something, I'm a good listener," I throw out to see if she'll spill what she's hiding.

"Thanks," she says meekly. "I have to get to class, but I'll see you at lunch, okay?"

"Okay." I add a fake smile to my face, but really, I want to grab her by the shoulders and demand she tell me what's going on.


Kara isn't at lunch. I text her and get no reply. I ask the table next to me if anyone has seen her, but they look at me blankly. Finally, Emma with the pink lips rolls her eyes and yells across the cafeteria that Kara went home sick. Her entourage laughs.

I'm texting Kara again when my homeroom teacher, Teresa, appears in front of me.

"Ready to go?" She radiates excitement. And she's wearing makeup. I've only ever seen her freshly scrubbed face in homeroom.

When she first handed me my packet about the free clinic, she said, "This one is so special to me," and clasped her hands over her heart.

I'm the sole student doing this project, so I've got no one to commiserate with about it. It's just me and flaky teacher Teresa.

The only good thing is that we get to leave school early on our project days.


We pull up to an old two-story Victorian house between several industrial buildings. People mill around out front. Shopping carts filled with dirty, cast-off objects line the side yard.

"We're here," Teresa announces. She unclicks her seat belt and bounces out of the car like we've arrived at an amusement park. She doesn't notice how the people outside stare at her. One man curls a lip in disgust at the wannabe-hippie do-gooder.

I hesitate to get out of the car. The look on the man's face changes. His eyes bore into me as he checks me out.

Note to self: change out of my uniform before coming next time.

The creep makes to follow us inside, but an older man wearing a dusty brown coat and a red baseball cap steps onto the porch, blocking his path. "I think you're fine out here." The creep glowers at him but slithers back to his spot along the wall.

"Good afternoon, Miss Teresa. Doc's waiting for you," the man says.

Inside, people sit in chairs or on worn sofas and flip through magazines or watch an old-school TV mounted to the ceiling. The floors are scuffed wood. Decorative sconces on the walls hide flickering light bulbs.

The air is filled with every smell a human body can produce, mixed with stale cigarette smoke and alcohol. I stagger back when it hits me. Teresa smiles sadly at me. "You'll get used to it."

It's not only people from the streets who are here. There's also a woman with two small children playing at her feet; a man dressed in thick jeans covered in mud, holding his arm against his body; a younger, clean-cut man in professional clothes.

I follow Teresa into an exam room with an office to the side. A man in a white lab coat is seated at the computer. His long graying hair is pulled back into a ponytail. Round reading glasses sit on his nose. When he turns and smiles at us, Teresa goes bright red.

He stands and takes off the glasses. Then he steps forward

and greets Teresa with a kiss on the cheek. She looks like she's about to pass out. I try to suppress a smile.

"This is Doc," she says.

He leans in to shake my hand. His grip is warm and soft, his eyes friendly. I instantly relax.

"Welcome, Jenny. We're so pleased to have you here."

"Let me give you the grand tour," Teresa says.

There isn't much that I haven't already seen. The exam room. The main floor, which is the waiting room and also a day shelter where people can come to get out of the cold and have a sandwich. Emergency exits: front door, back door. The second floor is room after room of donated clothes. Emergency exits: none—just the leap from a window.

Our last stop is the kitchen. It has industrial steel counters and shelves—almost all empty. "This is Jenny, our new volunteer," Teresa announces.

I pass through the door and see Ben. He gives me a huge smile.

Teresa glances back and forth between us. "So, I'll leave you with Ben. He can tell you what you're going to be doing around here."

I'm feeling overwhelmed, but I manage to squeak out a thank-you as the kitchen door closes.

"Are you following me?" I joke.

Ben laughs. "Well, I've lived here most of my life and you just got here, so no. You seem to be the one following me around." His eyes sparkle. It's enough to loosen some of the tension I've been holding in my gut all day.

"What should I do?" I ask.

Ben points to an industrial vat of peanut butter on a shelf. "In the afternoons we make sandwiches for people to take with them."

Ben leaves and comes back with his arms full of loaves of white bread. He tosses one to me. I almost catch it, but then it tumbles out of my arms and onto the floor. Great.

When I pop back up holding the bread, Ben has his lips rolled under like he's trying not to laugh. "I guess you're not going to Riverline on a football scholarship," he jokes.

"Riverline has a football team?" I ask with mock surprise.

Ben laughs now. I can't help but smile.

He dumps the rest of the loaves of bread onto the counter. The smile is wiped off my face when I see the expiration date on one. It was two weeks ago. I glance up at him.

"The grocery stores send us their expired food. We need all we can get. As long as it isn't moldy, we take it."

He hands me—carefully—a dull knife. "Don't use too much peanut butter. That's all we have for the next couple of months."

I slather thin strips of peanut butter on slice after slice of bread. Ben picks up a broom and starts sweeping. He's taken off his hoodie and is wearing a short-sleeved shirt underneath. He turns away from me, and I watch the muscles in his back and arms move gracefully under the fabric.

When he turns back around, I snap my head down and hope he didn't see me watching.

"I think you know my friend Kara," I say. Ever since Kara's

nonanswer about Ben, I've been dying to know what happened between them.

Ben stops sweeping. "How is she? Is she doing okay?" The caring concern in his voice is obvious. He's not inquiring about a casual friend.

"Yeah. She's great." I'm not going to tell him about what happened at her locker this morning.

"Good." He looks relieved. From both of their answers, I'm getting the impression that they dated at some point. Maybe they had one of those breakups where they say they're going to stay friends, but that doesn't work out and they end up avoiding each other. It would explain why Kara took off when she saw him in the truck.

Jealousy pricks inside me at the thought of the two of them together, which is stupid. I barely know Ben—or Kara. They had lives before me. They didn't pop into existence when I arrived.

Ben leans over the counter so that his eyes can meet mine. "I'm glad Kara has a friend like you."

And I'm hooked. I don't really know anything about Ben, but I want more. More smiles, more sparkly eyes.

My face is burning. I spin around to the sink and rinse the knife.

"So what do you do in this town when you're not making lattes or peanut butter sandwiches?" I ask, hoping it sounds flirtatious. It probably doesn't.

"I'm sure Cam has told you all about my past." His voice is still light.

I turn back around. "No. Cam doesn't talk much."

Ben shrugs. "I work at the coffee shop. I live in the apartments above it. I volunteer here."

"But you're Mike Vargas's nephew. Couldn't you be making tons of money working for him?" I remember too late what Cam said about Ben and his uncle not speaking.

Ben's body goes rigid. His face grows dark.

I focus back on the bread. "It's none of my business," I mumble.

"It's okay. I—"

Commotion fills the main room.

"Get Doc now!" a voice I recognize yells. It makes my hair stand on end.

Ben's eyes are wide with alarm. "Stay here."

I wait until he's gone before I creep forward to look out the kitchen door. Suds is flailing his arms, keeping Ben back several feet from him. The police didn't do anything about Suds looking in my window. They just took him to the hospital so he would stop making a scene on the sidewalk at the Los Ranchitos.

"Doc. Now!" Suds yells again.

Doc comes out of the exam room. He removes his reading glasses, folds them, and slides them into his front pocket.

Suds drops his arms. Doc nods to Ben, who steps back.

"What's the problem, Mr. Roybal?" Doc's voice is gentle and polite.

I cringe as Suds points to the shiner that Dad gave him. "The pain, Doc. I need something for the pain."

"I can give you ibuprofen and an ice pack. But that's it. You know I don't have anything stronger here."

Suds doesn't back away. "I know what you're hiding. You've got pills back there. The good ones."

A sudden coughing spasm shakes his whole body.

Doc places a hand on Suds's shoulder. "Mr. Roybal, that cough sounds bad. Let me help you."

Suds shrugs Doc's hand off. "You don't want to help me. You don't want to help any of us. You've got pills, but you're saving them all for yourself."

Doc flinches. Suds points an angry finger at Doc's chest. "That's right. I know all about you."

Ben leaps forward to place himself between Suds and Doc. Doc grabs his shoulder to hold him back.

Suds comes chest to chest with Ben. Ben's eyes shoot daggers at him. One of them is going to take a swing. But then Suds backs off. He must realize that he's no match for Ben.

"Fuck this," he says. He turns like he's going to leave, but his eyes meet mine, peeking out from the kitchen doorway.

Suds starts to laugh. "I seen you, girl."

Ben and Doc spin around and look at me.

Suds makes a flicking motion with his thumb. "I seen you in the trees."

My heart pounds so loudly in my ears that it mutes his cackle of laughter, which dissolves into another coughing fit.

Ben's fury can't be contained any longer. He puts both his hands on Suds, and pushes him out the door.

As soon as Suds is gone, everyone goes back to what they were doing. Doc gives Ben a light pat on the back that I think is supposed to be a signal for *Calm down now,* and walks into the exam room. Ben turns toward the kitchen. I jump back to my spot along the counter and pick up my peanut butter knife.

Ben crashes through the door. His face is red, and all his muscles tense. "Are you okay?" he asks.

I nod and try to come up with an explanation for why Suds would have seen me—one that doesn't involve the truth. But Ben seems too wrapped up in his own head to process what Suds said about me.

Ben picks up the broom and starts sweeping again. "Suds likes to make trouble. He's the kind of person who causes so much trouble that he eventually gets his way," he says. "Someone needs to put a stop to that," he adds to himself.

Doc sticks his head into the kitchen. "Jenny, your ride is here."

I wash the peanut butter residue off my hands and dry them with a paper towel. I expect to walk out alone, but Ben appears at my side.

When we enter the main room, all eyes lock onto me in my school uniform. Ben puts a protective hand on my back. My stomach flutters.

Outside, Cam is waiting in the truck. He looks momentarily startled to see Ben and me standing together—so close that Ben's body warms mine. I don't need my coat.

"Thanks," I say to Ben. "I'll see you next time? Or maybe

at the coffee shop?" My voice is full of expectation. It turns my cheeks hot. I walk fast over to the truck and get in before Ben can respond.

Cam glances over at me and wrinkles his nose. "Why do you smell like peanut butter?"

# 13

"You smell like peanut butter," Ro says. She's lounging on my bed watching TV. I pull the curtains aside and look out into the parking lot. Dad, Mike Vargas, and the lawyer are having a serious-looking discussion.

Ro sidles up beside me. "The police came back. Then some young, cheap-looking lawyer handed your dad a stack of papers."

I drop the curtains, close my eyes, and swallow hard to shove the bile down into my stomach. *What if they find something that incriminates me?*

"The motel will be fine," Ro reassures me.

She has no idea what I'm really thinking, but I nod in agreement.

"You never told me what was so bad in Ohio," she says.

I sigh and sit down. "My sister Hailey started a fire." Ro leans forward with keen interest. "She didn't mean to. She was trying to surprise Mom with dinner. A towel or something must have fallen onto the hot stove. She started screaming." I take a deep breath. At any moment, tears could spill out of my eyes. "It was like I was back at my friend's sleepover again. Like I was seven, hiding in the bathroom in that burning house, smelling the smoke, feeling the heat. Listening to everyone scream as they died."

I wipe the water off my cheeks. "Mom put out the fire in the kitchen and found me curled up in a corner. Now it's all I see whenever I close my eyes: Hailey being overcome by smoke and flames. I was completely powerless. I didn't try to save her. Anything could have happened, and it would have been my fault. I had to leave. I can't be around her."

"I'm glad you came here," Ro says with a smile. "I've never had a real friend like you."

I blink at the word "real." Both because it's a strange thing to say and because I'm lying to her. Would a *real* friend do that?

Hailey did start that fire, and I did have a panic attack. But watching those flames dance in front of me in the kitchen had awakened the monster. I split in half. One half is terrified of fire—of someone getting hurt or killed by it. The other half wants to possess it. Control it. Hold that power in my hands. Decide what it does.

The night of the kitchen fire is when my scar started to itch. I'd felt it before, but only in little bursts. We never had candles in the house. We didn't have a fireplace. Our jack-o'-lanterns were stuffed with LED lights at Halloween. There was no fire in my world. I started having nightmares after the house fire, and Mom didn't want to upset me.

One night, it was raining. A lightning storm. Everyone

was asleep. The thunder covered the sound of my footsteps as I crept through the house. Brian had an emergency kit. In it was a waterproof tube of matches. Mom probably didn't want me to know they were there, but Brian wanted to tell everyone what to do in case there was a disaster and he wasn't home. He'd showed me and Hailey the kit. He showed us what was inside.

I shuffled down the street in the rain with my hand covering my scar. I didn't know where I was going, but I followed my feet to the abandoned house.

The house was notorious for being a place to go get high on the weekends. It was a Tuesday night. I crawled through the broken back door.

I called out. No one answered. I went from room to room. I checked every closet and every bathtub. If someone had been there, I would have turned around and walked right back out into the rain. But no one was.

It was easy. I remembered how to do it from when I was seven: Light a match. Drop it on the carpet. Light another, toss it at the curtains. Soon the house was glowing around me. The flames chewed up the wall, and I felt something I never had before. I felt powerful. I had done that. I had decided when and where to summon the fire monster. I held him in my hands. I told him where he could go. I told him he couldn't hurt anyone.

When it was too hard to breathe, I slipped back outside. Fat raindrops sizzled as they hit the burning house. I heard sirens in the distance.

My feet skipped me home. I was elated and drained and satisfied. The itch in my scar had calmed. It was the most perfect I had ever felt.

Then I opened the door to my house. The light flipped on in the living room. My high disappeared. Brian sat on the couch in his uniform, holding the unzipped emergency kit.

It was a stupid mistake; in my haste to go do what I was going to do, I'd left it out.

"You're supposed to be asleep." My voice came out resigned. I was too spent from the excitement to fight for myself. I should have made up a secret boyfriend. Anything to explain why I was shivering and dripping water on the floor.

"One of the guys is out sick. I'm being called in for a two-alarm house fire." He zipped the bag and stood.

I watched in terrified silence as he walked to the hall closet and placed it back on the top shelf.

The memory brings a tear to my eye. I wipe it away.

Ro puts an arm around me. "It'll be okay." She rests her head on my shoulder. "You still smell like peanut butter."

I sniffle and wipe another tear away. Then we both start to laugh.

"Do you want to stay for dinner and watch a movie?" I ask when we have caught our breath.

"No." Ro sighs dramatically. "I have a test tomorrow. I have to go home and study."

"Oh. Okay." I try to hide the surprise in my voice. Ro never mentions school.

She collects her coat from the floor and bounces toward the bathroom.

"See you tomorrow," she announces, and slips out the window.

Then I'm all alone with my thoughts. I lie down and let fire and the image of Suds seeing me in the trees swirl around and around in my head.

# 14

I wake up in the morning to voices outside my room. "My client has nothing to say."

I jump up and rip open the curtains. Two police officers, a man and the woman I saw with Allen, stand outside the office. Dad's lawyer blocks them from going in.

"Sir," the woman says, "this is serious. A man is dead."

My heart starts to race. I can't see Dad. Only the lawyer.

"My client has nothing to say."

The male officer points over his shoulder. "We need to look in the toolshed, and then we'll be on our way."

The lawyer does not budge. "Do you have a warrant?"

The cop sighs. "We got information that the murder weapon was painted with a green logo. If you let us into the shed, this can all be over quickly."

"Let them look," Dad calls from the office. "I have nothing to hide."

When I hear his voice, my lungs relax and suck in air again. He's okay. The police won't find anything, and they'll leave. This is going to be okay.

The four of them make their way across the parking lot.

I grab my coat and open my door a crack. When they don't turn around, I open it all the way and run to a bulldozer that hasn't been put into place for the day's work yet. I peek over the tread of the back tire.

"Who has keys to this shed?" the female officer asks.

The lawyer glances a warning at Dad, but he doesn't pay attention. "Me; Mike Vargas; his son, Cam; and our architect. That's it."

The two cops walk around inspecting the shed and yank on the door. It's locked.

Dad produces his key. The lawyer takes it from him and makes a show of holding it up for the police.

The female cop unlocks the door. All four of them look inside. The two cops glance at one another. Dad gasps. I don't know what's going on, but in the line of hanging tools, only the shovel Cam had been using to dig holes around the property after he got in trouble is missing.

The cops look at the lawyer. His face is a solid wall, blank of emotion. "We'd like to talk to the others who have a key."

The cops and the lawyer walk away talking about appointments and police stations. Dad stands with his mouth open, looking into the shed. He rubs his hand over his face.

I creep forward. "Dad? What's going on?"

He spins around. "Everything's fine," he says. That doesn't answer my question. I don't move. "The guy who would protest outside the fence. He, uh, passed on last night."

Passed on. Dad is talking to me like I'm five. The police wouldn't be here if he had coughed himself to death.

I glance over my shoulder at the police car and lower my voice. "But what about—"

Dad cuts me off. "It'll be fine, Jenny. I'm not hiding anything."

"Okay," I say, but I'm not convinced. I point to my room. "I should get ready for school."

As soon as my door shuts, I flip on the TV. The reporter from before is parked in the lot near the cottonwoods where Cam takes his naps.

A picture of a better-kempt Suds fills the screen. ". . . where a man was brutally murdered last night. Police aren't releasing many details, but he seems to have been beaten to death with a shovel." She points over her shoulder to a flurry of activity and police tape behind her. "As you can see, this is still an active crime scene."

I flip the TV off. If Suds is no longer around to sue, that means my secret is safe. The Los Ranchitos is still a go.

Assuming no one here murdered him, of course.

I laugh out loud, imagining little blond Monica creeping through the woods at night. And Cam? Even though Suds got him in trouble, killing someone seems like it requires a lot more initiative than I've ever seen him take. Dad? No. Dad didn't do it. He wouldn't. Mike Vargas? I hardly know him, but I can't imagine he would take that kind of risk. He's a good businessman. He's built an empire; you don't do that by killing people—at least, not in such a public way.

Suds won't be missed. I smile in spite of myself. I don't have to worry about him trying to start something by telling the cops what he saw me do in the trees. I can sleep without worrying about someone standing outside my window.

When I'm ready for school, I go into the office to grab a bagel to eat on the way. Cam is seated across from the lawyer. His keys are on the table between them.

"When was the last time you saw it?" the lawyer asks, losing his patience with the heap of man-boy in front of him.

Cam shrugs. "I don't know. Maybe a couple days ago?"

"And you haven't left your keys unattended at any point?"

"No," Cam says with such confidence that it has to be a lie. I know it is. I've seen them lying on the seat next to him when he's asleep in the truck. He sleeps like the dead. It wouldn't take much to swipe them.

I press my back into the door. The Los Ranchitos isn't out of the woods yet—not if Cam's key is missing. Cam looks up at me and smiles. "Ready for school?" He wants to get away from the lawyer, who's inspecting his every facial expression.

When I climb into the truck, Cam's smile is gone.

Kara is standing in the middle of the hallway at school. She never answered any of my texts about why she disappeared after that paper fell out of her locker.

"Are you feeling better?" I ask.

She nods, but she doesn't step forward to open her locker.

"I went to my service project at the free clinic," I say. "It turns out Ben works there too."

I wait to see her reaction. I need to know more about the

two of them. Ben and I spent one afternoon together, so it's not like we have any sort of relationship, but the little spark of jealousy returns after thinking about them together.

Kara doesn't move. Her eyes are fixed on her locker door. "That's nice," she mumbles.

The bell rings.

Kara takes a breath and starts spinning her lock.

"Yeah. He seems really nice."

Still no reaction from her.

The locker pops open, and a piece of paper falls to the floor. This time it's faceup. Before Kara can dive for it, I see a stick figure drawing of a family: a mom, a dad, and a child in a dress. The mom is holding a baby that's been Xed out in red Sharpie.

"What *is* that?" I ask.

Kara shoves it into her locker. She turns to me and smiles with her lips, but the rest of her face is tight. She waves my question away. "Just a stupid assignment I have for one of my classes."

"What class?" It's just a question, but her eyes turn glassy. She looks away and fumbles with things in her locker.

"So you're working with Ben?" She changes the subject.

"Uh, yeah."

"That's good."

I have no idea what's happening. Kara closes her locker. "I'll see you at lunch."

"Sure," I say, and try to smile, but I'm getting annoyed with her for keeping things from me.

And being so blatantly obvious about it.

What is so bad that she just can't tell me? And what's with those papers falling out of her locker?

And—what I really care about—why is she avoiding talking about Ben?

My stomach flips over. She freaked after she saw him in the truck the day Cam took Ro and me for coffee.

At lunch, Kara's going to have to tell me what happened between them. Period.

Kara's not at lunch. A guy in her homeroom tells me she jumped up and ran out like she was going to puke. She never returned to class.

After school, I exit the building and stop dead in my tracks. Ro is across the street having an animated conversation with pink-lipped Emma. They're sharing a cigarette.

Emma sees me and glares.

I stomp across the street to Ro. Emma takes a drag from the cigarette and holds it next to her mouth. The filter's stained by her lipstick.

"Um, hi?" I say to them.

"I'll see you later," Emma says, handing the cigarette back to Ro.

I watch her walk away. "I thought you said you didn't smoke. And how do you know Emma? Why are you even here?" I whisper-scream.

"I don't, I don't, and waiting for you." She drops the cigarette and stamps it out. "That girl thinks she's bad, but it's an act. She wouldn't last five minutes on the street." Ro pulls another cigarette and a lighter out of her pocket. I flinch. "They're good for getting information."

"What could you possibly want to know from Emma?"

Ro gazes at the last of the students exiting the building. "She knows someone from my school. Where's your friend with the glasses?"

"She's sick. Why?"

Ro steps back from me. "I hope it's not contagious."

"I really don't think so," I mutter. "Where's Cam?"

Ro laughs. "Sleeping in his truck. That's why I came to meet you. So you wouldn't have to ride the bus by yourself." She smiles proudly, like this bit of unselfishness has made her day.

We walk to the bus stop. I'm mad at Cam for not showing up again. But then there's a part of me that's relieved. His lost key and the missing shovel—the weapon that could have killed Suds—make him look like a suspect. But that's ridiculous. Right now he's probably sleeping in his truck in broad daylight. Would someone guilty of a murder do that?

When we get off the bus at Henderson's, Ro grabs my arm. "I want to show you something."

We walk into the trees and turn away from the artists' colony. My uniform collects a million burrs as we clomp through the underbrush, sending birds and small animals scattering.

Ro stops in front of three large rocks about ten feet from the river. They look like they were moved here on purpose. There aren't any other rocks around.

Ro looks down at them. "I've never shown anyone this

before." I think I see a hint of redness in her cheeks, and she won't look up again and meet my eyes.

She kneels and pushes aside a pile of leaves. Under the rocks is a hole. If I had stumbled upon it, I would think it was some sort of animal den. Ro plunges her hand inside, making me cringe.

She pulls out a black plastic trash bag and sits down on the ground. I hesitate. If I sit, I'm going to get my uniform dirty. Ro looks up at me. Her eyes are glassy, like she's on the verge of tears. This is hard for her. I know what she expects me to do, so I plop down.

"These are my special things. All the things I have left over from before."

She opens the bag and pulls out a bright blue scarf with silhouettes of purple birds printed around the edges. She holds it up to her nose and breathes it in. "This was my mom's."

She hands it to me. It's polyester. Cheap, but made to look expensive. "It's pretty," I say, and hand it back to her.

"It's all I have of her. I have to keep it here so my aunt doesn't throw it out when she goes through my room." She looks up at me with searching eyes, like she's waiting for me to ask.

"What happened to your mom?"

Ro looks away. "She couldn't cope. Some bad things happened to us. We didn't have any place to go. There was this bench on the Plaza in Santa Fe. We were sleeping on it. When the cops came to tell us to leave, she was gone. I was all alone." She rubs her eyes with her palms. "I freaked out, thinking something had happened to her. I tried to get the cops to look for her, but they wouldn't. They told me she took off, and then they hauled me away to the group home."

I suck in a breath. "I'm sorry."

"One day my aunt showed up, and they handed me over to her. You know the rest." She takes the scarf and shoves it back into the bag. Then she ties the bag and folds it so that no dirt or water can get in and replaces it in the hole under the rocks.

I have my problems. I worry about Hailey, and I worry about Dad, but my whole family is around. No one has ever left me—not even Brian.

I need a second to myself. To breathe and to absorb what she told me. I stand up and take a step around the far side of the rocks.

Ro doesn't wait. She starts to head back toward the Los Ranchitos. I'm worried that she thinks I'm judging her or that I'll avoid her now that I've heard her story.

I jog to catch up to her. "I'm glad we met," I say. And I am. Being with Ro helps calm the itching in my scar. For a while, anyway.

"I used to have a friend," Ro says out of the blue. "A best friend. I told her all my secrets."

I wait for her to continue the story, but she doesn't.

"What happened?"

Ro shrugs. "She decided we weren't friends anymore."

After the fire when I was seven, I never got invited over to play at anyone's house. I don't think the parents meant to be mean. They just didn't know what to say, what to do with me. So I get it. Having friends and then not.

When we step onto the access road, motion in the trees

catches my attention. I spin around, but all I see is a flash of blue. The same blue I've seen behind me before.

"What?" Ro asks.

The trees are motionless, like it was my imagination. But it wasn't. I know it wasn't.

"Nothing," I say to Ro, and try to smile.

# 15

"...have a description of the person setting fires in the bosque."

I drop my curling iron onto the granite bathroom counter and run to the TV.

The fire chief appears on the screen. "A witness has come forward. A person in dark clothing was seen running from the area last night. This person was of slight build and did not have any other distinguishing characteristics that we know of. If you have any information, please call the police. Extra patrols will be out in the bosque night and day."

The screen snaps back to the anchor. I click off the TV. My skin crawls. I wanted the fires to get more attention. Now they are.

Last night the flash of blue in the trees kept running through my head over and over again. My scar took control. I watched my hands dig through the drawer and find the lighter. I watched them start the fire on the other side of the river.

I've put myself in a dangerous position. Someone saw me running away.

*It doesn't matter,* I tell myself. *I'm done.*

I tossed the lighter into the flames last night. There's nothing in my room to tempt me. Nothing to make me slip up again.

The anxiety and adrenaline of almost getting caught make my scar twinge. It makes my mind send me images from when I was seven, sitting in the bathtub of the burning house. Not knowing if I was going to live or die.

Hailey. The spike of fear I get when I think about something happening to her shoots through me. I need to talk to her.

Mom doesn't answer FaceTime. I can't breathe. My heart flutters with panic. Maybe the house burned down in the night and the police haven't come to notify me yet. My mind sees it—the fire. It races through the living room and kitchen, into Mom and Brian's room. Into Hailey's. I gasp for air. My lungs feel rough and scratchy, like they're filling with smoke.

I need Hailey's hat. I need to grip it between my fingers. Hold a piece of her.

I run to the dresser and dig through it. The hat's not there. I wasn't wearing it last night. My decision to go out was too impulsive to put on my whole disguise.

I throw everything out onto the floor. *Where is it?*

The bathroom window slides open. Ro thunks in and wanders into the bedroom. "I turned off your curling iron. It's not safe to leave it on like that." She stops in the doorway. "What are you doing?"

I run to her. "My hat. Do you have it?"

"What hat?"

I grab her arm and pull her into the mess on the floor. "My hat. It's pink with butterfly eyes."

"I don't know what you're talking about. I don't have a hat."

I collapse. They could be dead. Burned to death. Hailey and Mom. They might have screamed for me. But I never came.

"Are you going to school today?" Ro asks.

I glance at the clock. It's seven-fifteen. My head snaps over to Ro. "It's nine-fifteen in Ohio."

"If you say so."

"It's nine-fifteen in Ohio. Hailey's at school. Mom's at work. That's why they aren't answering." My lungs open and let oxygen in again. My family is okay. I grab Ro and pull her into a big, relieved hug. She smells like outside air with the slightest hint of woodsmoke. I pull away from her.

"Are you high?" she asks.

I shake my head. "I need to get to school." I grab my bag. "If you find my hat, leave it on the bed, okay?"

Then I walk out the door before she can respond.

My job at the clinic today is to greet people coming in, take their names, and offer them one of the many pamphlets on the table in front of me.

Every moment I sit here, I'm painfully aware that I'm not in the kitchen with Ben.

I straighten the birth control pamphlets and rest my head in my hands. This is so boring.

Ben comes out of the kitchen and stops behind me. His warmth brushes across my back. He's wearing a T-shirt again today, and when he reaches out to take the sign-in clipboard, the muscles in his arms contract. I feel a little buzz.

The door opens. The men milling around the room scatter to the far corners. I sit up straighter and draw in a sharp breath. Ben puts the clipboard down.

"Can I help you?" he asks the two police officers—the ones who were at the Los Ranchitos.

"We need to speak to Dr. Moreno," the male cop says. In my peripheral vision, I see Ben's fist clench.

"He's with a patient."

The male cop smiles. "We'll wait."

Ben leaves and goes into the exam room.

"So, what's your job here?" the male cop asks me, and picks up a diabetes pamphlet. The woman is still looking at me, like she knows me from somewhere but can't place me.

"I volunteer. For school."

"That's great. They need help around here." He puts the pamphlet down and looks at the people in the waiting room. Most of them pretend to be locked in conversation or reading magazines. Some simply face the wall.

Doc comes out of the clinic drying his hands with a paper towel. Ben is on his heels. "What can I do for you, Officers?"

"We're investigating the murder of Jonathan Roybal, also known as Suds. We'd like to ask you some questions," the woman says.

Doc's face falls. "That was a terrible thing. Please, come

to my office." He gives Ben a pointed look before leading the officers away.

"Suds got what was coming to him," Ben says under his breath. I turn around, surprised by the bitterness in his voice.

"Why?"

"Your first day wasn't the only time he came in here looking for pills. He threatened us more times than I can count. Doc's worked too hard to be treated like that."

"Do the police think Doc did it?" I can't believe Doc would even squish a spider.

"Probably not, but they have to talk to him, like every other time Suds came in here and caused trouble."

Ben stands guard by the clinic door. No one is coming in with the cop car parked outside.

When Doc walks the officers out, the look of pain is still on his face. I don't know what the cops think, but I believe he's truly upset by Suds's death.

He gives Ben a reassuring pat on the shoulder. "Who's next?"


"Did you know your dad is a criminal?" Ro asks when I open my door.

I freeze. "What?"

"It was on the early news." She points to the TV. "He almost killed someone. They showed his mug shot and everything."

I let my bag drop to the floor. This can't be happening. Not now. Not with the murder investigation. Not with this being Dad's chance. Everyone's going to know. What will happen to the Los Ranchitos once they do? My stomach contracts, sending its contents upward.

I run to the bathroom and fall to my knees on the floor, but nothing happens. Ro follows me in.

"So does this mean you knew or not?"

"I know," I squeak. "It happened before the fire, when I was five. My mom tried to hide it from me. She said that Dad was going to work on a job far away, and I wouldn't be able to see him for a while. I could tell that something was wrong by the look on her face, but I was too young to understand. I just remember worrying that something bad was going to happen to Dad while he was gone. As soon as I was able to go on the internet by myself, I figured out he had been in prison for assault."

I lay my head down on the towel covering the cold marble floor and look up at Ro. "My dad didn't kill Suds."

Ro puts her hands up. "Whoa. I never said he did."

"He's not violent. He beat that guy up to save a woman." He just didn't stop throwing punches once the woman was safe. "My mom testified in his defense at the trial, even though they were already divorced."

Ro sits down next to me and shrugs. "Everyone has a past. Plus, the world needs fewer perverts. I'm glad Suds is dead."

She says it so calmly that I'm taken aback. I sit up. Her face is completely blank. Then it breaks into a smile. "I think I found your hat," she says.

She jumps up and pulls it from the dresser drawer. Her nose wrinkles. "Have you been wearing it outside? It smells like smoke."

I grab the hat from her and nod. "Everything outside smells like smoke." I put on my saddest, most pathetic face, and hold the bridge of my nose like my head suddenly hurts.

Ro cringes and looks away. "Sorry," she says.

I believe that she really is. She won't bring up smoke—or my hat—again.

# 16

I don't want to go into the office. I've been standing outside the door for so long that the winter cold has seeped through my clothes. My hands are numb, but I can't face Dad.

"Go inside, Jenny," Monica says behind me. "He wants to talk to you."

I don't want to talk to him.

Monica steps around me and opens the door. She puts a hand on my back and pushes. "Go."

Dad is seated at the table. Two plates of spaghetti sit in front of him. I slide into the chair across from him and look down at the congealing pasta. My stomach churns. The last thing I want to do right now is eat.

"I'm sorry you have to go through this again, Jenny," Dad says. His voice is soft and caring. There's no anger in it. He made peace with his past a long time ago. He sighs. "It follows me everywhere. It's why I had to build my own company. No one wanted to hire a convicted felon."

I pick up a fork and poke at the spaghetti—anything to avoid eye contact with him. If I get caught setting fires, that could be me one day. Who would want to employ someone who might burn down their business?

"Now that it's on the news, is Mr. Vargas going to fire you?"

"No. I never hid anything from him. He's known since our first meeting. The work is coming along well. The investors are happy. And luckily," he says with a chuckle, "no one else wants to work on this motel."

"What about the police?" I suck in a shaky breath and will myself not to cry. "Do they think you killed Suds?" Are they going to come bursting in with handcuffs for Dad and a plane ticket back to Ohio for me?

Dad reaches across the table and covers my hand with his. "No. This is going to turn out fine. Mike's lawyer is the best around. The police had to come check things out because of my past, but they've left us alone since then." He pauses and looks away, blinking hard. "Jenny, I want you to know that I didn't do it. I didn't kill him."

"I know," I whisper. I reclaim my hand and pick up the plates. "We should reheat these." I whip around to face the microwave before he has time to see what I'm thinking. He's not guilty of anything, but I am.


I take a sleeping pill. My heart won't stop pounding. My scar won't stop itching. Every sound sends my eyes to the window. I'm being ridiculous. There's no one there. It was always Suds. Ro saw him trying to look inside the day Dad punched him.

But my mind won't let go of the image of someone stand-ing outside.

Before I let chemical-induced sleep take me, I have to check. I creep up to the curtain and lift it just enough to see out.

No one is standing on the sidewalk under the bare bulb.

Motion in the blackness beyond the blub.

A flash of blue disappearing into the night.


School is horrible. Even after popping the sleeping pill, I didn't sleep much. Now I'm fuzzy-headed and exhausted.

Kara is out sick, so I have to face the pointing and whispers about my dad in the hallways alone. This school isn't for kids like me. The other students have two-parent homes in the hills. They go on family vacations to Florida. They get cars for birthday presents.

I get looks like I'm a criminal. Like I'm the daughter of the guy who killed a man. Like I'm back to being seven and a museum specimen on display.


Cam actually shows after school. He is fully awake and parked across the street.

A group of girls standing in the doorway of Riverline Prep point at the logo on the side of the truck and start to whisper. Cam rolls down his window, sticks his blue-coated arm out, and gives them the finger.

I flinch—not at him flipping them the bird; those girls deserved it. It's his blue coat. Why do I keep seeing that shade of blue everywhere? I saw it last night. Or did I? The pill was already in my system. It could have been my imagination.

But then why do I keep imagining the same thing?

I go back into school and dash out the back emergency exit.

At the bus stop, I hide in the shadows of a building. Cam's truck drives by, his eyes scanning the empty bench. I rub my scar.

When the bus drops me off near the Los Ranchitos, Cam's truck isn't in the parking lot. He could still be out looking for me. But if there's really nothing more going on and he's just trying to be a good employee, he'll give up soon and come back.

I wait, but his truck never shows. He's not looking for me here. I start to head toward the river. If I'm right, I know exactly where I'll find Cam. If he really was outside my window last night, if it's his coat I've been seeing everywhere, he'll look for me in the trees.

Even though I don't have on my special soft-soled shoes, I've learned how to walk quietly through the leaves and underbrush. If anyone were ahead of me, they would hear nothing more than the birds and the squirrels hunting for food.

When I get to the river, I sit down and wait.

Most of me is scared that Cam is going to come through the trees in front of me. Part of me is terrified that he won't. If it's not him, it's someone else.

Heavy tromping footsteps. I get ready to jump up. Jump up to confront Cam, or jump up and run.

The crackle of a police radio.

Dammit.

I stand as soon as I see Allen the police intern approach. He starts, but then a smile cuts across his face.

"Hi, Jenny. Are you out here bird-watching?"

I nod. "Why are you here?" My tone is not friendly.

He doesn't seem to notice. "The arsonist. I'm on patrol."

My lack of sleep makes it impossible to hide my frustration with him being here. "You are not a cop." My voice is shrill. He's messing up my whole plan. If Cam sees us together, he'll hightail it out of here.

Allen shrugs. "I'm a concerned citizen."

I put a hand on my hip and glare at him.

He sighs. "I'm failing the program. My supervisor said in her review that I was"—he makes finger quotes—"'arrogant and uncooperative.' She's a bitch." He doesn't apologize when he sees me flinch. "I can't fail out of the program. My family will never let me live it down. This is what I was born to do."

"So you're going to catch the arsonist?" My tongue trips on that word: "arsonist." It's such a harsh, grimy-sounding word. A word for criminals. Criminals who hurt people.

"I've been tracking him. It's only a matter of time until he screws up."

My body goes tense. "What do you mean you've been tracking him?"

Allen winks. "I know where he's going to set the next fire. He picks the same kind of place every time. There's only one place like that left within walking distance. No one's seen a car drive away from the burn sites, so he must be on foot."

I will myself to stop moving, even though every cell in my body is yelling at me to run away.

"I'll be waiting the next time he shows."

"How are you going to be out here all night? Don't you have school?" My voice shakes. I don't let my hand reach up for my scar.

He shrugs. "When I catch the arsonist, no one is going to care that I fell asleep in history class."

"Do you have a blue coat?" The words burst out, as if my mouth can't hold back my panic any longer.

Allen raises an eyebrow. "No. Why?" *Yeah, Jenny. Why?*

"I, uh . . ." *Think faster.* "I found one the other day, and I thought it might be yours." I suck down a gulp of air. "I should go." I take two steps forward, and I point to the Los Ranchitos, but my brain can't come up with anything else.

Allen crouches to look at the ground. The ground where my footprints are.

I walk away casually, even though my heart is leaping from my body with each beat. No matter how badly my scar itches, I have to stop my nighttime forays across the river. I'm too close to getting caught.

I lean against a tree to catch my breath. A flock of birds suddenly lifts off from a tree behind me.

Every hair on my body stands on end. My breath speeds up again. It's not Allen.

I slowly turn around. There it is. In the spaces between bare branches.

Blue.

It takes off.

I'm faster.

I have so much adrenaline coursing through me that if I lifted my arms, I could fly.

He stumbles, and I'm right there. Right there sinking my nails into Cam's puffy blue coat.

"Why the fuck are you following me?" I yell.

He puts his hands up in surrender. He looks like he's trying to come up with something. I see the wheels turning. Then I see them stop. He's got nothing.

I'm not letting go until I get an answer.

"Monica," he says. "She's paying me a hundred bucks a week to keep an eye on you."

I don't let go. "Why?" I snarl.

He holds his hands up again. "I don't know. She said you're a threat to the project. I'm supposed to report back if you do anything suspicious."

I release him. Monica? There's no way Monica could know anything. Dad knows about my panic attacks around Hailey, that's it. Mom wouldn't have told him more than that, not after she gave Hailey and me a lecture about how the police asking about Brian was "private" and not to be discussed with anyone.

Maybe Monica just assumes that my sudden arrival at the Los Ranchitos means I'm trouble?

"What have you told her?" I ask softly.

Cam smooths out his coat. "Just that you're generally annoying. But I'm done. I'll find another way to make money. This"—he flashes a hand at me—"isn't worth it."

"You put a hundred-dollar bill in the tip jar at the coffee

shop." When I glance up at him, he turns red and looks down at his feet. "You gave that to Ben. Have you been giving all Monica's money to Ben?"

"It's none of your business."

I think that's a yes. I lean against a tree to hold myself up. I'm flooded with feelings—so many I can't identify them all.

"I'm not a threat," I whisper. Then I look up at him. "Keep taking Monica's money. You don't have to worry about me. I'll behave."

I feel myself flinch at my own words. A strange look passes over Cam's face. "You'll *behave*?"

He's not asking for confirmation; he's asking why I said that. Why I need to reassure him. Like maybe there's really a reason Monica is having him follow me.

"You don't need to watch me. I like to go for walks. You like to sleep in your truck. There's no reason for Monica or my dad—or Mike Vargas—to know every little thing we do."

Cam rolls his lips under. I see the debate raging in his head. He doesn't want his father to know about his work-time naps.

"Okay," he says. "But you have to show after school."

"You too." Our eyes meet. A deal is reached.

We walk back to his truck without speaking. I get in. We have appearances to keep up now.


When the truck pulls up to the office, Cam and I both inhale sharply. The lawyer is getting out of his car. He turns and waves at us, all smiles.

We scramble out and follow the lawyer inside. Dad and Mr. Vargas look up from the plans on the table.

"All clear," the lawyer announces. "That son of a bitch Suds caused trouble all around town. The police will never figure out who killed him. And since there's no evidence against anyone here, it's all good." He looks at Dad. "And the assault charges have been dropped."

Dad glances over at me before standing to shake the lawyer's hand. Maybe now the cops will stay away, and we can pretend like none of this ever happened.

"Excellent," Mike Vargas chimes in. "And we're right on schedule. We should have this place ready for business by the beginning of June."

My stomach twists. Once the motel is ready for paying customers, Dad will have to move somewhere else. I don't know what will happen to me. One thing is for sure: I can't go back to Ohio. Not with Brian there watching my every move . . . if he even lets me come back at all.

# 17

I tried texting Kara first. Really, I did. I was going to ask her point-blank what happened with Ben. If, to be a good friend, I should stay away from him.

She ignored me. Again.

I know she saw my text. It's the weekend—there's no way she's gone hours without checking her phone. I don't know what her problem is, but I'm not going to let it bother me. It's a beautiful March day. The sun is out and little buds are starting to appear on trees.

And I'm going to see Ben, whether she wants me to or not.

I got Cam to tell me that Ben works on Saturdays. Ever since the arrangement we came to in the cottonwoods, things have been much more cordial between us.

I take the bus as close as I can to the coffee shop and walk the rest of the way. I feel silly doing this, but my job at the clinic has been working the front table, so I never get to talk to Ben. Every glimpse of him I get makes me feel equal parts happy and excited and sick to my stomach with nerves.

In the coffee shop, a couple of people are lounging in the

soft chairs in the corner. Ben is leaning on the counter reading a flyer from the stack next to the register. "Can I help you?" he asks without looking up.

My cheeks are hot before I even open my mouth. This was a dumb idea. I'm not one of those giggly girls who goes out of her way to get a guy's attention.

And yet, here I am.

"Hi."

Ben's head snaps up. His cheeks flush. The woman at the espresso machine tries to hide a smile. He glances around. "It's just me," I say.

"What can I get you?"

He smiles, sending a surge of energy through me. My usual coffee order slips right out of my head, and the shop suddenly feels like it's a million degrees. Great. So much for being casual.

"Uh . . ." I point randomly at the specials chalkboard propped up on the counter. Ben raises an eyebrow and punches a button on the register. I look at where I'm pointing. Apparently, I'm also a girl who drinks limited-edition green tea.

The woman gives me a smile and winks, which sends all the blood back to my cheeks. She hands me my cup. I sit down at a table, unsure of what—if anything—happens now.

"It's time for your lunch, Benjamin." The authority in the woman's voice is unmistakable. Ben doesn't have a choice but to do as she says, even though, from my first trip here, I know that he's the one in charge.

Without thinking, I take a sip of the tea. My face twists

at the taste. There isn't enough sugar in the world to make it drinkable.

Ben laughs and places another cup in front of me. "Vanilla latte," he says. "That tea's gross. We have it for the kind of people from the hills who get a kick out of correcting our pronunciation because, you know, we're all bums here." He smiles. I don't know if I should smile back.

I take a gulp of the coffee and think about what I'm going to ask next.

Although Ben has a magnetic pull on me, I did come here with another purpose. Everyone at the Los Ranchitos was cleared because there wasn't any evidence to connect them to the murder. After the huge scene Suds made at the clinic right before he was killed, I want to know if the police cleared Doc too.

"How's Doc?" I ask. "Is everything okay with the police?"

"Doc's fine. The police know him. Those questions were a formality. He's still upset about Suds. Doc has a big heart. He wants to save everyone. Sometime he can. Sometimes he can't."

Ben points at the ceiling. "I was going to go up and eat something. Do you want to come?"

I nod, my cheeks burning again. He leads me to a back staircase by the side emergency exit. I try to take a deep breath without him noticing. If I don't get it together, I'm going to trip and fall flat on my face.

When we get to the second floor, I expect it to be dark and dingy, but I'm surprised by what I see. Doors painted a rainbow of colors line the hallway. The carpet smells new and has a bounce to it.

Ben pulls his keys out of his pocket and unlocks a purple door. Inside, the apartment is small, but a big window that overlooks the parking lot floods it with light. It has a bed, a kitchenette, and a bathroom. Against one wall is a bookcase filled with well-loved paperbacks.

"Pretty nice digs for a junkie, huh?" Ben says, and I flinch. Is he joking? I really know nothing about him.

But he knows nothing about me, either.

He walks to the fridge. "Do you want something? There's no peanut butter, I swear." He laughs.

"No, thanks." I wander over to the bookcase so I can avoid his eyes.

He holds up a package of turkey lunch meat. I decline again. I don't want to eat his food—especially now that I know Cam is giving him money. His expression changes. I bite my lip.

I lean in to examine the paperbacks. When I reach out for one, my hand snaps back. I spin around.

Ben munches on his sandwich, watching me.

"What's that?" I point to an engraved lighter like Cam's. This one has the letters *BCA* on it. I try to seem calm, like I'm asking to make conversation.

"My uncle gave me that when I was fourteen. He went through a monogramming phase." Ben scoffs. "He said he had extra lighters left over from a box he bought to advertise the business, but I think that he was trying to convince me to change my last name to match his and Cam's." Ben shakes his head. "Who gives a kid a lighter?"

I run my fingers over the engraved *A*. I don't know what Ben's last name is. I assumed it was Vargas, like his uncle's.

Ben stands next to me and watches my finger. I look at him. "Arellano. My mother is my uncle's sister. My father—the Arellano—was a name on the long list of people my uncle didn't approve of. He took off before I was born, but my mother gave me his name. Sometimes I think it was just to spite her brother."

Ben picks the lighter up and flips the top. Open, closed. Open, closed. I will my hand to stay by my side. My scar sears across my arm.

"Then my mom took off and left me on my uncle's doorstep when I was eight. I was raised a Vargas. My uncle thought I should take the name, follow him into the business, and live happily ever after as his lackey."

He puts the lighter back down on the bookshelf. "But he kicked me out when I had an unfortunate run-in with a bottle and a syringe." My eyes widen. "Don't look so shocked, Jenny."

I try to smile as if I'm not surprised, but it isn't working.

"I can talk about it. It's not like it's a secret. I wasn't proud of who I was then, but I'm proud of who I am now." He opens his hands, gesturing to the apartment.

"I, uh . . ." I have no idea what to say. He wears his past on his sleeve. That's something I could never do. I smile tightly and hope he doesn't notice the discomfort radiating off me.

"You can breathe. It isn't contagious." His voice is still light. He's not mad at me for the way I'm acting.

Every piece of skin on my body must be red. "I'm glad you're doing better," I say, parroting what Kara told me. It makes sense now.

Ben nods a thank-you.

He waves the other half of his turkey sandwich under my nose. "Are you sure you don't want it?" My stomach betrays me by growling. I accept it. Ben goes to the sink to wash his plate.

I nibble at the sandwich and look around. I see everything differently now. It isn't a small, sparsely furnished space. It's an achievement, something to be viewed with pride.

I turn around and smile at Ben. He smiles back. A pulse of electricity passes between us. He blushes and looks away.

I slide my hand over the bookcase and slip his lighter into my pocket.

So Ben has a past. Who am *I* to judge him?

Ten minutes later, Ben retakes his spot in front of the register. I wave goodbye and let my eyes linger on him longer than is comfortable for two people who have only shared a sandwich. Then I step outside the coffee shop and sigh. I'm not ready to go back to the Los Ranchitos.

My phone bleeps. I fish it out of my pocket.

It's a text from Kara. A simple *Hey*.

I know more of Ben's story, but I still don't know how Kara would feel about the maybe-flirtation Ben and I have going on. That's really all it is right now—a maybe. I could see it being more.

The thought makes me feel hot and shivery and excited and anxious all at the same time, like lighting a match.

I plunge my fingers into my pocket and feel the lighter, heavy and cold between them. It centers me.

I text Kara back.

*Just had lunch with Ben.*

My phone immediately rings. I wait to pick up until right before it goes to voice mail. I don't know what she's going to say. But if she tells me to stay away from Ben, it's too late.

"Hi," I say, my voice chipper.

"Do you want to meet somewhere?" Kara asks. "Just you and me," she quickly adds.

"Sure. Is that going to be okay? Your parents are all right with that?"

"They're working today. It will just be for a little while. They'll never know." She pauses. "I have something to tell you."

"Okay. I'm at the coffee shop right now."

"No. Not there," she says. My heart lurches. *She's going to tell me something awful about Ben.* "There's a park a couple blocks away."

Kara gives me directions, and I start walking. The streets are quiet on this Saturday afternoon, but I feel like there's someone behind me.

I spin around, expecting to see Allen pretending to be a cop or Cam in his blue coat, but no one's there.

I look back three or four more times. I keep my hand on Ben's lighter. Rubbing my fingers over his initials makes me feel guilty for taking it. But I need it. I need it more than he does.

At the park, the grass is still brown from the winter, but little purple crocuses line the sidewalk. I sit down on a newly painted bench next to a pot of blooming daffodils. The play structure is also freshly painted in bright primary colors. It feels happy here. Like a place you would want to hang out.

Kara pulls up and parks along the street behind the bench a few minutes later. She's wearing giant dark glasses and a baseball cap, like she's a movie star who doesn't want to get recognized.

"How are you feeling?" I ask.

"I'm okay." She glances over her shoulder and opens her mouth to say something. But I put my hand up to stop her.

"I like Ben," I say. She closes her mouth. "I know he has a past, but I don't care. But I do care about you. About our friendship. If something happened between you two—"

"No," she cuts in. Even under her dark glasses, Kara looks stunned. "You should like Ben. He deserves to be with someone like you."

I feel the lighter in my pocket, and I have a moment's doubt. Does he deserve to be with someone like *me*?

Kara lowers her voice and looks away. "I want him to be happy."

Something definitely happened between them.

"Are you sure? I mean, I don't even know if he likes me back. But if something did happen between me and Ben . . ."

She nods, but I don't have her complete attention. Her sunglass-covered eyes drift over the edge of the park behind me. She tenses and stands up quickly. "I should go. My parents will be home soon." She takes off fast toward her car.

"Wait," I call. "What were you going to tell me?"

She gets to her car and freezes in place. I jog up behind her. Stuck under her windshield wiper is a photo of fuzzy, black-and-white lumps—something that would be recognizable to anyone who has a sister who is ten years younger and saw a similar ultrasound photo stuck to the fridge for months.

Kara grabs it and stuffs it under her arm as she fumbles with her keys. "It's probably a political ad or something from a church," she says before I can ask. I glance toward another car parked on the street. There's nothing under the wipers.

She's lying. It was left for her to find.

Kara slams the car door.

"See you on Monday?" I yell through the window, but she doesn't respond before peeling away from the curb.

The things in her locker, that ultrasound photo, the way she's been acting.

I'm trying to be her friend, but she's making it really hard with all her secrets and lies.

Plus, she doesn't realize who she's lying to.


Later, when I get off the bus at Henderson's, I see a car like Kara's in the parking lot. But it can't be hers. After the way she looked at the park, I figured she would go straight home. And there's no way her parents would let her come to this side of town.

I'm curious—and ready to straight-up confront her about

what she's hiding from me. It's probably not even her car, but since I need to refill my snack stash, I go inside.

The clerk I usually see is manning the front checkout. She gives me a wave. I wave back and grab a basket. On my way to the snacks, I see a cashier in the separate liquor section resting his chin in his hands on the counter. That must be the famous Joey the kids at school say will sell anything to anyone.

Henderson's doesn't have a great selection of snacks. So I have to get the same ones over and over again. Ro likes the chocolate-covered granola bars the best, so I dump two boxes into my basket. It's my good deed for the day.

"Kara?" It comes from the front of the store. I dash to the end of the aisle and see that the clerk has come out from behind the register. Her hands are clasped under her chin. "Is that you?"

The girl in front of her, who is definitely Kara, shakes her head. She has her arms wrapped around a paper bag from the liquor section and a receipt in her hand. At the register there, Joey leans way over to see what's going on.

Kara's buying booze now? She doesn't hold the bag sheepishly, like someone who got caught on their way to a party. She clings to the bag like it's a lifeline—something she'll never give up.

She looks terrified.

"No," Kara whispers, and hightails it out of the store, her bag clinking with each step.

I should go after her. If whatever is going on with her has gotten *this* bad, she needs help. I drop my basket and move toward the door, but I'm too slow. Her car is already pulling away.

I retrieve my basket, toss in a final package of Oreos, and take it up to the front. The clerk is standing in the doorway watching Kara drive away.

She looks at me waiting with my food. "Sorry. I thought that was a girl I used to know. A long time ago."

I don't want to say something that will out Kara. I fake a chuckle. "She must have one of those faces."

The clerk nods. "That must be it." But her eyes move back to the window and the now-empty parking lot.

# 18

On Monday morning, Kara isn't in school. But this time, instead of ignoring my texts, she writes me back and asks me to pick up her homework. She still wants to talk.

I can't concentrate on anything. I want to know what's up with Kara, even if it is none of my business. Someone's been leaving her notes, that's all I know. Maybe someone is bullying her and she's too embarrassed to tell me?

And I still want to know her story with Ben.

Ben. He occupied my thoughts all weekend. I'm afraid he got the wrong idea from my reaction when he told me about his past. I don't care who he used to be. I was uncomfortable because I'm not like him. I'm not shiny and new and better.

I'll have to find a way to tell him that his past doesn't matter to me. Tell him that I hope we can be friends—more than friends.

I hid the lighter in my bottom dresser drawer. I'm not going to use it. I want to be better for Ben. Be the kind of person he is; one he deserves to be with. Next time I'm at his apartment—and I really hope there is a next time—I'll put the lighter back like I never took it.

．．．

Cam shows up after school, just like he's supposed to. He's brought Ro with him—probably not by choice. He stares straight ahead while she chats away at him.

Kara's homework and books are in my arms. I was going to have Cam drop me off at Kara's house so she and I could talk, but I can't do that with Ro here. Ro and I are real friends now. She's never outright said anything, but I think she's a little jealous of Kara.

I open the truck door. "We're going for ice cream," Ro says. "We can have all the toppings we want." She gives Cam a challenging glare.

"We have to run an errand first." I maneuver myself and the stack into the truck and pull out my phone. "I need to drop these off at Kara's. She texted me the address."

Cam looks surprised. Then his entire face changes. It's softer, concerned. "Kara? What's wrong with her?"

"You know her?" Of course he knows her. She had *something* going on with his cousin. From his dramatic change of expression, I wonder if Cam and Kara might also have a history.

He shrugs and sits up straighter. He pulls away from the curb with a stomp on the gas. His expression is a mixture of worried, excited, and confused. All part of the puzzle that I'm not getting the pieces to.

Cam doesn't ask for Kara's address. He seems to know where he's going. "How do you know Kara?" I ask again, hoping for some details. Details about anything. Him. Ben. The past.

"She lives down the street. We used to hang out." His lips close. That's all he's going to say.

We pull up to a swanky gated neighborhood. Cam punches in the code to make the wrought-iron gate slide open. This is my first time coming to the hills. It looks so different from the area around the Los Ranchitos. The houses are giant and surrounded by lots of land dotted with native plants and cacti.

Cam pulls into the driveway of a two-story, light stuccoed house with a red-tile roof. The front yard is covered with pink rocks and artful, scraggly bushes.

I slide out of the truck. Ro follows. "This will only take a second," I say, hoping she will climb back in.

"I never get to visit the fancy houses. I want to see the inside."

"But—"

She's too fast for me. She's already ringing the doorbell.

No one answers. I stand behind Ro with the books. "Try again."

This time there's movement in the peephole, like someone is looking out at us, but the door doesn't open. I knock.

"Kara, it's Jenny. I have your homework."

The dead bolt disengages. Kara opens the door with a fake smile on her face. She looks like crap. Her hair is all over the place. She's wearing sweats with a hole in one of the arms. Her eyes dart to Ro.

I hold up the books and give her an apologetic smile. We won't be talking today. "I have these for you."

Ro pushes past Kara and makes her way inside.

"Ro," I snap under my breath, then look back at Kara. "Sorry. That's Ro." I point behind me at the truck. "She came with Cam to pick me up from school."

"Where's your room?" Ro asks.

"Ro, we can't stay. We're getting ice cream, remember?"

"It's okay," Kara says, still with the fake smile. "My room's upstairs."

We all tromp up the stairs. Kara's room isn't as nice as I would have thought—it certainly isn't as fancy as mine. I put her homework down on her blue-and-white-striped comforter.

Ro wanders around the room picking up random objects and putting them back down again. Kara watches her.

Tacked to the wall is a wooden sign that says "Friends." It looks like it was hand-painted by a young child. Ro slowly runs her finger over it. A weird tension fills the room.

"We should go," I say. Neither girl pays attention to me.

Ro picks up a candle and takes a deep sniff. She wrinkles her nose and looks at Kara. "Huh. Citrusy."

Kara's face goes pale. Her knees buckle. "Are you okay?" I ask.

She pushes me out of the way and runs down the hall to the bathroom. She slams the door.

Even from her room, I can hear her gagging. "I guess she's still sick. We should go before we catch something," I say to Ro.

Ro opens Kara's jewelry box and peers inside. That's the last straw. I grab her by the arm and pull her into the hallway. I point her to the stairs and push.

"Fine. I'm going," she protests.

"I hope you feel better," I call to the bathroom. "Text me if you need anything." I hope Kara understands that for what it is: Another invitation to talk. To tell me what's going on.

I close her front door behind us. Ro slides into the truck next to Cam and points to the house. "She was puking."

Cam grips his door handle like he's going to get out. But he doesn't. Once I'm inside, he starts the truck and puts it in reverse.

Another day with zero answers.

Ro claps her hands. "Ice cream time!"

Today I *am* one of those giggly girls who tries to get a boy's attention. It's a new thing. I'm not sure I like it.

Ben wipes down the table next to me. I have my books spread out like I'm doing work. Homework is my cover story. I told Cam I couldn't concentrate at the Los Ranchitos. He agreed to drop me off at the coffee shop after school and pick me up later. But I think he's figured out that I like Ben.

I watch the muscles in Ben's arms move back and forth. He looks up and smiles. I do *not* giggle—but I feel my face go red.

"Ben?" I ask like I need to get his attention—like his attention isn't already completely focused on me. "I wanted to tell you that I don't care about your past." Once the words are out of my mouth, I feel a weight lifted off my shoulders. But then the weight moves to my stomach when he doesn't respond.

I look down at my books. That was an okay thing to say, right? Is he going to walk away?

The chair pulls out across from me. Ben sits down.

"I know," he says matter-of-factly.

I look up at him. "You do?"

He smiles. "I know because you're here."

And just like those giggly girls, I melt into a puddle in my chair.

This feels so right. When I'm with Ben, it's like my scar doesn't exist. I feel like someone who doesn't have to hide. Someone who wants to be better.

My phone bleeps. I glance at it and see a text from Kara. Ben's still across from me, his eyes still staring into mine. I don't want this to end, but I know Kara needs me.

"It's my friend." I point at the phone. "She's having a hard time." I can't bring myself to tell him it's Kara. I know he'll be concerned.

I don't want to share him.

He stands up as Cam walks through the door. I'm sure my face is still flushed. Ben is smiling more brightly than usual.

For just a second, I think I see a hint of a smile on Cam's face.


I read Kara's text in the truck on the way back to the Los Ranchitos. It's a question about our history assignment. That's it. Nothing personal. No hints at her secret.

I turn to Cam. "How well do you know Kara?"

145

He shakes his head.

"You don't really know her, or you don't want to tell me?"

He throws his hands up in exasperation. "It's been a long time, okay?"

He looks away and blinks hard, like he's feeling something big, but with Cam, it's impossible to say what.

"Okay," I say softly.

Cam drops me off at the gate. As I walk through the construction zone, my mind is so busy swirling with thoughts about Kara that it takes me a second to realize that someone is standing in front of my door. He turns around.

You have got to be kidding me.

"Hi, Allen." I want to tell him to go away and leave me alone. But I can't. I don't want to do anything that seems suspicious. He still has that police radio on his hip.

"Um, hi." He rubs the back of his neck with one hand. He holds up a book with the other. "I saw this and thought of you." His face goes bright red.

"How did you know I live here?" My adrenaline is rising again. Who is this guy? And just how serious is he taking this wannabe-cop thing? Did he track his "arsonist" to the Los Ranchitos? To my room?

Allen laughs. "Everyone in town knows about the girl living in the motel."

Great.

But it's also a relief. He isn't here on "official" business.

I step forward and take the book. It's a field guide to birds.

"Thanks." I realize that I'm holding the book between two fingers like it might bite.

"Because you like to bird-watch," he says, and rubs his neck again.

Right. *I'm a bird-watcher.* That's what I told him I was doing in the trees.

"So, I'll see you around?" he asks. His smile dazzles.

I give a noncommittal nod. He turns and walks away. I hope this is just a passing crush. I'm going to have to talk to him. Tell him I'm not interested . . . unless . . . unless he really is tracking the arsonist. If he starts getting too close, I might have to become really interested, really fast.

The thought turns my stomach.

# 19

The sirens scream outside. The towel I'm lying on doesn't soften the cold marble under my back or head. Looking up through the bathroom window, I see the smoke billowing into the sky.

I don't feel high or calmed. I feel horrible. I was going to be better. Better so I would be worthy of Ben.

With Kara and Allen—and Ben—the stress and nerves and excitement were too much for me to handle. The lighter was in the bottom drawer.

Even as I was clicking it to life, I hated what I was doing; I hated myself for doing it. Now I have to stay here in the bathroom, by the exit. Where someone can pull me out.

As soon as I heard the sirens, I stumbled back to the Los Ranchitos with tears and snot running down my face. The fire is close. Too close. On this side of the river, far away from where Allen might be camped out.

The bathroom window screeches open. When I was seven, it was Brian's arms that reached for me through that tiny, frosted-glass window. I jumped into them, and in one swift motion, I was out in the sweet night air. A hundred hands held me, stroked my hair, said soothing things. Then they put me in the ambulance and drove me away. I escaped.

It's not a savior coming through this time. It's Ro.

I scramble up off the floor and wipe my eyes.

"Did you see the fire?" she asks with amazement in her voice. She plops down into the bathtub. "Why are you dirty?"

I look down at myself. My special shoes and pants are covered in dust. Hailey's hat lies cast off on the floor.

I'm worn to the bone, but my mouth begins to move. "I was looking for you. I was afraid that you were out at the spot where your mom's things are and near the fire."

Ro seems surprised I remembered. I'm surprised too. I don't know where my tired, self-loathing brain pulled that out from.

"You were worried about me?"

"Of course. You're my friend." I'm on a roll.

A huge smile cuts across Ro's face. She's bought my explanation.

My scar gives me a brief buzz of delight.


My eyes are red. My throat is scratchy. I got maybe two hours of sleep, and I look like it. I consider telling Dad that I'm sick and staying home from school, but it's a project day. The thought of seeing Ben this afternoon is enough to get me up and into my bee uniform.

When I open my door, Cam isn't waiting for me; Mike Vargas is. He's leaning against his shiny black BMW.

"Good morning," I say as politely as possible. I don't know what to think of this man. He's given Dad a great opportunity, but I saw the way he talked to his son. I know that he kicked Ben out onto the street when he was still a kid.

"Come on, I'll give you a ride to school." He opens his car door. I look around the parking lot. Dad and Monica are huddled in a corner. Dad waves to me, which I guess is permission to get into the car. Cam's nowhere to be seen. If I have to wait for a bus, I'll be late. I get in.

We pull out onto the street in uncomfortable silence. When we stop at the light in front of Henderson's, he turns to me. Emergency exits: jumping out the door into traffic.

"I hear you've made friends with my nephew."

I swallow hard. His tone is so even, I don't know where this is going. "Yeah, I see him at my project site. For school."

Mike Vargas turns his attention forward when the light changes. "I can't get through to him. I sent my son to do it, but that didn't work." He sneers on the word "son." It sets my heart racing remembering what he said to Cam after Suds came onto the property. How angry he was. How capable of *anything* he seemed. I look out the window, mentally pushing the cars in front of us to make them go faster.

"Will you talk to him?"

"What?"

"Cam says that Ben likes you. I want Ben to come back home. He doesn't have to work in that coffee place. I have a job for him, a real one. I want him to be part of the business. I want it to be his someday." Mike Vargas's voice is different now. Gone is the composed, charming businessman. In his place is a diminished, broken-hearted uncle.

"I made a lot of mistakes. I let pride get in the way. I know that now. If I could do it again, I would have gotten him help. Made him accept it. It never should have happened like it did. If he had died . . ."

I don't know what I'm supposed to say. I'm overwhelmed by the outpouring of emotion from this adult man—from Dad's *boss*. Plus, *Ben likes me*.

"Will you tell him that? Tell him I'm sorry?"

"Okay," I say to make this stop. He nods, and his stoic professional persona is back when we pull up to school.

Kara is waiting for me. She glares at the tinted windows of the BMW. When I get out, she jumps back.

"What were you doing with Mr. Vargas?"

"He wants me to apologize to Ben for him."

"Oh." It's one syllable, but Kara's face says so many more things.

"Tell me," I say. *Tell me anything.*

She shakes her head. "He's Cam's dad. I've been to his house a couple times. A long time ago."

I risk asking for more. "Cam's worried about you." I let it hang in the air between us.

"Hmm."

I see so much roiling under her surface. Why she's been sick, what happened with her and Cam and Ben. But she isn't budging. And she's my friend—one of my only friends. I can't jeopardize that by pushing too hard. Maybe we're the kind of friends who hide things from each other. I'm certainly hiding things from her.

My stomach is all fluttery when I get to the clinic. I want to see Ben so badly, but I also dread having to talk to him about his uncle. I hate being in this position. It's not my business, but what am I supposed to do? Lie to Mike Vargas and say I did it when I didn't? What if Ben does want to go back and join the business? He would make a lot more money. He could be set for life.

I'm disappointed when I see the registration table set up. I'm not going to get to say much of anything to Ben. I'll be taking names while he shuffles back and forth to the exam room.

"Good afternoon, Jenny," Doc says when I sit down at the table. He has the kindest eyes I have ever seen. They make you want to spill all your problems. As he helps a limping man, he doesn't flinch at the man's smell or his dirty clothes. He just takes his arm, and they move slowly across the room.

"Hey." Ben comes up behind me with a clipboard. "It's been a busy day because of the fire last night."

I jump to the edge of my folding chair. It threatens to tip. Ben grabs my arm, almost touching my scar to keep me from falling on the floor. "Did they get burned?"

"No. It's the smoke. A lot of these people have bad lungs."

"Oh." I try to catch my racing heart, and reposition myself in the chair. Ben still holds on to my arm. His thumb makes soft circles on it.

"I wish they'd catch the asshole doing this," he says.

When Doc calls for him and he lets go of my arm, his warmth evaporates. I settle back into the folding chair. Today my pamphlet stack features a new one about wound care. I pick it up and am greeted by photos of seeping green lesions. My stomach churns.

The door flies open. The incoming wind scatters my pamphlets. I try to catch them, but some hit the floor.

"Can I help you?" I ask with my head under the table. When I sit up clutching the pamphlets, the man in front of me screams.

I jump, causing my chair to slide back and screech on the floor. The man's wearing a long trench coat. His hair is matted and wild. He screams again and points. "Monster!" he yells.

I'm too stunned to stand up and move away. All I can do is wrap my arms around myself, protecting my heart and midsection.

Doc rushes out of the exam room. "Good afternoon, friend. What can we help you with today?"

The man paces back and forth, tearing at the hair on the sides of his head. "Monster. Fire monster. Big eyes." He leans into Doc, points at me, and whispers, "She saw me."

My heart is going to explode in my chest. *I saw him? Saw him where? In the trees while wearing Hailey's hat? The one with the butterfly eyes?*

"Tell me more about it. Let me see if I can help." Doc grabs my arm and pulls me to my feet and away from the man.

"She's after me!" the man shrieks.

I stop breathing. The waiting room goes blurry.

Ben comes up behind us.

"Ben, why don't you and Jenny make this gentleman a sandwich?" Doc says.

Ben puts a protective hand on my shoulder. He leads me to the kitchen door. I look back before we go inside. Doc nods at another man, who walks down the hallway.

"This kills Doc. When there are people he can't help, it chips away at him," Ben says.

I want to creep forward and look out a crack in the kitchen door. I need to hear what the man is saying about me.

Before I can, the door swings back open. Doc comes into the kitchen. He glances at me and then turns to Ben. "Take Jenny home." He pulls a set of keys out of his pocket. I must look as rattled as I feel.

"What's going to happen to that man?" I ask.

"He needs more care than we can provide here. Don't worry. I'll do everything I can to get him help."

My stomach twists up in knots. No one is going to believe this poor man, but I have to be more careful. The next time I get seen, it might be by someone they will believe. Someone like Allen.

An ambulance pulls up outside as Doc leaves the kitchen.

Ben puts a gentle hand on my shoulder. I look up at him. "I don't want to go home. Can we walk for a while?"

Ben gets our coats and follows me out the back exit. A few puffy clouds float around the otherwise blue sky, but the wind blows. It bites at my cheeks and ears. Ben doesn't even zip up his coat.

"Here," he says, and pulls a black beanie out of his pocket. He smooshes it down on my head. I laugh, but my chest is tight.

I want to ask Ben if he heard what that man said about me being a fire monster. But I don't, and Ben doesn't say anything.

We continue down the sidewalk, and our arms keep bumping, like two magnets that can't help but be attracted to each other. Ben takes my hand. My icy fingers are wrapped in his warmth. I give him a reassuring squeeze to let him know that I want him to keep holding on.

I smell coffee. I look up and realize we're standing in front of the coffee shop. In front of Ben's apartment.

He swipes his free hand over his head and vibrates, as if he's nervous. It's cute. I haven't seen him act like this before. I try to suppress a smile, but I can't. I'm feeling the nervous vibrations too.

"Do you want to come up?"

I nod. Through the coffee shop window, the woman who works with Ben gives me a smile and a wink.

Ben takes me to an outside entrance—an additional emergency exit. He doesn't let go of my hand as we climb the stairs to his purple door.

I hesitate for a second before I go in. Ben notices. He jumps back. "I can take you home, if you want. I'll go get Doc's car."

I put my hand on his arm to stop him. "I don't want to go home." I hope it conveys everything I want to say. That I like him. That I want to be with him.

We go inside. Ben's bed is a mess of twisted covers. There are dishes in the sink. He glances around apologetically. Now that I'm here, I can't look at him. There's too much energy between us. I don't know what to say or do.

"Do you want sit down?" He motions toward a little two-person sofa in front of the TV.

I take off my coat and the beanie and sit. Ben sits next to me. The couch is so small that we can't not be touching.

I turn and wrap my leg under me so that I can see his face. I have to get this out of the way.

I take a deep breath. "I don't want to get involved. It's none of my business. But your uncle is my dad's boss, and . . ."

Ben's head flops back against the couch. "Let me guess, he wants you to convince me to move back to the hills, join the business, and live happily ever after?"

I nod. Great. I've ruined the nice moment we were having. "Sorry," I whisper.

He lifts my hand and starts making lazy circles on it with his thumb. "It's not your fault. My uncle has sent everyone he knows to try to convince me. The only person who hasn't tried to convince me is my uncle himself."

"Do you want to go back?"

Ben shakes his head. "I know I don't drive a Beamer or anything, but the life I have is *mine*. I'm proud of that."

I lean in closer to him. I want to put my hand on his face, feel the stubble on his chin, press my lips to his.

His phone rings. We jerk apart. He answers, and I look away toward the bookshelf. The one with the empty space

156

where the lighter was. The lighter that's still in my drawer, despite my pledge to return it. I stare down at the floor. Why is this so hard? Why can't I kick this?

"I've been instructed by Doc, in no uncertain terms, to take you home now." There's a smile in his voice, but I don't turn to look at him. I can't face him knowing that I failed *again*. I'm not the person he deserves. He deserves far better.

I bury my hands in my pockets as we walk in silence back to the clinic. I haven't said a word since we left the apartment. I know Ben is wondering what he did wrong.

The clinic is going to close soon. Ben unlocks the car, and I get inside. When I reach over my shoulder for the seat belt, I catch a glimpse of a girl who looks like Kara dashing into the clinic as Doc steps out to lock the door.

I spin around to look, but the clinic door closes.

"What?" Ben asks.

"I thought I saw Kara."

"Oh. Maybe," he says.

"Maybe? What does that mean?" My voice is screechy.

He shakes his head. "Nothing."

"Whatever," I mutter, and look out the window.

Ben sighs. "It's not my story to tell."

Which means he knows something. It seems like everyone but me does.

· · ·

Ben drops me off outside of Henderson's to avoid running into his uncle at the Los Ranchitos. My whole body is shaky, like I threw back a hundred Pixy Stix. It's aggravation and anxiety with a little whisper of hope underneath.

When I cross the street and approach the gate, one of the construction guys nods at me. I don't recognize him, but his hard hat is casting a shadow over his face, so it's hard to tell. Plus, there are always different people coming in and out with each new phase of the project.

I see something in front of my door. I take a couple of running steps, but then slow way down and creep forward. The kitten is bigger now—in a leggy, awkward stage. He gobbles up a pile of treats.

When I open my door, he follows me inside and jumps up onto the bed.

"You found him!" The kitten cuddles up to Ro and purrs.

"He was right outside. Where do you think he's been all this time?" He looks healthy, and his fur is neat. Someone must be taking care of him.

Ro shrugs. "Maybe he has a real home and comes here to visit?"

I join her on the bed and scratch the cat behind the ears. "I'm glad he came back. I've missed him."

Ro's smile can't get any bigger. "Me too."

When we first met the kitten, Ro and I were complete strangers. Now we're friends. She wasn't someone my parents organized a playdate with; she wasn't someone from school. Ro is a friend I made all by myself. I'm proud of that.

# 20

Kara's hair flops over her face, and her glasses shield her eyes, but I find a smile under there.

I won't press her for an explanation for her recent behavior. She seems so much better today. I don't want to send her crashing down again.

We're supposed to be working on a history project, but so far, we've spent the last hour tearing through the unhealthy snacks and gossip rags I brought to her house. Or at least Kara has; my eyes have been searching every bit of her room for clues. I haven't found any.

"Check this out." Kara licks fluorescent orange cheese dust off her fingers and hands me the magazine. "Why would she wear that outfit when she knew there were paparazzi around?"

Ro already pointed out that same picture when I brought the magazine home last night. She wanted to come with me to Kara's. I told her it would be boring, but in case she appeared outside Riverline Prep, Kara and I skipped going to our lockers after school and ran straight to her car.

There's no way it could have been Kara at the clinic.

Looking at her house, I'm sure her parents have good insurance. As nice as Doc is, no one would go to that clinic if they didn't have to.

"This is fun," Kara says. She looks at me with such a hopeful expression, I wonder how often she gets to have people over.

I glance at her bedside clock. "I guess we should get to work." I open my bag and pull out my history book.

"Okay," Kara sighs.

We don't get far. The call of the chips is too much. I gulp a mouthful of water to wash them down. Water's all there is to drink in Kara's house—other than some slimy-looking green juice.

"Are your parents total health nuts or something?"

"They want me to be healthy and safe," she says softly.

"Oh. That's nice." I try to dislodge my foot from my mouth. "I could invite half the colony to my room for a pizza party and my dad wouldn't notice. Not if Monica was around." I laugh. I mean it as a joke, but Kara's face is blank. Then she looks like she wants to say something, but she turns back to her history book.

"So tell me what's going on with you and Ben," she asks after a moment.

"We almost kissed." The words are out before I can stop them.

Kara's head snaps up. "That's so great."

"It is?"

"Well, yeah. Don't you like Ben? I'm sure he likes you."

My face goes warm. "That's a really nice thing to say, but I'm not so sure. I acted kind of strange after the almost-kiss."

"It will be fine. I know Ben. He doesn't give up easily when he wants something."

There's a sparkle in her eyes, which makes doubt flood into me. I'm sure Ben really liked her, too. Maybe he still does.

It grows quiet between us. I know she wants to say whatever it is that she's been working up to. I wait. I will wait all night if I have to.

"We moved here from Santa Fe when I was thirteen," she whispers. I look up with interest. I thought she had always lived here.

"I had a little sister, but she died. That's why my parents want to keep me safe. Why they're so strict with me."

The whole room changes. Kara's eyes are glassy. The chips in my stomach lurch toward my throat. "I'm sorry," I say. "I have a little sister too." My hand goes to my scar. "I don't know what I would do if anything happened to her."

Kara nods and rubs her eyes. She smiles. Now that she's opening up, I want to finally ask about the notes she has been receiving.

But then the doorbell rings, making us both jump. I follow Kara down the stairs and notice something I didn't before: there aren't any family photos on the walls. I get that it would be impossibly hard to lose a child, but you would think that there would be some trace of Kara's little sister. Some happy family portrait from before.

Kara pauses before she looks through the peephole, like

she has to psych herself up for whoever might be outside. She turns to me and shrugs. When she opens the door, Cam is standing there.

I can't put my finger on it, but he looks neater than usual. And he's smiling. At Kara. I rarely get a smile.

"Hi," he says, and looks down at his feet.

Kara doesn't respond to him. "Jenny, it's for you." She steps out of the way to let Cam in. She doesn't look irritated, but she's also not as happy that he's here as he seems to be.

They are killing me with all the secrecy.

I gather up my stuff from Kara's room, being careful to collect all evidence of unhealthy snacks. "Do you want to keep these?" I hold out an unopened bag of Doritos. "You can hide them in your closet and eat them after your parents go to bed."

"No," Kara says, turning on a dime again. One moment she was happy and relaxed, and now she's back to tense and nervous. I'm even more worried that something is going on in her house.

When I get into Cam's truck, Kara waves from the doorway. Cam goes red.

"You like her," I tease.

Cam turns away, but before he does, I see pain on his face. Ah. I'm guessing Kara never liked him back. She broke his heart.

We drive along in silence. I can't help but glance down at the cup holder. It's still empty. "Where's your lighter?"

"I was going to ask you the same thing," he says under his breath. "You kept staring at it like you were waiting for the chance to swipe it."

I jerk back in surprise. "I'm the last person who would steal your lighter."

"Uh-huh," he says, and focuses on the road.

Great. I told Cam that I would behave in exchange for him not following me around. I don't need him thinking I stole his lighter. Am I going to have to start checking for flashes of blue behind me again?

Ben wanders in and out of the clinic's kitchen while I make sandwiches. Since I'm not sure where we stand right now, I don't say much.

He steps forward to open a drawer. His body passes closer to mine than is necessary.

"I'm sorry about the other day," I say. He looks confused. Maybe he didn't notice my change in attitude. Maybe all this is in my head. Maybe there's a real chance for us.

He takes a deep breath and reaches for my hand. "I have to tell you something."

I don't want to have a hand-holding conversation—one that means I'm going to need comforting—but I let him take it anyway.

"I really like you. I wanted to kiss you more than anything when you were at my place." He's saying the words I want to hear, but his face doesn't match them. He looks disappointed. "But . . ."

And here it comes. The reason he's holding my hand.

"I can't be in a relationship right now."

"Why?" There's a desperation in my voice that I can't hide.

He releases my hand and scrubs his face with his palms. "I've been sober for ten months now. I go to AA. I see a counselor. Everyone agrees that I need to be on my own for a while. Learn how to be me. The new sober me."

I look away. "I understand," I say, because what choice do I have? I have no right to interfere with that. It would be selfish beyond belief.

"I'm sorry," he says. "But I felt like I should tell you. I didn't want you to think I was leading you on."

"It's okay." I pick up my peanut butter knife and will my eyes to stay dry.

"So, um, Doc's waiting for me." He places a gentle hand on my shoulder. "I hope we can still be friends."

I nod, but my heart is breaking.

I see the flames all the way from the street in front of the Los Ranchitos. Everyone in the neighborhood has come out to watch. Some wring their hands. Others have faces full of wonder. Then the wind shifts, sending us into coughing fits.

The wind. I've heard people talking about it blowing all spring. It's gotten an early start this year. It's pushing the fire toward the colony.

I completely lost control this time. I didn't think about where I was or what the consequences might be. All I could see in my head was Ben and what might have been. What will never be.

Dad eyes me with worry. I rub my scar. He's tried to

convince me three times to go back inside, but my feet won't move.

"Are they going to be okay?"

If someone gets hurt, I will turn myself in.

Dad wraps his arm around me. "They'll evacuate the colony if the fire gets too close. They have lots of practice with this. The fire will be out before you know it." The false cheer in his voice is like nails on a chalkboard.

He maneuvers me around until we're facing the Los Ranchitos. "Let's go inside. I'll make you some hot chocolate."

When I was seven and got out of the hospital, my burn wrapped in so much gauze that I couldn't wear a regular shirt, Dad made me hot chocolate. He had just gotten out of prison, and he and Mom stood in the kitchen in uncomfortable silence, watching me drink it and looking at me with fear—like I was going to break into a million pieces in front of them.

Dad leads me into the office. "I'm okay. I don't need hot chocolate. I just want to go to bed," I say.

He pulls two mugs out of the cabinet. "Sit."

I slide into one of the chairs and watch in silence as he fills up the mugs and pops them into the microwave.

A couple of minutes later, he joins me at the table and places the cup of watery instant hot chocolate in front of me. I lift it to my lips and take a sip. Then I put the cup down and place my hand over my scar.

Dad nods at my arm. "For me it feels like I've been shot up with a syringe."

I drop my hand. "What?"

He points to his gut. "Right here. The anger. This is where it starts, and then it radiates until it's everywhere. Like a drug. It should feel awful, but it feels kind of good. Powerful." He takes a slurp of his hot chocolate. I have no idea what's going on.

"In prison—" His voice is emotionless, but I have to look away. I've never allowed myself to imagine him in an orange jumpsuit.

"In prison I had to learn to control it. It would have gotten me killed otherwise. When the burn starts, I think about you. I think about all that I have to lose."

My cup shakes as I try to bring it to my lips again. I don't know if I'm about to cry or laugh. I'm confused and exhausted and sick to my stomach.

"I'm not perfect, obviously." Dad chuckles. "But I want you to know that it can be controlled. I don't want anyone to get hurt."

"Okay?" I say hesitantly. Does he think I'm afraid of him? That I think his punching Suds is some sort of backslide, and he'll go to prison again? Or is this his way of telling me that he knows I have anger inside me too. That he knows about me and what I do.

"Your mom called." He looks me straight in the eye. My heart speeds up. "She said something about an arson case. Her husband's been cleared of any wrongdoing."

I blink hard. Mom told Dad about Brian? Why? Why would she do that?

"So that's good," Dad says, standing and picking up our

mugs. "I'm sorry your mother had to go through something like that again." He put the mugs in the sink and turns back to me. There's guilt in his eyes. He's the reason she had to go through it the first time.

I point my head at the table so he won't see the guilt filling me. I never thought about Mom—how Brian forging those reports to save me would affect her. I was too worried about getting out of Ohio. About getting away from Hailey.

Dad leans over and kisses me on the head. "Love you, sweet pea."

"Love you too," I say, and try to smile.

I have to stop. No more fires.

# 21

Ro drops in through the window and goes straight to the wardrobe. She rips open the door and starts riffling through my clothes.

"Hi?"

She pulls out a pink sundress and holds it up to me. "No," she says. Then she holds it up against herself. "Maybe."

It's Saturday night, but I have my homework spread out on my bed. There's nothing else to do around here. I can walk around Henderson's for only so long. The mall isn't really a mall, so . . .

Ro tosses a black skirt and red sweater at me. "Do you want leggings, too? Or do you want to go au naturel?"

"Where am I going?"

Ro puts a hand on her hip and cocks her head. "To a party. Emma is going to be here in about half an hour."

"Emma from my school? Why would I go anywhere with her?"

"She invited us—well, me—to a party. Now I'm inviting you. She's picking us up. I told her to come here to see the motel."

"When did you arrange all this?"

"Yesterday, when you were at school. That Emma has a real habit." Ro pops a cigarette out of her pocket. "She was smoking behind the dumpster during lunch."

"Why were you at my school during lunch?"

"I was going to the dollar store," she says.

"For lunch?"

Ro ignores me and digs through my underwear drawer. "Leggings or no leggings?"

I glance at my homework on the bed. I'm facing another night watching bad TV and feeling heartsick over Ben. "Fine. Give me the leggings."

The pink sundress is dangerously short on Ro. She's wearing the ultradown coat over it. Once the sun goes down, the winter-like chill comes back, and even though her legs are bare, she doesn't shiver like I do.

We're waiting outside the gate for Emma. Since I definitely wasn't invited, she's going to be surprised to see me standing here. Maybe she'll refuse to take us, and Ro and I can watch a movie or something instead.

Her car pulls up. It's an old silver Honda Civic. I expected her to drive something snazzy—I know she lives in the hills.

Ro jumps to the street and pops open the front passenger-side door. She pauses. "You coming?"

I look at Emma. She glares.

I go around to the back.

"You said I could see inside," Emma whispers under her breath to Ro.

Ro shrugs. "The gate is closed."

Emma glances over her shoulder at me, now seated behind her. Her eyes are like knives.

Ro throws her arms up into the air. "Paaarrrty!"

Emma makes a U-turn in the middle of the road, and we head off to the hills.


Ro's beer sloshes over the side of its red cup as she bounces up and down in the middle of a sweaty bunch of drunk dancers. She's been holding the cup all night, but I haven't seen her take a sip.

I'm sitting on the floor in a dark corner, nursing my second can of Coke. I don't like drinking. I never feel buzzed, just dizzy and out of control. Things I don't want to feel.

Homework would have been better than this. I know only a few people here. One of the guys from my homeroom thought it would be hilarious to call me Motel Girl, and then explain to everyone that I'm the legendary girl living in the Los Ranchitos. So that's who I am now. Motel Girl.

We're in the hills, but not the gated, exclusive part. If the hills had a low-rent district, this would be it. The house has been used for parties before. The carpet is stained; the couch pillows are dented from being sat on, jumped on, and made out on. It's filled with people, but has only two doors, and a few windows for emergency exits.

"Motel Girl!" A guy walks by and points at me. I tip my can at him. I need to get Ro and find a way back to the Los

Ranchitos. When we got in the car with Emma, neither one of us was thinking about how we would get home—especially since, from the moment we walked in, Emma had a beer in her hand and her tongue down some guy's throat. They've since disappeared into a back bedroom.

I have to pee. I've been trying not to think about it for the last hour, but I can't wait anymore. I stand up and push my way through the bodies to a hallway. All the doors are shut, and I'm afraid of what I'll see if I open one.

The door at the end of the hallway looks the most promising. I knock. No one yells at me to go away. I knock again. No answer. "I'm coming in," I announce.

The door isn't locked. The lights are off. I slap my hand over the wall, looking for the switch.

The lights click on.

Kara, of all people, is sitting in the bathtub, sucking on an almost-empty bottle of vodka. She blinks at me while her eyes try to focus.

"Kara! What are you doing here?"

She raises the bottle. "Drinking."

"I see that."

She takes another slug from the bottle and doesn't answer.

"I want to talk to you," I say. "But I kind of have to pee." I motion to the door.

She points to the toilet. "Have at it." She pulls the shower curtain closed.

Great. This isn't uncomfortable or anything. But my odds of finding another bathroom are slim. I shut the door.

"I would never hurt anyone," Kara says. Her head thumps against the wall.

"That's good to hear," I say, humoring her. She's super-drunk. If she's polished most of the bottle off, she's not going to remember anything tomorrow. I'm surprised she's still conscious.

I flush and go to the sink to wash my hands. The shower curtain slides open. "It was an accident." There are tears in her eyes now. She rests the bottle on her stomach and gazes down at it. "But you can't tell anyone."

"Tell anyone what, Kara?"

"Why is this happening?"

"Kara, you have to tell me what's going on."

"The pictures. The pictures in my locker and on my car. I want it to stop forever."

"The pictures? The family with the baby, and the ultra-sound? What are they, Kara? Who's leaving them?"

Instead of answering, she takes another slug off the bottle and starts to cry.

"You've had enough." I rip the bottle away from her and pour the rest down the sink.

She shifts around like she wants to get to her feet. Her keys fall out of her pocket.

She tries to pick them up, but I'm faster. "No. Absolutely not. I'm taking you home."

With her arm thrown over my shoulder, I get her out of the tub and into the hallway. We stumble toward the pounding bass. I prop her up against a wall. "Stay here!" I yell over the music. "Don't move."

I wade into the dancers. Aerosolized sweat and beer envelop me. I grab Ro's arm and pull her out before I start to gag.

"Hey!" she protests. Ro thinks she can take care of herself, but I'm not leaving her alone in a house full of drunk strangers.

I point at Kara. "We have to take her home."

When we approach, Kara shrieks. "No, no, no!"

Ro laughs. "I don't think she wants to go home."

I hoist Kara off the wall, and Ro takes her other arm. "I don't care. That's where she's going."

We stumble outside. I shift Kara's weight to Ro. "I'll go find her car."

This street is packed with cars, and I find Kara's parked on the next one over. It takes me four tries to shimmy it out of its spot.

When I pull up to the party house, Kara is staggering at full drunken speed down the sidewalk. Ro is chasing after her. "What happened?" I yell as I open the car window.

"I don't know. Some random dude walked out of the house across the street, and she took off."

I drive to the end of the street, put the car in park, and jump out. Kara crashes into my arms. She looks terrified. "Help me," she whispers.

Ro runs up and shakes her head in irritated confusion.

"I'm going to help you, and take you home," I say gently to Kara.

She nods and lets me maneuver her into the car. She lies down in the backseat. Ro gets into the front. "Your friend is totally wasted."

Kara whimpers.

I don't remember how to get to Kara's house. We drive up and down the quiet, dark streets of the hills looking for it. Kara is asleep. Ro looks out the window like we're taking a nice Sunday drive.

I finally find the heavy iron gate that surrounds Kara's neighborhood. I pull up to the keypad and look at Ro.

Ro twists around and pokes Kara. Kara moans. Ro pokes her again. "You have to give us the code."

Kara opens one bleary eye. "Hi," I say. "Can you tell us what the code is so that we can take you home?"

"5-7-0-4-3," she mumbles.

I punch it in, and the gate slides open.

When we pull up to Kara's house, there are no cars in the driveway and no lights on inside. I say a silent prayer that her parents are out of town. I don't know how I would explain why I am bringing their very precious daughter home drunk in the early-morning hours.

Ro helps me get Kara out of the car. I use her keys to open the door. I remembered seeing an alarm when I was here before. I cringe and wait for something to start beeping or wailing, but nothing happens. No alarms, no parents thundering down the stairs.

We flop Kara down onto her bed. I roll her onto her side and prop a pillow under her to keep her from rolling onto her back, just in case. She's so far gone that if she were to throw up, she might choke to death.

"I'm going to get her a glass of water for when she wakes up. Don't touch anything."

Ro throws her arms out to her sides in defense.

When I come back upstairs, Ro is leaning against the wall with her hands in her pockets. "Can we go now?"

"We can't just leave." I pull Ro out of the bedroom and whisper, "Someone's been following her and leaving stuff, like pictures. She's really scared."

"Huh," Ro says, and glances back into the bedroom. "So you think we should stay here and wait and see if some creep shows up? Good plan. She's got a giant gate with a code. No one can get in here."

She's got a point.

"Take her house key to lock the door," Ro says, and motions to the set of keys I left on the dresser. "If the front door is locked and the gate closed, it will be like any other night she's here alone."

I hesitate, but I reach for the key and scribble Kara a quick note saying that I have it. I'll call her first thing in the morning to make sure she's okay.

Ro follows me down the stairs. I hesitate again. Maybe I should stay; that's what a friend would do.

"Cam can take us home." Ro has opened the front door and is pointing to Cam's Breland Construction truck parked in front of the Vargas's house.

"Fine," I say. I won't win this argument with Ro. I lock Kara's door behind us and pull out my phone to text Cam.

He doesn't reply. I call. It goes to voice mail. I call again and again and again. There's a light on in one of the windows. Someone's up.

"What?" he finally barks into the phone.

"You need to take us home."

"No."

"We're right outside your house."

The curtains move in the window with the light. Ro waves.

"It's Kara. She was drunk. We had to drive her home."

"Dammit, Kara," he says to himself. He hangs up. A couple of seconds later, the front door opens.

Cam doesn't say anything or even look at us as he marches to the truck and gets in. Ro and I scrabble to jump in before he starts it and throws it into gear.

He slows as we pass Kara's. "She's in bed. I locked her door."

He shakes his head, and under the white streetlights, I see real pain on his face.

# 22

"I'm guessing you don't remember much," I say when Kara groggily answers the phone.

"Thank you for the water by my bed." She takes a deep breath. "I'm sorry."

"You know you can talk to me, right? About anything?" *You can tell me who's leaving you the pictures.*

"I know. And I will, but not right now. My head is pounding. I haven't even made it downstairs yet."

"Okay. Feel better. We'll talk tomorrow. For real."

"For real," she says.


I lie on my bed and stare at the ceiling until I can't stand it anymore. Ro's off doing whatever she does on Sundays. Dad and Monica are tucked away in their room—I do not want to know. And besides, I've been giving them, especially Monica, a wide berth. I don't know how much Dad told her about the investigation into Brian, but I'm guessing she knows something. Enough to pay Cam to follow me around.

I pull on my shoes. Even though we can't be in a relationship and my heart's still sore, I can't stay away from Ben. He's
the person I want to see more than anyone else. He's like the
fires: I want to stop, but I can't. And he said he wanted to be
friends, right?

The coffee shop is packed. I've never seen it so busy. The
warm day has brought everyone out. A man and a woman in
full bicycling spandex lounge at a table outside and sip that
horrible tea while they guard their bikes. As I step past, the
man reaches out and places a protective hand on his.

The line almost stretches to the door. I get in back of it.
It'll be worth the wait to see Ben's face light up when I get to
the front, but right now, he's not paying attention to anything
other than the register and the espresso machine.

A few other people join the line while I'm in the middle.
It's moving slowly. The woman who isn't good with the register needs Ben's help, so he jumps back and forth between
taking money and making drinks.

The door whooshes open hard. The line turns to look at the
motion. Kara sweeps in, pushing the hair out of her eyes with
one hand and holding a plastic grocery sack in the other. She's
wearing her old sweats. Her face is puffy. She looks like hell.

I call her name, but she keeps going.

"Hey!" someone shouts as Kara elbows her way to the first
position. She leans over the counter and says something into
Ben's ear. He doesn't punch anything into the register or write

on a cup. His eyes narrow. He motions with his head to the corner where the emergency exit and the stairs that lead up to his apartment are.

A second later, he comes out of the back and meets her there. I step out of line to see what's going on. As I'm walking toward them, I see that Kara is crying. Ben puts a hand on her shoulder, like the man who put his hand on the bike outside. Protective and caring. I stop in my tracks.

Kara holds open the bag. Ben gasps.

"It was *inside* my house," she says.

I step forward to join them, but Ben puts his arm around Kara. It is a practiced, loving gesture—not awkward or spur-of-the-moment. It's something he's done before. Many times.

He leads her up the back stairs to his apartment. I dash out to the parking lot and shield my eyes as I look up at his window. Soon the two of them are standing in it, arms around each other in an intimate embrace. He kisses the top of her head.

The itch cuts across my scar with such ferocity that it almost brings me to my knees. I rub it as I go back inside. There's no need to panic. They have a past; I knew that. It doesn't mean they have a present. Ben's known what's going on with Kara from the beginning. There's a perfectly reasonable explanation for what I just saw.

They'll come back down soon, and I'll ask. We will work it out together. The three of us.

. . .

I finish my fourth latte. Ben's coworker is wiping down the counter. It's closing time, and I'm the only one left.

All day I sat here waiting for them to come down. I told myself over and over again that there was a reasonable explanation for what was taking so long.

I told myself I wasn't jealous.

Ben's coworker approaches me. "Um . . ." She points to the door and the growing darkness outside.

I scoop up my empty cup and stand. My legs are stiff. I hobble to the door and trash my cup.

One last look up the stairs. They're not coming down.

I tell myself once again that I'm not jealous. Besides, Ben was very clear about not having a girlfriend right now. He and Kara are just friends. He's just helping her out.

Ben's coworker smiles apologetically as she locks the door, leaving me outside in the dark.

I text Cam. When he pulls up, he takes one look at my face and keeps his mouth shut the whole ride back to the Los Ranchitos.


The next morning, I struggle to get ready for school. I have a plan. I'm going to ask Kara ever so casually about her day with Ben. She'll give me the reasonable explanation, and everything will be fine.

I flop back down onto my bed. Or she won't, and it won't.

Cam pounds on the door. I have no choice but to face this.

In the truck, we don't talk. Cam sips from his travel mug and bobs his head to the song on the radio.

We cruise up to the road that runs past the coffee shop. The light turns red. I gaze down the street toward Ben's building until the light turns green.

"Wait."

Cam slams on the brakes. New plan. I'll ask Ben. He'll be more forthcoming than Kara. He'll reassure me, and then life can go back to normal.

"Drop me off at the coffee shop. I'll walk the rest of the way," I say.

"You'll be late."

I scoff. Like Cam cares if I'm late to school. I shift around in my bee uniform and try again. "It will take five minutes. I just want to get a coffee before school."

"Yeah, right," he mumbles.

"What's that supposed to mean?" I snap.

He rolls his eyes, but he flips on his blinker and makes the turn toward the coffee shop.

Five minutes. I will take five minutes to ask Ben about yesterday. Then I will run to school.

I wait until Cam pulls away before I go inside. The smell of freshly brewed coffee hits my nose. A woman in a suit uses her chin to balance several cups as she walks away from the counter. The counter that Ben isn't behind.

I've never seen this guy before. I smile. "Hi. Is Ben here?" The guy looks over his shoulder and then back at me like I'm an idiot.

"Nope."

"Do you know what time he works today?"

"Nope."

"Okay. Thanks." For nothing.

I really am going to be late for school. I walk to the corner. Kara's car is parked on the side street. I cross over to examine it. There's nothing on the windshield. Nothing amiss inside.

I jump as the door to Ben's apartment building opens. He steps outside and looks around. I'm about to wave, when I see Kara come out from behind him.

Her hair is wet. She's wearing a T-shirt I've seen Ben in at the clinic, and too-long black jogging pants that are bunched up at her ankles.

Ben puts his arms around her again. She looks up at him.

I can't watch. I know what's going to come next.

I spin on my toes and hightail it down the street.

# 23

Fine. I admit it. I'm jealous. And hurt. And mad. Maybe when Ben said he couldn't be in a relationship, he meant that he couldn't be in one with *me*.

Was this part of Kara's big secret? That she's been sleeping with Ben behind my back? That she's been playing me?

When I got to school, I took Kara's house key and slipped it through the vent in her locker. Then I went straight to the nurse. It wasn't hard to convince her to send me home.

Once I was tucked back into bed, I told Dad to leave me alone. Then, thinking I had some sort of "girl problem," he sent Monica. She only stuck around long enough to look at me suspiciously.

The duvet is too hot, but I don't care. I want to be wrapped in its warm puffiness, where nothing bad can reach me.

The bathroom window slides open. "Go away, Ro!" I yell. She doesn't. She walks in with her hands held up.

"Whoa," she says. "Why aren't you at school?"

I pull the duvet over my head. Ro crawls onto the bed next to me and leans against the headboard.

"Do you want to talk about it?"

If I talk about it, my anger is going to turn to sadness and I'm going to cry. I would rather be angry.

"Why aren't *you* at school?" I grumble.

"First period is boring."

She peels the duvet back. My staticky hair clings to it. "Did that boy you like do something to you?" Ro's eyes are dead serious. She clenches a fist. "I'll take care of him." I've never seen this look on Ro's face before. I believe she would stop at nothing to protect someone she cares about. It's something we have in common.

I sit up. "No, it's not like that." Her fist unclenches. "He didn't do anything to me. He was too busy doing Kara."

Ro crinkle's her face in disgust. "Your drunk friend from school?" Her eyes trace my face up and down, like she's mentally comparing Kara and me. I come out on top. "I don't understand."

"I don't either. She knew how I felt about him. She's the one who told me I should go for it."

"That bitch," Ro says. "You were nice to her. We hauled her stinky ass halfway across town and tucked her in like Sleeping Beauty."

She stands up and walks toward the bathroom. "Today calls for ice cream and bad eighties movies."

"I don't want you to get in trouble for ditching school."

She waves me away. "This is way more important than school."

My heart warms. I don't think Ro has many friends, which is why she hangs around me so much. Sometimes I wish she were less clingy, but then there are moments like this when I'm happy having her around.

She's really the best friend I've ever had.

"You can go out the front door," I call when I hear the window slide open, but her feet are already hitting the ground.

Thirty minutes later, Ro comes back with a Henderson's bag full of what she calls "the broken heart special." I don't know where she got the money for it, and I don't ask. She looks so proud to be able to help me.

She dumps the bag out onto the bed. Inside are two pints of ice cream, three bags of M&M's, a package of Oreos, and two Slim Jims. She holds up one of the jerkies. "For lunch." I laugh and her face glows.

By lunch time, I'm feeling better—queasy, but better. Ro seems to be having fun too. She picks another movie. We only watch the ones with explosions. "No soppy romantic comedies," she declared as one of the rules of the day. That was fine by me.

Later, my phone buzzes. A text from Kara asking why I'm not at school and another one saying she still wants to talk. I ignore them.


In the late afternoon, when Ro and I are both on a sugar crash with bleary eyes from so much TV, a stern knock sounds on my door. I don't want to answer it, but I can't ignore the outside world forever—the longer I do, the more likely Dad is to call Mom, and then I'll have to deal with her.

I stand up, while Ro stays in her nest of wrappers on the bed. I look through the peephole. Cam shifts his weight from foot to foot, like he wants to run away.

When I open the door, Cam thrusts a stack of books and papers at me. "Your homework."

"Dad sent you for my homework?" That doesn't sound like something Dad would even think of.

"No. Kara texted."

I narrow my eyes and stare him down. "I know," I say. He glances around like he's looking for an emergency exit from this situation. "I know about Kara and Ben."

"Oh," he says. "That."

"Yes, that." I feel my anger rising to atomic levels. Am I the only one who *didn't* know about them?

Ro creeps up behind me. She takes the books. "Goodbye, man-boy," she says, and closes the door.

I'm still standing facing the closed door. Cam's footsteps retreat into the distance.

"Time for *Terminator Three*," Ro announces.


I have to go to school. I can't let on to Kara that I know about her and Ben. She can't see that she's gotten to me.

My scar is killing me. It didn't get its release last night because Ro stayed too late. There wasn't time to prepare. I've learned my lesson about not preparing. I can't get seen again.

Kara meets me at my locker. "Are you feeling better? I texted you yesterday."

"I guess my phone is broken." I slam my locker door and push past her to class.

At lunch, she's sitting at our table, looking down at a bowl of brown rice. She has deep, deep dark circles peeking out from under her glasses. Her hair's even more of a mess than usual.

I make a left toward Emma's table. I shove in beside her and give her a fierce glare that says *Don't mess with me today*. She starts to protest but backs down. "Whatever," she mumbles.

"Did I do something?" Ben asks. I haven't said a word to him since I got to the clinic. I've handed him the clipboard and taken it back. That's been the extent of our contact.

I press the clipboard into his stomach. "Here's your next patient."

I shouldn't be mad at Ben. He didn't lead me on. It's not like we were dating and he slept with Kara behind my back. He's a free agent. He can do whatever he wants.

But the jealousy comes roaring back and fills my veins. Why would he pick Kara over me?

On Ben's third attempt to quiz me on what's wrong, the door opens. A man helps Ro inside. She's hopping on one foot. I jump up. "What happened?"

Ro turns toward me and away from Ben. She winks. "Ow, ow, ow," she says.

"We'll get you in to see Doc," the man says, and starts to hand her over to Ben.

"No," Ro says. "Not him." She points to me. "Her."

I step forward and take her arm. She wraps it around my shoulders. "I thought you could use some moral support," she whispers into my ear.

I have never loved a friend as much as I love Ro in that moment.

We hobble into the exam room, and Doc helps her onto the exam table. She holds my hand. "I want her to stay." She twists her face like she's terrified to be alone with Doc. If her school has a drama program, she should be in it.

"Okay," Doc says. He glances at me. I nod.

He takes her shoe off and starts twisting and squeezing her ankle. She lets out an "ow," but otherwise looks around the room with disinterest.

Doc finishes his exam. "I only have ibuprofen," he says.

Ro gets his meaning and looks offended.

"It's strained. I'll get you an ice pack. Stay off it for the rest of the night, and you should be good as new tomorrow." He leaves to go to the kitchen.

Ro puts a hand on her hip. "Does he think I'm some kind of pill whore?"

"Don't take it personally. He sees a lot of that. Thanks for coming. It's been awful with Ben today."

A smile lights up Ro's face. She drops it when Doc comes back in with her ice pack and ibuprofen.

I help her back out to the porch. It's later than I thought. Cam is waiting, wide-awake, outside. Ben's at the truck window, hands out to his sides, pleading with him.

Ro gives up the hobble and walks over to the truck. She glares at Ben. He's taken aback. She climbs inside, putting the ice pack on the dash.

"Jenny," Ben says. But I don't look at him as I crawl in behind Ro.

We pull away. Cam turns to me and opens his mouth.

I stop him. "I don't want to hear it."

Ro crosses her arms and glares at him in solidarity.

Cam's mouth clamps shut.

# 24

The wind has wrapped my hair halfway around my head in the three steps between my room and the office. I peel it out of my eyes.

"Apparently, the wind blows a lot here in April," Monica says, looking over the paper. It's also hot one day and cold the next. The plants are confused. They start to bloom only to be pulverized by the frost.

I sit down across from her. "You aren't from here?"

She laughs. "No. I was living in Colorado with—" With my dad.

"It's okay," I say. It's not like I ever harbored any dreams of my parents getting back together. My mom is happy with Brian.

The jury's still out on Monica. I think I could like her, but it'll take a long time to get over her paying Cam to watch me. And I still don't know how much she's figured out about my past—or my present.

I take my coffee back to my room and stare at my bee uniform. I'm going to have to put it on and go to school. I'm going to have to see Kara again.

FaceTime rings. I check the time. It's too late in Ohio. My heart starts to pound. My fingers shake as I answer.

Hailey's head pops up on the screen. No adults hover behind her.

"What's wrong? Why aren't you at school? Where's Mom?"

She jerks back at my barrage. "It's in-service day for the teachers. Mom's at work. Mrs. Jenkins is here."

Mrs. Jenkins is our elderly neighbor who sits for Hailey when Mom can't find anyone else.

"You're not supposed to be on the computer without an adult." My tone comes out far harsher than I intend—a product of the adrenaline still coursing through me. "But I'm glad to see you," I say, and hope that makes up for it.

Hailey looks worried. "Do you have your hat? I don't want you to be scared."

"Of course I have my hat. Why would I be scared?"

She leans into the screen until her eyes and nose are giant. "Because of the fires."

My heart sets off at a gallop again. "What fires, Hailey?"

"I wasn't supposed to be listening, but I was." She glances over her shoulder, but no one has entered the room. "Mom and Dad were talking about fires near your motel. I don't want you to be scared."

Her eyes are glassy. My heart breaks into a million pieces. We all tried to shelter her from what happened to me when I was her age, but it was impossible. People in our town are still talking about it ten years later.

"I don't want you to be scared either. Those fires were

in the woods a long way from here. They didn't hurt any people or burn any houses. Besides, our firefighters are the best."

Hailey's little chest swells with pride. Her father's a fire-fighter. That's how Brian got dragged into everything in the first place.

"If I ever get scared, I'll put my hat on, and it will make me feel better. I promise." I try not to cringe. Of all the things I own, why did I have to wear Hailey's hat on my midnight walks? Why couldn't I have picked something else? Now the hat is tainted. It will never be a sweet, innocent gift from my little sister again. I did that. No one else is to blame.

"Okay," Hailey says. But she doesn't smile. I have to look away to regain my composure.

I look back, a smile on my face. "Mrs. Jenkins is going to notice that you're gone. Why don't you go ask her to make her famous chocolate chip cookies? Then when you eat one, think really hard about me. I bet I'll be able to taste it."

Hailey nods.

"I love you, bug," I say.

"Love you too." The screen goes black on her side.



"Huh," Ro says. She's flopped over on my bed, messing with my phone. "Huh," she says again.

"What?" I ask since it's pretty clear that's her desired response.

"The bitch posted a picture of herself."

"Kara? No. Her parents don't let her do social media."

Ro sits up and shoves the phone in my face. On it is someone I don't recognize. "That's not Kara."

Ro pokes the phone and pushes it at me again. In the time I have before the picture disappears, I see that it is Kara. A Kara I've never seen before. Her glasses are off; her hair is curled and teased; she's wearing a ton of makeup—but she must know what she's doing, since it looks professional and effortless. Her top is low-cut.

"Wow."

"Yeah. But her earrings don't match her necklace," Ro says with disgust. I laugh. Ro has never let on that she cared a thing about jewelry—or hair or makeup. Only clothes. Ro loves clothes.

One more shove of the phone in my face, and I see that Kara's silver necklace with a turquoise pendant indeed does not match her gold hoop earrings.

"How'd you find that photo?"

Ro flops back down onto the bed. "Emma shared it. Kara's going to a club tonight. That skeevy all-ages one with the glow-in-the-dark, over-twenty-one wristbands. I've heard everybody gets one whether you show ID or not."

"Good for her."

"We could go, and you could tell her what a bitch she is."

"If I wanted to call Kara names, I could have done that a hundred times now at school."

"You're right. Let that jerk take her sorry drunk ass home."

I look up at Ro. "Ben? Is he going to be there too?"

Ro shrugs. "We could go and find out. You could catch them red-handed."

Do I really want to see them together? No. But part of me wants to let them know that I know. To stand next to Kara so that Ben can see what he could have had, but won't now. Ever.

"Let's go to the club."

Ro bounces to the wardrobe and starts tossing everything out onto the bed. I know better than to interfere. She's going to dress me however she wants, whether I like it or not.

The club is called Legit—which it definitely is not.

"This is too many people, Ro," I say as we join the line outside. They aren't waiting for anyone to come out before letting others in. The guy at the door just takes the money, and more people jam themselves inside.

"It's fine," Ro says. Cam sulks behind her. He drove us here, but I think the only reason he came was to keep up the show for Monica. So she wouldn't find out that that juvenile delinquent Jenny was at a club.

I bounce on my toes in the heels Ro picked out. I'm also wearing a fuchsia dress with a blue flower print. It's long-sleeved and cinched around the waist with a matching belt. It's cute. I don't remember which of my binge-shopping-with-Mom's-money trips I bought it on, but Ro pulled it out of the wardrobe and declared it to be "the one." She's wearing a simple black dress with a black leather jacket.

She didn't dress Cam. He's got on jeans and a maroon polo

shirt—tucked in. The preppiest-looking hoodie I have ever seen is *tied over his shoulders*. If he wasn't such a big guy, he'd get beaten up by this crowd.

When we get to the front of the line, I glance inside. Way too many people. I wipe a sweaty palm against my dress over and over again. There's no way everyone would make it out in an emergency.

This isn't worth it just to confront Kara and Ben. I try to back away, but Ro pulls the money I'm holding out of my hand. Ninety bucks. Thirty for each of us. That's the I-don't-have-a-fake-ID admission to this club. It buys us three glowing over-twenty-one wristbands. Thanks, Mom.

Ro seals my wristband around my arm. "No," I whisper. I can't go in. Too many people.

Ro pushes me from behind. Cam follows her. Soon we're standing in the hot, humid room with hundreds of people jumping up and down in the flashing strobe lights.

My head starts to spin. Too hot. Too loud. Too many people. Once I find Ben and Kara, I'm out of here.

Ro grabs me by the hand and Cam by the shirtsleeve. She pulls us farther into the pulsating throng. I'm jostled and grabbed by the crowd. My back is against Ro, who is bouncing to the beat. A woman in a silver minidress gyrates against Cam. Somewhere along the way he's lost his hoodie.

Emergency exits: I have to find them.

I shove my way through to the bar. My dress is twisted around one way and then the other. My feet are stepped on, my toes mashed.

I see one glowing exit sign in the back. Only one exit sign for all these people. I slap my hand over my mouth. I'm going to throw up.

I catch a glimpse of Kara, but no Ben. I follow her around the perimeter of the club, but every time I make a move toward her, another sweaty, drunken body crosses in front of me. I see another exit. A door painted black to match the walls. Another way out. Another chance at life for these people. A chance that's blocked by a heavy amplifier.

I run up to the amp and try to shove it out of the way. It's half as tall as I am, and it doesn't budge. I look around. Kara is gone. I have to tell someone. Tell them about the blocked exit.

I work my way back to the bar. I'm sweating through my dress, but not because of the heat. My heart is racing. I can't catch my breath.

"The exit!" I yell to the bartender, and point. He raises a hand to his ear, trying to hear me. "The exit is blocked!" I scream. He glances to where I'm pointing and shrugs. He tries to hand me a beer.

"No! The exit."

He turns away. I have to get Ro and Cam out of here.

I start to wade back into the bodies, but it's too late. I already smell smoke.

"Ro!" I scream. "Cam!"

I see Kara, but she can't hear me. She's heading for the back exit. Relief floods through me when I see the door close behind her. She's out. As mad as I am, I don't want her to die in a fire.

I call for Ro and Cam over and over again. It's getting hard to breathe.

They never appear. *Fire spreads fast.* I'm going to have to leave them. When all these people start rushing the exits, they'll jam up. Anyone who falls will be trampled. I look frantically around the club. Most of these people don't stand a chance.

I make a run for it. I'll get help. That's all I can do.

I push through the crowd and tear out the front entrance. They're still letting in more people.

"No," I grab the money-taker's arm. "Don't let them in. Fire."

He shakes me off. "What did you take?"

"Fire," I whimper.

A bouncer appears in the corner of my eye. He lifts me to my feet. "Time to go home," he says.

I kick at him. "Those people in there. They're going to die!" Why won't anyone listen to me? "Smoke. There's smoke."

"I'll bet," the bouncer says. He half carries and half drags me to the corner and dumps me at the base of a traffic light.

I look over my shoulder, and I see it. Smoke rising from the building. I can't breathe. My lungs don't want to take it in. Ro has my phone in her jacket pocket. There's nothing I can do. I stumble away, their screams echoing through the night behind me.

I keep a lookout for the fire trucks as I stumble to the Los Ranchitos, but they never come. I hiccup and gasp for air. My shoes are shredded. Someone whistles at me when I cross through the underpass below the interstate.

Ro has—had—my key. I want to scream and pound on Dad's door. Make him get up and do something to help those people. But it will be too late. By now it will just be a story for the morning news.

I push myself through the bathroom window and fall headfirst into a heap in the bathtub. There's a shoe print near my nose. A print from Ro's shoe. Ro. She's gone. And Ben. I don't know if he was there. But if he was . . .

My tears flow like they're never going to stop.

I can make them stop. I hoist myself up and stumble to the dresser. I pull the lighter out and flick it on. I hold the fire now. I'm in control.

"No!" I say out loud to myself, and click the top shut. I would be diverting resources away from the fire at the club. They're going to need every fire truck in town to try to save those people. I stuff the lighter back in its spot and open the nightstand drawer.

I dump two little blue pills into my hand. Nights like tonight are what the pills are for. I toss them into my mouth with such force that I almost choke.

I lie down on my bed. I smell like sweat and smoky night air. I get up, peel the dress off, and toss it into the corner. I crawl into bed in my underwear.

Then I pull the duvet over my head and black out the world.

# 25

I peek my sweating head out from under the duvet. Light spills in through the window. The construction equipment rumbles and crunches outside. I don't know what day it is. Did I sleep through Sunday?

A snore next to me. I leap out of bed. Ro rolls over and opens one eye. She closes it. "Where the fuck did you go last night?"

I lean over and poke her to make sure she's real. Her eye opens again. I jump back against the dresser. My palm knocks into something on the otherwise clear surface. I glance down and gasp. Under my hand is a silver lighter. Ben's lighter.

I wouldn't have left it out, would I? No. It wasn't there last night, I'm sure.

Ro sits up. I sweep the lighter into my hand and shove it behind me. She blinks the sleep out of her eyes and then turns away. "Why are you naked?"

I look down at my bra and underwear, and the hazy memories of last night start to flood back to me. My eyes water. I grab my coat off the chair and wrap it around me. I pop the lighter into the pocket.

"What happened? Where were the fire trucks?" I demand.

Ro rubs her eyes like my being in focus will increase her understanding of me. "Why would there be fire trucks?"

I pace back and forth. "The emergency exit was blocked. The room was filling with smoke. I tried to find you and get you out."

Ro doesn't say anything.

"There was a fire at the club. I saw the smoke."

Ro sits up on her knees. "They had one of those dry-ice fog machines. Plus, people there were smoking everything you can smoke, and some things that you can't. I don't know if you noticed, but it's not exactly a reputable establishment." She holds up her wrist, still wrapped with the over-twenty-one wristband.

I collapse into the chair. "There wasn't a fire."

"No. You took off. Then I lost Cam. I waited until the whole club cleared out. He came back, but you were just gone. Cam freaked out about having to explain to your dad and the blond lady that he lost you."

I finger the lighter in my pocket. There wasn't a fire. But I was so sure. I could hear them screaming.

"What's that?" Ro points to my coat. The lingering pills in my system make me slow to react. I look down for a whole beat before I realize that she can see the top of the lighter.

I drop it and send it into the bottom of the pocket. "Nothing."

Ro's face goes serious. "You can tell me your secret. It's okay. I already know."

The whole world stops. I slowly remove my hand from my

pocket. What should I do? Confess? Let someone else carry part of this burden? Ro won't go to the police.

My mouth opens, but no sound comes out.

Ro looks annoyed again. She flops back down on the bed. "Fine. Don't tell me that you started again."

"Started what?" My heart hummingbirds in my chest.

"You told me that you were trying to quit when we first met, remember? Then I found that lighter in your drawer. You don't have to be Sherlock Holmes to figure out you started smoking again."

I can't contain the gasp that's released from my mouth, but I quickly roll my lips under and nod. I look down like I'm ashamed.

Shouldn't I feel ashamed after all I've done?

What does it say about me that I don't?

"Are you at least going to tell me what happened last night? Did you find Kara and Ben?"

It's a blur. I remember seeing Kara leave. I remember stumbling home. I remember taking the sleeping pills.

Ro is staring at me, awaiting an answer.

"I got scared."

"Whatever," Ro says. She rolls onto her side and pulls the duvet over her head.


"Late night?" Monica asks. I glance at my reflection in the microwave. She probably thinks that I'm hungover or stoned or both. I lift the coffeepot and see that I'm still wearing my neon wristband.

It's too late to try to hide it, and my slow brain can't come up with an excuse. I look back at Monica. She holds up her hands. "I'm not your mother."

She peels the color comics section out of the fat paper on the table. "Why are they working on a Sunday?" I point outside, and the wristband floats in front of my face. *Come on, brain. Wake up.*

"There are some protestors threating to get an injunction to stop the project," Monica says as I dig through the drawers, looking for scissors.

"Can they do that?" I ask.

Monica stands up, walks to the last drawer, pulls out a pair of scissors, takes my arm, and cuts the band off. She holds it in front of my face. "Put it in the bottom of the trash can." She drops it into my palm. "The protestors don't have a real case. The paperwork was filed correctly. But if they're obnoxious enough, they can get a judge to halt the project while it's all reviewed. Or they can go straight to the city and try to get our permits pulled."

She must read the alarm on my face. "Don't worry. No one in the city wants to go up against Mike. But the sooner the motel is done, the sooner all this foolishness is over with."

Cam opens the door. When he sees me, he jumps. Then he glares. Glares like he's trying to strangle me with his eyes.

"Good morning," I say.

"It's two o'clock in the afternoon."

"I guess I better go do my homework, then." I push past him before he has a chance to say anything else. Something tells me that after my disappearing act at the club, I'm going to be riding the bus home from school all week.

Ro's in the shower when I get back to my room. I open a bottom drawer of the dresser and shove Ben's lighter way in the back.

My crumpled heap of a dress smells like that horrible club. I scoop it up and open the wardrobe to toss it into the laundry.

Ro comes out of the bathroom drying her hair with a towel. She points to my hands. "I love that dress."

I look down at it. After last night, I never want to see it again.

Ro takes it from me and shakes it out. She holds it up against her and stands in front of the mirror. "Where's the belt?"

I search through my still-drugged brain. I don't remember taking it off last night.

I shrug. "I must have lost it at the club."

# 26

Ro's playing a game on my phone, while I try to concentrate on my homework. I still feel underwater. I'm never taking two sleeping pills again.

The construction crew has left for the day. The wind whips sand and construction dust into swirls that glow in the orangey light of the setting sun.

The curtains are open, so I see Dad approach. He has his phone in his hand. He stops in front of the door and takes a breath. He knocks. "Come in," I call.

Dad pops the door open. He glances over at Ro. "I need to talk to Jenny."

Ro looks back and forth between the bathroom and the door, unsure of how to exit. She decides on the door.

"What's going on?" The look on Dad's face is unreadable. Did Monica rat me out about the club? Or did Cam? I bet it was Cam.

"Sit down," he says, and points to the chair. He sits on the bed across from me. I steel myself for whatever kind of discipline Dad is going to hand out. We've never crossed this bridge before. Ro is leaning against the window, hands cupped around her face to see through the reflection. I give her a little shrug.

"Last night—" Dad says, and then stops to take another breath. Next time Cam is asleep in his truck, I am personally escorting Mike Vargas over to catch him.

He starts over again. "Your teacher Teresa called. . . . I don't know how to do this." He rakes his hand over his face.

"Your friend Kara died last night."

"*What?*"

I couldn't have heard him right.

"Your teacher Teresa called. She said that last night Kara died."

I jump to my feet. "How? Was it in a fire?" I knew that smoke wasn't dry ice. There was a fire somewhere in the club.

Dad stands up too. He reaches out like he's going to hug me, but isn't sure how to grab my panicked figure.

"No. It wasn't a fire." He gulps. "She was murdered."

"What?" I ask again. It has to be the pills. None of this is real. It's my brain having a reaction to the stupid sleeping pills. In a second, I'm going to realize that Dad came in to ask if I want pizza for dinner.

"They found her body this morning behind a club. That's all I know."

I collapse back into the chair. Behind a club. The club I was at last night. The club I ran away from.

Everything in my body goes still. For a moment, I feel absolutely nothing. But then the pain starts to flow from the bottom of my feet up through my legs and my stomach and my heart.

I scream like a rabid animal. Dad backs away. Ro charges in and runs over. She puts her arms around me and looks daggers at Dad.

"I'm sorry. I'll let you two be alone," he whispers, and leaves.

The pain reaches my eyes, and they start to spill tears down my face.

"Kara died, Ro," I say in between sobbing gasps. "She was murdered. If I hadn't been so mad at her, I could have ... I could have been there with her. This wouldn't have happened."

Ro's arms tighten around me. I don't feel comforted. My lungs are being squeezed of all their air. I want her to release me.

"We should watch the news." I jump up so quickly that Ro is knocked over. "We have to find out what happened."

I don't have control anymore. My hands shake. My knees wobble. I stab at the remote and stab at it and stab at it, but the TV stays black.

"We have to know what happened." My knees give out, and I hit the floor. I can't breathe. The tears are coming too fast. My stomach is sick. I clap my hand over my mouth.

Ro takes the remote away from me and turns on the TV. It plays a commercial for some wonder drug with side effects that are worse than what it's trying to cure. My tears slow. I start to feel nothing. Nothing but cold and dried out. A frozen husk of a person.

The commercial switches to a breaking-news graphic, and

the anchor puts on his serious expression. "We are getting reports that the body of a teenage girl has been found outside the Legit Night Club in Las Piedras. Let's go live to the scene."

The screen flashes to the same reporter who's been covering the Los Ranchitos. "Police aren't releasing much information, but we know that the body of a seventeen-year-old girl was found here in the early hours of the morning. Police don't have a motive, but we know that her ID, bank card, and cash were still in her possession."

The screen jumps back to the anchor. His stiff hair glows under the lights. His eyes are wider than before. He tries not to betray what he's thinking. But it's the same thing we're all thinking: Drunk girl found behind a club. Wasn't robbed. He knows exactly what happened to her.

So do I, and I could have stopped it. But my brain was spinning. I couldn't tell what was real. I thought there was a fire. I remember looking for Kara and Ben, but the rest is blurry.

And someone was leaving those strange pictures for Kara. I could have made her tell me what was going on. Who was doing it. Is that another thing I could have done to prevent this?

My body is not dried out. I continue crying with a ferocity I haven't felt since I listened to my friends die in that fire. I crawl onto the bed and curl up into a ball. I slap my hand over my screaming scar and pull the fluffy duvet over my head so that nothing else bad can reach me.

# 27

School's been canceled today. Instead, an army of counselors fills the halls of Riverline Prep for anyone who wants to talk. Dad showed up at my door and offered to take me there and sit with me. I declined.

Mom calls three times. Three times I hit ignore. I don't want to talk. I don't want to share my feelings. They are too big, too many. If I let them out, they might not go back in again.

I pass the office door without going inside. I can't stand sitting across from Monica and seeing the awkward sympathy on her face.

I walk out the front gate and down to the cottonwoods. Even though Kara's dead, the construction workers keep doing their thing. The sun keeps shining. The wind keeps blowing.

Ro left sometime in the night. She didn't come back this morning. She must be at school by now, so I'm by myself for the whole day.

I wander through the trees, away from the colony, and pass the site of my last fire. I look away. I'm not in the mood. I've found a feeling worse than the itch in my scar.

I sit on a tree stump in plain view of the access road. And I wait.

The sun is moving toward the horizon, and my stomach is growling by the time he comes.

"Hello, Jenny," Allen calls with a huge smile on his face. As he approaches me and sees my face, his smile fades.

"Do you need help?" He reaches for his radio. I put a hand out to stop him.

"No. I'm okay." I scooch over on the tree stump so he can sit. "The girl"—I suck in a lungful of dusty air—"the girl who was killed, she was my friend."

"Oh," he says. "I'm sorry." Awkward.

"I wish I knew what happened to her." I glance up ever so slightly to make sure that he's watching me. "I keep thinking over and over again that maybe I missed something. Something that could have saved her." I rub my eyes with the back of my hand.

I know it's wrong to take advantage of his liking me— even worse to encourage it—but I have to know what happened to Kara.

"It's not your fault," he says, and hesitantly puts a comforting arm around my shoulders. "Is there anything I can do?"

He means it as an empty nicety, but I do need something from him. If Allen wants to play cop, here's his chance.

"Can you find out how she died? Like from the police reports?" I have to know what happened. Was it a random attack, or was it more than that? Planned by a killer she knew? The guilt of what I could have maybe prevented surges through me again. I wish I could remember more of what happened after I saw the smoke.

Allen drags his foot through the dirt. He rubs a hand over the back of his neck. "I'm not supposed to access those kinds of reports."

I look away and exaggerate the disappointment in my voice. "It's okay. I understand."

He stands up. I look up at him through my lashes, like I'm a damsel in distress. I know he'll go for it. He's wanted to impress me from the first time we met.

"Give me your number. I'll see what I can do."


Ro is in Henderson's parking lot. She runs over when she sees me coming up the sidewalk. "What are you doing here?" I ask.

Ro scrunches up her eyebrows like I've hurt her. "I came to check on you, but you weren't home."

I jut a thumb over my shoulder. "I was walking." I step into the street to get around her, since she's planted herself in the middle of the sidewalk.

"Where are you going?"

I point at Henderson's. "I was all out of tampons this morning." I turn and look at her. "Which is funny since I still had half a box left last month." I don't know why I'm being mean to Ro. I couldn't care less about tampons. But I'm feeling angry now. Angry at her. Angry at Kara for being at the club in the first place. Angry at me.

"Do you want to come?" I try to soften my voice as an apology.

Ro trudges along behind me. When the doors of Henderson's whoosh open, she stops. "I'll wait outside." She crosses her arms indignantly.

"Fine." My irritation with her increases.

I march straight to the tampons and pick out what I need. Then I decide that I'm going to make Ro wait awhile, so I browse the other aisles and dump random impulse buys into my basket.

The familiar clerk is at the register. She smiles, but it doesn't reach her puffy eyes. I've never seen her wear a name tag before, but today, she's pinned one on that says "Ruby." Hovering over it is a silver necklace with a turquoise pendant. It sparks something in my memory.

"That's a beautiful necklace," I say.

She grabs it and holds it between two fingers. "It's been in my family for generations."

"Oh." I remember where I saw one like it. In the photo of Kara, before the club. My stomach sinks. Kara. The club.

I try to shake it out of my head. This is the Southwest. I bet every woman within a five-hundred-mile radius has a turquoise necklace like that in her jewelry box. Ruby probably wears it every day and I never noticed before.

I punch in my PIN and ask for ten dollars cash back. Ruby gives me my receipt and money. I'm too distracted by the necklace to stuff them into my pocket. They're clutched in my hand when I get to the door. Ro is waiting outside, arms still crossed.

I sigh and look down at the money. It's a twenty. I look back up at Ro, and then turn on my heels and walk back to Ruby.

She's surprised to see me come back. I hold up the twenty. "I think you gave me too much." I hold up the receipt. "I only asked for ten."

I expect Ruby to be flustered, to be apologetic, to maybe even be mad. What I don't expect is for her to burst into tears.

I glance behind me. There are no other customers. "It's okay. I just don't want you to get in trouble."

She wipes her eyes on the green smock she wears over her clothes. "I'm sorry. I'm having a bad day. That girl who was killed? I knew her when she was little. All I can think about are her poor parents losing another child. And like that . . ." She tears up again.

I remember Kara's trip to visit Joey at Henderson's when she was buying alcohol. No wonder she looked so scared when Ruby recognized her. She probably thought Ruby was going to call her parents.

Ruby takes the twenty from my outstretched hand and sniffles.

"Is everything all right here?" a voice asks. I turn around. A man—if you can call him that; he can't be more than a few years older than me—in a green vest embroidered with "Manager" stands behind me. He crosses his arms and looks at Ruby sternly.

She wipes her face with her smock again.

I smile. "Everything is fine. Thanks." He doesn't believe me. "I just needed some change." Ruby hands me the ten.

I look at Ruby. "I hope your allergies get better. I keep sneezing too." I glance over at the manager. He doesn't seem convinced, but since I'm not going to complain, I'm not worth his time. He gives Ruby one more glare and wanders back to whatever hole he crawled out of.

"I'm sorry about that." Ruby has regained her composure and motions to the bill in my hand. "And thank you."

I fold up the money and shove it into my pocket. I give Ruby a half wave and leave.

"Ro?" I call out. The sidewalk is empty. I walk down into the parking lot. "Ro?" She's gone.

I feel superdrained—like I could crawl into bed and sleep for a week. I shuffle back to the Los Ranchitos. When I open my door, I expect Ro to be on the bed, snapping at me for taking so long, but she's not here, either.

I go into the bathroom and check the window. It's unlocked, as usual. I guess Ro is mad at me.

I kick off my shoes and crawl into bed. She'll come back. She always does.


I'm startled awake by my phone ringing. My room is in shadows. It must be dinnertime. Ro still hasn't shown up.

I don't recognize the number, but it's a local area code.

"Hello?"

"I have to do this fast," the voice on the other end says. "My supervisor is in the bathroom."

"Allen?"

"I have the autopsy report."

Adrenaline shoots through me. Do I want to know what

the investigators found when they put my friend on the table and cut her into pieces? My stomach flips over. If it weren't so empty, its contents would be on the floor.

Allen doesn't wait for me to decide. "She died from asphyxiation. An object one point five inches wide—like a belt or something—was wrapped around her neck. She wasn't, uh"—he clears his throat—"sexually assaulted. Her ID and debit card and fifty dollars in cash were found on her body."

I can't process this. My mind keeps skipping around. "What about her jewelry? Her necklace?"

He flips pages. "Gold hoop earrings." Through the phone I hear footsteps approaching him. Something slams down.

"What did I tell you about making personal calls?" I can hear a muffled voice say.

The phone goes dead.

# 28

School is ... awkward. The halls are quiet. We don't know what to say. We don't know what to do with our hands. Do we look one another in the eye? Or keep our heads down and pretend nothing happened? Whenever anyone makes a joke or laughs, someone glares at them.

In homeroom, Teresa talks to us about expressing our grief. Emma bursts into tears and has to go to the nurse's office. I roll my eyes. She wasn't nice to Kara once in the time I've been here.

By lunch, the rumors have started. Someone heard that a guy was seen hanging around the club. He didn't belong there. He was scruffy, like he lived in the colony. He could have killed Kara. He probably did.

The police aren't commenting.

But I have to believe the rumors are true. If it was someone from the colony, then it was probably random. There's less I could have done to stop it.

But Kara's killer didn't take her money, and the autopsy report said he used a belt.

The belt from my dress went missing that night.

Why can't I remember more?

After school, I feel numb. The world goes by in blurry flashes of colors. Ro's being pissy to me. I'm being pissy to her, too, but my friend died. I have an excuse.

I didn't go to the clinic. I couldn't sit at the table and look cheerful. I couldn't see Ben. Everything hurts too much.


The night before Kara's funeral, the sirens blare. From my spot on the sidewalk that ends just beyond the Los Ranchitos, I see what must be every fire truck in town. The fire is close. It's moving toward the colony.

I weigh the lighter in my pocket. They deserve it.

Orange flames jump over the tops of trees and race through the underbrush. Smoke and fluffy bits of ash blow over me, but I don't move. I stand tall and watch it. Watch it eat away at the trees on its way to get Kara's killer.

"What are you doing out here, Jenny?" Dad grabs my shoulder and twists me around. "I went to your room, but you weren't there." The light from the flames shows me the fear in his eyes. I push my hands deeper into my jacket pockets.

Dad loops his arm through mine and moves me along the sidewalk, as if we're taking an evening stroll. But only I know how tight his arm clamps down. The force with which he moves me back to the Los Ranchitos.

When we cross through the gate, a new man is standing there waiting for us. He has on a security uniform. He leans against a knockoff police car. Dad nods to him. "I'm not taking any more chances around here."

The security guard follows us to my room. Dad shoves me inside.

Even after Dad is long gone and I've turned off my light, I see the shadow of the stationary security guard posted outside my door.

*I wish Ro had dressed me.* That's what I'm thinking as I walk into the church for Kara's funeral. This dress feels wrong. It's too tight, then too loose. It chafes. Dad and Monica offered to come with me, but I refused. The new security guard drove me. He'll wait outside until I'm ready to go home.

I walk down the aisle toward the box covered in flowers. The box that contains my friend. My friend who I was horrible to in her last days.

Most of Riverline Prep has come. Some look sad; some look like this is the social event of the year. They point and whisper to one another.

I hear my name. Doc waves me to where he and Teresa are sitting and pats the pew between them. He's wearing a dark suit with a red tie. His hair is pulled back. Teresa, in her usual long skirt and loose blouse, half smiles and gives me a nod.

As I sit down next to my teacher, it suddenly occurs to me that I'm back to having zero friends. Ben was my friend. Ro was my friend. Kara was my friend. But now . . .

I glance back up at the flower-covered box. Guilt floods

me. How can I be feeling sorry for myself? Kara will never have a friend again. If I had been a better one, none of us would be here.

Emergency exits: I can't even care right now.

Doc glances over his shoulder. "I haven't seen Ben in a week. I'm getting worried." His eyes stop moving and focus on me like I'm supposed to say something reassuring.

"Will you go check in on him after this? I know he'd like to see you." Doc's kind voice is pleading. I want to say no. But I can't disappoint anyone else.

"Okay."

Whispers fill the church as the next mourners enter. Mike Vargas walks down the aisle like this is an important business meeting. Cam shuffles behind him.

Cam's whole face is different. His eyes are glazed over and bloodshot. The skin around his mouth droops, but the rest of his muscles are held so tightly that I'm not sure he's actually breathing.

He looks the way I feel, and for a brief moment, I want to stand up and give him a hug.

Mike Vargas walks to the front of the church. A man in the first pew stands up to shake his hand. The woman next to him clutches a tissue and accepts a kiss on the cheek from Mike. Those must be Kara's parents. I turn away. I can't look at them. I can't see their faces. They remind me of other parents and grandparents and aunts and uncles at the funerals when I was seven. The ones where I sat in the front pew in an itchy black dress, flanked by my blank-eyed parents.

I hold my head in my hands. Teresa puts a sympathetic arm around me.

As soon as the funeral is over, I take off. I can't go through the line and tell Kara's overprotective parents how sorry I am. If I do, I might confess: *I was there. I could have stopped it.*

I dash outside. The security guard perks up. "I'm going out with friends," I tell him.

"No. I'm supposed to take you straight home."

I pull my phone out and send a quick text to Dad. Even though he's been watching me like he's suspicious of something, he's acting awkward, too. I know he'll say yes to me being with friends right now.

A few seconds later, the security guard gets a text. He pulls out a business card. "Call me when you need to be picked up."

I shove his card into my purse and walk back to the church. When I see him drive away, I make a quick turn to the right and keep going.

# 29

I walk for a long time. Spring has set in. Baby birds chirp in trees that are starting to explode with leaves. Tulips bloom in beds along the nicer streets. The wind blows. Hard.

The coffee shop is closed when I get there. The sign on the front says it'll be opening late today due to a funeral.

How many people knew Kara? She mostly kept to herself at school, but there was a part of her she didn't tell me about—the part that didn't care what her parents thought. It's why she was drunk at the party and why she was at that club. She must have known more people than I realized. She knew Ben—*really* knew him—the whole time.

I can't forget that, even now.

When I turn from the coffee shop, I see a woman walking out of Ben's building. I dart toward her, hoping that when I climb the stairs, I'll find Ben safe at home. She smiles and holds the door open so that I can go in.

I knock on Ben's purple door, but he doesn't answer. I keep knocking until dread fills me. What if something has happened to him? What if he's lying cold and dead on the floor? I pull out my phone. Who do I call? The police? Doc?

The door rattles as the dead bolt unlocks. It opens, and Ben stands before me. From the way he looks, I expect him to reek of alcohol—to have gone on a bender and crashed off the wagon—but he doesn't. He moves aside to let me pass.

His apartment is messy, but I don't see any bottles, pills, pipes, or syringes. I turn back and look at him. All I see is grief.

"Hey." I don't know what else to say. Seeing his face makes me feel like I'm being stabbed in the gut a thousand times. But I came here to do something.

"I'm sorry." I don't give him a chance to respond. "I'm sorry about Kara. I saw you two coming out of the building together and I was blindsided. I shouldn't have treated you the way I did." I shouldn't have treated Kara the way I did.

The tears that didn't fall during the funeral fall now. I make my way back to the door. I can report back to Doc that I have checked on Ben. I've apologized. There's no other reason for me to be here.

"Wait," Ben says. "You saw us that morning?"

My heart stops cold in my chest. Something about his saying it out loud brings the pain and humiliation back. I feel my face burn. I can't look at him.

"I saw her come into the coffee shop. You took her up to your apartment. She came out the next morning in your clothes."

Ben places both hands on my shoulders and gently turns me around to face him. "And you thought Kara spent the night. That we were together?"

He wraps his arms around me in a hug I don't reciprocate.

It makes so much more sense now. When he pulls away, there's relief in his eyes, but it quickly goes back to grief.

"Sit down." He points to the little couch—the one we almost kissed on.

I'm feeling numb again. I don't know what's going on, but I sit. He positions himself next to me so that I can see his face.

"I was never with Kara—not like that. She moved in down the street from my uncle's at the end of middle school. She was a wreck. I was a wreck. We became wrecks together."

I shake my head. I still don't understand.

Ben takes a deep breath. "Cam started at Riverline Prep the year before I did. He made friends who were juniors and seniors. They drank and smoked and did any drug they could get their hands on. I wanted so much to be like Cam." He laughs at the involuntary scowl I feel on my face. "He was different then. He was cool—like an older brother to me. He invited me to go out with him once, and his friends adopted me like I was their mascot.

"One night on our way home from a party, the guy driving got pulled over for DWI. My uncle had to pick us up from the side of the road. He convinced the cops not to charge us with anything, but he was really disappointed in us. We were grounded for forever. Cam stopped partying. I . . . I couldn't stop."

Ben's eyes look off in the distance. I can't help but take his hand and squeeze. He squeezes back and doesn't let go.

"Kara"—he chokes on her name—"moved here about then. We both were at Riverline. She found me during third period behind the dumpster with a bottle in my hand. She sat down and took the bottle from me. That's the day we became drinking buddies."

Kara? She doesn't seem like the kind of person who would get away with that—not given the way her parents treated her. Or maybe that's *why* her parents treated her the way they did.

Ben looks at me. "Does this make you uncomfortable?" It's not a challenge. He's asking. *Yes, of course it does.* But I shake my head. I want him to keep talking. I need to know. These are the things I wanted to know from the beginning. The things no one would tell me.

He takes a breath to steel himself. I can tell that this story is one he's told before. It's smooth and emotionless, but when he talks about Kara, there's something more there. Something hidden.

"One day we ditched school. My uncle was working. Cam was out being the dutiful son. I'd scored some pills. We were up in my room. I'd already taken some, but Kara hesitated. Pills were something new for her. She held one between her fingers, and it was like something broke inside her. She confessed."

"Confessed to what?"

Ben shakes his head. Even though she's dead, he won't tell me her story.

I don't want Ben to know that I might have been able to prevent Kara's death, but I have information that he doesn't. Maybe together we have all the pieces.

"Before she died"—I blink hard to clear my eyes—"Kara

got some strange pictures. In her locker and on her car. One of the pictures was from an ultrasound."

Ben sucks in a breath. Was that Kara's secret? Was she pregnant? Did she have an abortion? Give a baby up for adoption?

Ben grips my hand as if he's drowning and I'm the only person keeping his head above water. He shakes his head, like he's fighting with himself. Then he comes to a decision.

"When they lived in Santa Fe, Kara's mom was pregnant. After years of trying, something finally worked. The doctors wanted her to stay in bed. They lived in a massive house, so her parents hired a housekeeper to come during the day to clean, and to watch Kara. It went bad fast. The housekeeper accused Kara of stealing from her. Kara swore she didn't do it, but the housekeeper was going to tell her mother.

"Have you met Kara's mom?" he asks. I shake my head. "She was obsessed with safety. She was always afraid something was going to happen to Kara. The housekeeper left a bucket out once, and Kara's mom reamed her for creating a tripping hazard.

"Kara wanted the housekeeper gone. After she had left for the day, Kara spilled furniture polish on the wood floor at the top of the stairs. She called her mother over to look at it and blamed the housekeeper. Her mother was furious and cleaned it up—but she didn't get it all. A little while later, she was walking in socks on the wood, and she slipped.

"Kara found her mom crumpled at the bottom of the stairs. She was in the hospital for a long time. She lost the baby."

"Oh my God."

"Kara thought she had killed that baby."

"But it was an accident."

He nods. "The housekeeper was fired. The police were called, but they couldn't find any evidence of a crime. Kara never told anyone what she had done. After she confessed to me, something changed in her. She started talking to Doc about her drinking. I wasn't ready for that yet, so while she got better, I got worse. She was doing well for a long time. Until . . ."

"Until someone found out what she did."

Ben rolls his lips under and looks away like he's trying to stop himself from crying. "We hadn't really talked in years. But that night, she was terrified. Someone had been in her house and left a bottle of lemon furniture polish with the word 'killer' written on it in her kitchen. Since I was the only one who knew, I was the only one she could come to. Her parents were out of town. She didn't want to stay in her house alone, so she spent the night."

"Do you think the person who left her those strange pictures is the person who killed her?"

Ben closes his eyes like he's trying to maintain his composure. He nods.

"Oh my God," I whisper. "I was so horrible to her. I let her suffer. I left her to die." Ben's eyes snap open, and he jerks away from me, but I keep going. "I was at the club looking for her, but I freaked out. I left. I left without her."

Ben stands up. My head drops into my hands, and I block

out the world with my fingers. I wait for him to yell at me and tell me to leave and never come back. It's what I deserve.

He sits back down. I feel his arm wrap around me. "Why was she there in the first place? Kara drank, but she would never hang out in a club like that."

Maybe Ben didn't know the real Kara either.

"She posted a picture saying she was going to be there."

Ben's quiet. His arm stays around me. I drop my hands from my eyes and stare at a sock lying in the middle of the carpet.

"It's not your fault. She started drinking again. She was getting reckless. Doc was worried that she was going to do something stupid. She told him she wanted to confront the stalker and get it over with. If I had known she was going to go through with it . . ."

I look up at him. "You think she confronted him at the club?" Did she have a gun? A knife? How was she going to stop him?

"I don't know. But obviously she got the guy to come." He chokes on the words. I turn until I can put my arms around him, and we hold each other on the little sofa.


As the sun sets, we're still entwined on the couch. A crappy old movie that neither of us is watching plays on the TV. I feel Ben's heart beating, his breath warm against my neck.

I don't want this to end; every moment here makes it harder to leave.

"I should go. My dad will be worried."

Ben sits up.

Our eyes meet.

I know what's going to come next. We shouldn't do it. We should find ways to deal with our pain separately.

But I want this so badly—even more than I want to go out into the trees and pacify my searing scar.

Our lips come together. It's rough and desperate, as if we're trying to pour all our hurt out in that kiss.

I pull away. It's the right thing to do. "I don't want to mess up all you've worked for."

He threads his fingers through my hair. "I need this right now."

So do I.

# 30

I have four missed calls from Dad, two from the security guard, and one from Allen. I don't know how long I've been lying in Ben's arms, but he's asleep and it's dark outside.

I untangle myself from him and take my phone into the bathroom.

Dad picks up after the first ring. I speak before he can. "Sorry, I never turned my phone back on after the funeral. I'm at a friend's house. She's having a hard time. I'm going to spend the night."

I hear his breathing on the other end. I can tell he wants to yell at me. I've scared him, and I'm sorry. I know I've been doing that a lot lately, but I can't go back to the Los Ranchitos. Not tonight.

"Okay," he finally says. "But keep your phone on."

I step out of the bathroom, and Ben looks up at me with sleepy eyes. I lie back down in his arms.

"How did you do it?" I ask.

"Do what?"

"Get better. Make all the urges go away."

He laughs softly. "They never go away. Not completely.

Doc found me half dead in an alley. He told me he could help me, that I could get better. I didn't believe him, but he offered me a meal and a place to sleep. No one had ever been that selflessly kind to me. He made me want to get better. I went into treatment, and when I got out, I surrounded myself with people who loved me."

His fingers trace up and down my arm.

"I still take it day by day. But helping out at the clinic, that's really what keeps me going. They're like my family there. It feels good to give back. I don't know where I'd be without it."

His finger touches my scar. He's seen me grip my arm through my clothes, but I've never told him what was underneath.

"I was in a fire when I was seven."

His fingers turn featherlight against my skin.

"Does it hurt?"

"Yes." It's the first time I've ever admitted that—even to myself. What I do—setting fires—it hurts. A little piece of me dies every time.

Ben has his own scars. Lots of them. He doesn't try to hide them from me. I put my finger over a round one on his chest.

"There's a reason I ended up living with my uncle. I was mad for so long. I felt abandoned by my mother. But now I know she did the best she could. Dumping me on his doorstep saved my life. Until I did my best to destroy it."

"My sister's the reason I don't do those things. I wanted to. I wanted the pain to stop. But she looks at me like I'm the most important person in the world. I can't hurt her."

He places his hand over my scar, like he's erasing it.

I want to be better. He makes me want to be better.

"It was me," I blurt out. The deep brown of his eyes in the light from the street makes me want to tell him. To confess. "I did it."

Ben sits up and faces me.

"When I was seven, I started the fire. It was my first sleepover. I had to go to the bathroom, but the house was so dark. I couldn't flip on the light or wake up any of the other girls. I didn't want them to think I was a baby.

"There was a chunky red candle and a book of matches on the mantel over the fireplace. I'd seen a movie where the girls carried around candles in their long white nightgowns. I thought I could do that." I cringe and wait for Ben to say something, to look uncomfortable, but his face doesn't change. He's listening.

"I didn't know how to use matches. It took me four tries. When one finally lit, I couldn't move. I was mesmerized by the flame dancing at the end of the stick. I had made that happen. Then I got scared and shook it out.

"I have dreams where I crawl back into my sleeping bag and nothing happens. We all wake up in the morning. That's what I should have done. But the matches . . . I wanted to see if I could do it again.

"The next time, I didn't shake it out. I dropped it. The carpet started to smolder. I lit another one and dropped it on the curtains. They went up almost instantly. That's when I realized what I had done. I knew I was going to get in big trouble. I wanted to put it out, but I didn't know how.

"I ran down the hallway until I found the bathroom. I hid

in there, curled up in the bathtub, waiting for the smoke detectors to go off and for my friend's parents to come in and yell at me. But that never happened. The house was silent for so long. Then I heard the screaming. The parents must have gone in to get the other girls. They were all trapped. It was too late. I tried to go out to find them." I motion with my head down to the scar.

Ben's lip twitches slightly. I don't know if it is sympathy or disgust. A sudden fear fills me. "You can't tell anyone. No one knows what I did."

No one except my stepfather, Brian. He suspected me from the moment he pulled me to safety through the bathroom window.

Ben doesn't jump up and demand I leave. He kisses my shoulder, lies back down, and holds me in his arms. He doesn't try to make me feel better or tell me I was too young to know what I was doing when I started the house fire.

As his chest moves in and out against me, I realize that for the first time in ten years, I can't feel my scar.

Ben's warmth and acceptance makes me want to confess *everything*. I open my mouth, but no sound comes out.

Some secrets are too big to turn into words.


Ben nuzzles my ear. "You talk in your sleep."

I roll over and smile. "About what?"

Ben looks away, cringing at having mentioned it.

Fire. I must talk about fire.

I turn his chin toward me. Our lips meet. Sun is pouring

in the window. It's like the last few weeks have melted away. I feel happy.

There's a sharp knock on the door. "Benjamin?" a voice calls from outside. I jump up and scramble for my clothes, but Ben seems unconcerned. He pulls on his jeans and opens the door.

The woman Ben usually works with is on the other side. I try to smooth my hair and pretend I just got here.

"Good morning," she says.

I give her a little wave. My face must be atomic red. She focuses her attention on Ben.

"Will you be coming to work today?" Her tone is teasing.

Ben glances over his shoulder at me. There's more life in his eyes today. I feel buzzed too. "Yeah, I'll be down soon." She nods and gives me a wink before walking back down the hallway. Ben closes the door. I'm still red. "Don't worry about it," he says. "She's not going to judge you—either of us."

"What's her story? She doesn't really seem like the barista type."

"Jackie?" Ben rubs his hand along the back of his neck and glances around the room, like he's not sure he should tell me. "Doc found her, like he did me. He helped us both get clean and find jobs and places to live. He pays it forward by doing that."

"What does Doc have to pay forward?"

Ben wanders into the kitchen and digs through the refrigerator. He pulls out bread and pops two slices into the toaster. "Prescription pills. He was a big-time surgeon in Albuquerque. I don't know what happened, but he had a prescription pad, and soon he had an addiction. He got fired. The state almost pulled his medical license. Somehow he found his way to Las Piedras and someone who helped him."

The toast pops up. He smears jelly on it and presents it to me on a blue plastic plate. "Doc saved me; now I work at the clinic so *I* can pay it forward. It keeps me centered. Keeps me healthy."

I look around. The whole world seems a different color now. So many people have stories I didn't know.

The knock sounds on the door again. Ben gives me an apologetic look. "They must be busy downstairs. You can stay here if you want." He holds his toast between his teeth as he ties on his work apron.

I want to stay. I want Ben to stay. Want both of us to stay wrapped in this cocoon a little longer.

"I should go home before my dad sends the National Guard out to find me."

Ben opens the door with me on his heels. It isn't Jackie standing there. It's Cam, holding a stack of textbooks. His eyes widen in surprise when he sees me.

"Hey." Ben takes the books from him. "We're doing college classes online. It's cheaper to share the books."

Cam turns red. Ben's face falls. "You probably weren't supposed to know that," he says.

Ben puts the books on the table and locks the door behind us. Cam is already several steps down the hallway. When we get to the bottom of the outside stairs, Ben kisses me. "I'll see you later?"

"Definitely."

He enters the coffee shop, and I chase after Cam, who's opening the truck door. "Wait!" I call.

He gets into the truck but doesn't start it. I crawl into the passenger side.

"You're taking classes? That's why you're so tired all the time? Why you were awake that night when I took Kara home?" Saying her name stabs me in the gut and lets all my guilt flow into the wound. After my night with Ben, I forgot about her.

Cam looks like he's been stabbed too. "You can't tell anyone. I don't want my father to know."

"Why? Isn't that the kind of thing parents are proud of?"

Cam turns toward me. "Not when you won't take business classes and you're supposed to be upholding the family legacy." He sighs. "Since Ben won't come back, it's my job now."

Ah. I get it. The way this father treats him. His general lack of enthusiasm about his job.

I examine his face, and I realize something else. The look on it when he says Ben's name—it's shame. Cam's the reason Ben got hooked on drugs—or at least, that's what Cam thinks. He's been trying to help Ben. The hundred-dollar tips are part of that.

Another piece of the puzzle that is someone's complicated life.

I feel a sudden and surprising warmness for Cam.

"I like biology," he says. I shake my head in confusion. "The subject. I want to get a degree in biology and maybe work for the Forest Service. Do something outside."

"That's great." I look out the window. "I won't say anything."

He starts the truck and drives me back to the motel.


I wave to Dad when we pull up. Since he's still being awkward over Kara's death, he's not going to push me for details about which friend's house I was at last night.

When I open the door to my room, Ro is sitting on the bed with her arms crossed. Her brow is wrinkled, and she stares at me like she's trying to make lasers come out of her eyes.

"You were with that boy, weren't you?" she snarls. "The boy from the coffee shop. Kara's boyfriend."

I glance around the room, trying to feign innocence.

I don't know why she's so mad. Is she jealous of me? Does she think I'm taking advantage of a dead girl's boyfriend? That would be strange for Ro. She should be pushing me at Ben now that Kara's out of the way.

"I stayed at a friend's house," I lie, sort of.

She stands up and points a finger at me. "No. You have two friends. One sat here all night waiting for you. The other is dead." I flinch. "A dude who thinks he's a cop came by. He told the guy at the gate he needed to talk to you. Why?"

I don't know why she's attacking me. I step back from her. "Ro. Sit down and I'll tell you."

She sits and crosses her arms again. She turns her head and glares.

"Yes, I was at Ben's last night. He wasn't Kara's boyfriend.

And Allen"—I roll my eyes—"is getting really obnoxious. He has a crush on me."

Ro's face is still stormy. I tell her about the stalker leaving things for Kara, but that's all. The rest was entrusted to me by Ben. It's not my story to tell.

"You should go to the police," Ro says firmly.

"No." I wave her comment away. "We'd be wasting their time. The guy could have known Kara in Santa Fe, or it could have been random. We don't have any real information." *And if I go to the police, I'll be on their radar. They might start asking questions. About me.*

"Hmm . . . ," Ro says. "We should go shopping."

"What?"

"You need a new dress for your new boyfriend, since you can't wear the one you wore to the club without the belt."

A chill runs up my spine. My missing belt hasn't resurfaced.

"You're right," I say. "I'll go tell Cam he needs to drive us to the mall."

# 31

Ben convinced Doc that the donations needed to be sorted right away and that he needed my help.

But mostly, we've been kissing.

Kara's death still hangs over us. When we catch each other's eyes, I know we're both thinking about it.

I shouldn't ask and ruin the nice time we've been having, but I've wanted to know for so long. "What happened between Cam and Kara?"

Ben shakes his head. "Cam liked her from the day she moved in. They went out once. I don't know all the details, but he tried to kiss her, and it didn't go well. Cam was really angry and hurt, but he never got over her."

I nod. That's what I figured. It explains the awkwardness between them, and his concern for her.

"Cam wants to study biology," I say as I toss a pair of jeans with a giant hole in the back into the trash pile. *Seriously, people? If you wouldn't wear it, why would someone else want to?*

Ben laughs. "Cam has always liked being outside. He loves

the bosque. He cried once when there was a fire. He was worried about all the animals losing their homes."

"He doesn't seem all that touchy-feely."

"You learn to hide it when you grow up with Mike Vargas." That weird warmth for Cam spreads through me again.

"What do you want to do? Do you think you'll ever join your uncle's business?"

"I don't know. I try not to worry too much about the future." He stands up. "I have to be at work early. Someone called in. Are you good to finish this?" He points to the mound of old clothes surrounding me.

I lift a giant flowered shirt and roll my eyes. Ben laughs. His eyes sparkle. When he kisses me goodbye, I can't let go. So I don't. Not until I hear the creak of someone coming up the stairs.

We separate as Doc enters the room. Ben leaves, and Doc pats him on the shoulder as he goes by.

"At least we're still getting clothes," Doc says.

I hold up an old bathrobe. "Really?"

Doc's face twitches into a sad smile. "That's about all we're getting in donations. We're going to try cutting open hours to save on utilities. After that . . . ?" He gazes off into the distance.

"You don't get medical donations from the hospitals or the government?"

Doc shakes his head. "There isn't enough to go around."

"Oh." I look down at the pathetic pile I'm sitting in. "Sorry."

Doc forces his face into a truer smile. "I'm glad you're

here to help. Ben's glad too." He winks at me, and my face goes hot.


Cam has to help pick up a shipment of drywall, so he drops me off at the gate. I'm still feeling high from my afternoon with Ben. The site is quiet—most of the crew has gone home for the day—so I spin around with my arms out in the middle of the parking lot.

I'm still laughing at myself as I approach my door. A folded piece of paper is taped to it. It would be strange for Dad to leave me a note. I check my phone. I don't have any texts or missed calls from him.

I pull the paper off and unfold it. I drop it. I don't have to read it to know what it is. I've seen it a hundred times.

It's a printout of the front page of the Ohio newspaper from ten years ago. A photo of smoldering ruins with only the brick chimney still intact. The headline reads "Accidental House Fire Kills Four."

The word "accidental" has been circled and Xed out in red ink.

I grab the paper off the ground, crumple it, and stuff it into my bag. I whip around, looking for whoever could have left it. Looking for anyone who could have seen.

The red ink is Sharpie. The giant X is just like the one on the picture that was left for Kara.

How could the guy who stalked her—I gulp—killed her, know about me? I've only told one person in my whole life.

He's also the same person Kara told her story to.

*No, it can't be.* I was with Ben this afternoon—until he left the clinic in plenty of time to get to the Los Ranchitos before me.

Am I about to find out that Ben is the biggest liar of us all?

# 32

"The blond lady will be pissed if you make a hole in her new carpet," Ro says when she finds me pacing frantically in my room. The newspaper article is still wadded up in my bag. I can't help but glance at it. Ro follows my eyes but doesn't know what I'm looking at.

"What's wrong? Did you have a fight with the boy?"

I stop pacing and shake my head.

"You can tell me anything," she says. "Anything at all."

I *do* want to tell her. Discuss it with someone. Have her reassure me that I'm crazy for suspecting Ben for a single moment. But I can't. I can't tell anyone else my childhood secret.

I ignore the adrenaline that makes me want to jump out of my skin. "I have an assignment for school that I can't figure out."

"Right," she says. "An assignment."

I have to confront Ben. I have to know if he did this. He was so obvious about leaving the clinic before me. Did he do that on purpose? Is he trying to lure me in?

I can't go alone to see him.

"Will you meet me after school tomorrow?" I blurt out. Ro leans back at the force of my words. "I'll buy you a coffee."

She raises her hands in front of her. "As long as it has whipped cream."

The next afternoon, Cam drops Ro off in front of me and drives away. "I told him he wasn't invited," she says.

I've already had too much coffee. I didn't sleep at all last night. My whole body vibrates from caffeine and nerves. I feel nauseated.

I don't want to confront Ben. I don't want to be wrong and ruin what we have.

I also don't want to be right.

"Is this a booty call?" Ro asks when we're a block away from the coffee shop.

"What?"

"Is that why we're going for coffee? So you can have an after-school booty call?"

"No! I need to talk to Ben about something, and I thought you'd like to have coffee. That's it."

Two is safer than one, but I also need the moral support. Someone to smile at in relief when I find out it isn't Ben.

Someone to pick me up off the floor if I find out it is.

Ro raises an eyebrow. "I'm getting the big cup."

"Get whatever you want," I mumble. Ro bounces ahead and through the coffee shop doorway.

I have to take a deep breath before I go inside. The

newspaper article is still wadded up in my bag. I don't know if I should whip it out and press it to his nose or be more subtle about it. Hint around and watch his reaction.

Ro is already at the counter listing the things she wants in her drink. Ben punches it into the register while Jackie tries to mark it all down on the cup.

Ben looks at me. His whole face lights up. Ro clears her throat to get his attention back on her. "And extra whipped cream."

I hand over my debit card. "I need to talk to you," I whisper to Ben.

He hesitates, reading the expression on my face. "Okay?"

"Why don't you get us a table, Ro?" I say.

She rolls her eyes and mumbles, "Booty call."

I meet Ben by the emergency exit next to the stairs. I fumble through my bag and pull out the wad of crumpled paper. I'm going to hand it to him and watch his face. That will tell me what I need to know. Or it won't. I have no idea what I'm doing.

He takes the paper from me and unfolds it. He sucks in a sharp breath. "What's going on, Jenny?"

"I found this on my door yesterday."

His eyes look concerned. They look innocent. But I persevere.

"You're the only person who knows."

He flinches. He gets my accusation. I feel horrible. I shouldn't have said that.

"You think I did this?"

"No!" This is it. What I say next is going to determine whether I lose Ben forever. Tears fill my eyes. I'm too tired to think straight. I glance over my shoulder at Ro chatting with Jackie.

"Maybe it was one of the protestors Monica told me about. Or someone from the colony who's mad about Suds." As soon as I say it out loud, I realize it could be true. It must be true. I want to bang my head against the wall for not thinking of that. For jumping to my first conclusion.

"If they researched Dad, it wouldn't take long before they found out I was in that fire. Maybe they were trying to rile him up and guessed?" Guessed the truth.

"Why would they put it on your door, then? Wouldn't they send it to him directly? Or to my uncle?"

I look down at my feet planted on the thick tiles. "I don't know."

"You should go to the police. After what happened to Kara, you shouldn't take any chances."

"No. I'm sure it's fine. Just a prank." I take the paper back from him. I can't go to the police. The article, the investigation in Ohio, the fires in the trees that started when I got here. Everything points directly to me.

"Sorry I bothered you at work."

I believe that he had nothing to do with the article, and I know that if I stay, he'll give me a concerned and caring kiss. He'll tell me again to go to the police. He'll talk more about Kara and make my stomach roil. I turn on the balls of my feet. "Come on, Ro," I call. "I need to get home."

We step outside. Ro holds her massive cup with both hands. With her head, she nods at the paper I still have clutched in front of me. "What's that?"

"Nothing." I stuff it back into my bag.

Cam drops me off at the gate after school the next day. Before I get to my room, I stop dead in my tracks. There's something in front of my door. I step lightly over to it, as if it's a rattlesnake that will strike if I make any sudden moves.

It's a collection of sticks piled on the sidewalk. I look around. Most of the outside construction is finished, so the crew has moved inside. No one is in the parking lot.

I crouch down. The sticks are standing up in a teepee shape, with dried leaves stuffed at the base. It looks like what Hailey showed me after one of her Girl Scout meetings. They had had a class on how to build a fire.

I kick the fire starter over and brush everything away until the sidewalk is clean and the pieces are spread across the parking lot.

The person who did this is nowhere in sight.

I get my key out and stick it in the door, but I don't need the key. My room is unlocked.

My heart races. What am I going to find inside? Will it be even worse? Like my wall spray-painted with "murderer"? A candle and matches in the middle of my bed?

I find nothing. The room is exactly how I left it this morning.

The bathroom window slides open. Ro wanders in holding a magazine.

"What do you think of these shoes?" She shoves the magazine in my face, but then she drops it. "What's wrong?"

"Did you see anyone outside my door?"

Ro glances over her shoulder. "No. I came around the back, like always."

"Why do you keep doing that?" I yell.

"Whoa. What's going on with you?"

"Nothing." I turn away from her so she won't see the lie.

Ro opens the door and looks back and forth. "I don't see anything." She sits on the bed. "What's really going on with you? You're acting all jumpy and nervous, like you're doing something wrong and you're afraid of getting caught."

Even though my heart is pounding, I force my body to go still. I can't let on that she's guessed right. "It's really nothing. I'm just not feeling well today." I fake cough. "You should go home. I don't want you to catch it, if I'm coming down with something."

Ro raises her hands like she's surrendering. "Fine. I'll go." She walks with heavy, angry steps to the bathroom.

I flop down onto the bed. The pile of sticks twists around and around in my brain. That newspaper article wasn't a lucky guess.

Someone knows.

And if I don't start hiding my feelings better, Ro's going to know too.

. . .

The flames are near the colony. So close that they could have been started by a campfire. The wind is bad, but the police and the fire department were already on alert.

They were on the other side of the river, looking in the wrong place.

I stand on the sidewalk in front of the Los Ranchitos and watch the fire trucks race up the access road. The wind pushes the smoke away from me and wraps my hair around my face. It's too chilly to be out in my pajama tank top and shorts, but I don't feel the cold. I feel numb.

It has to have been Suds. It's the only explanation I can come up with. He must have told someone that he saw me in the trees. Someone who wanted Kara dead. Someone who is now looking for revenge on me.

I'm still hearing the whispers around school about the colony. That the guy who killed Kara lives there. The same place Suds used to hang out.

I wonder if the guy's there now, worried about the fire coming to gobble him up. I wonder if he's *squirming*.

I hope so.

"The motel's not done yet," a voice says behind me. I turn to see Monica with a sweatshirt pulled over her pajamas. "There's still another round of inspections and more permits pending. The protestors might have backed down, but that doesn't mean that there aren't plenty of people who want to see this project fail."

She steps around to face me and looks me square in the eye. "All they need is an excuse." I try to look away from her, but she moves with me to keep eye contact. "Don't be that excuse."

My mouth opens like it wants to say something. I close it. Monica walks away, leaving me alone as the wind changes and blows smoke into my watering eyes.

# 33

I thought it would be weird with Ben—that I would have to fall to my knees and beg his forgiveness after I pseudo-accused him of leaving the article. But mostly he looks worried when I show up at his door.

"Are you sure you're okay?" he asks for the twelfth time. We sit on his little couch. My head is on his shoulder.

"I just wish there was more we could do. For Kara."

"I want to know who killed Kara as much as you do, but let the police do their jobs."

No. The police are too slow. Someone out there knows about me. They killed Kara. I've got to figure it out before they end my life, one way or another.

I look up at Ben. He seems even more concerned now.

"Doc told me he's worried about the clinic," I say to change the subject. Ben's body tenses next to me.

I sit up and face him. "Maybe we can have a fund-raiser." I take a deep breath. "Your uncle really seems like he wants to mend his relationship with you. Maybe he would sponsor something."

Ben's face is stony—but he doesn't say no.

I settle back into his arms. "I was just brainstorming," I mumble.

Ben's quiet for a long time. "Maybe," he finally says. I try to hide a smile. "But the people with money in the hills have never been too fond of Doc. Suds went around telling them that Doc sells pills in the colony."

I snap to sitting again. "What? Doc wouldn't do that."

"I know. Suds made it up. But the people in the hills will believe anything that might get the clinic shut down. It's easier to make Doc out as a drug dealer than to think about all those people who need help. And now, with what happened to Kara . . ." His voice drifts off. The pain is back in his eyes.

"Do you think her killer lives in the colony?"

"Most of those guys from the colony have come into the clinic at some point. They may not be the hills' idea of *desirable*, but I don't think any of them are killers." He shrugs. "But there are always people passing through. Even the regulars are afraid of some of them."

I know that people in the hills whisper about the man from the colony who murdered Kara, but I wonder what the guys in the colony whisper about. Do they talk about me? The girl who lives in the Los Ranchitos? The one who likes to start fires?

"What do they say when they come into the clinic? Has anyone said anything about Kara?"

Ben doesn't look away or cast his eyes down. That's a good sign. If he had heard anything about me, he would have reacted.

He still looks at me with concern, so I don't tell him what I'm really thinking: That someone's out there waiting for me. That I can feel it.

The same thing that happened to Kara is happening to me. First she received a threatening message, and then . . .

Sooner or later, I'll have to face him.

But I'll be ready.

What happened to Kara won't happen to me.


I'm in my black clothes and soft shoes. The lighter is in my pocket. I'm going to use it. Use it as a weapon to save myself if tonight's the night I meet Kara's killer.

I lift the curtains to make sure the coast is clear.

Ro's face appears in front of me. Her fist is raised, ready to knock on the door. I jump back and let out a startled scream.

When I open the door, she takes me in. "Going somewhere?" she asks.

"I, uh . . . I'm going to the colony." A half-truth.

Her eyes widen. "Why?"

My mouth kicks into overdrive. Words start flowing. "There's a rumor that Doc is selling pills in the colony at night. I want to see if it's true. For Ben. The clinic means everything to him. If it's true, I need to know so I can protect him."

I smile in spite of myself. That was good. It sounded believable.

Ro purses her lips and considers what I just said. "Okay. Let's go."

"What? No, you can't come with me. It's dangerous."

A serious misstep. Ro laughs. "I am way scrappier than you."

I have no response to that. Not one that I can give her. She doesn't know about my soft-soled shoes or the lighter, heavy against my side.

I guess we're going to the colony.

We'll take a quick look around, Ro will see that I was wrong about Doc, and we'll come back to the Los Ranchitos. I'll send Ro home. I'll try again.

The formerly condemned room where I first met Ro has been transformed. It's solid now. No more holes or cracks or signs that say it's going to fall down.

But no one has spotted the secret gap in the fence yet. The overgrown weeds have concealed it—and me—from detection so far.

We push through it, and I follow Ro out to the street. Henderson's is open twenty-four hours. The sign and windows blaze in the darkness, even though there are only a couple of cars in the parking lot. Probably the poor employees who have to stand there all night waiting on kids who have the munchies after a night of partying.

Ro doesn't cross the street into the shopping center's parking lot. She keeps going down our side. "Ro," I whisper-snap. I try to catch up with her to tell her we need to cross. We can't walk past the gate. Dad has the security guard posted there. If he catches us, trouble doesn't even begin to describe what I'll be in.

Ro stands up straight and walks past the guard like she

owns the sidewalk. There's no hesitation in her step. No nerves. The guard glances up but quickly goes back to his phone. She owns it so well, she's completely unsuspicious.

Once she's out of the guard's sight, she motions for me to come.

I can't do it like she did. I crouch down and run.

I don't stop until I reach the trees. Ro laughs at me as I try to catch my breath.

"You are so bad at sneaking out," she says.

I smile. She has no idea how good I am.

We pick our way through the darkness, tripping over exposed roots and hidden holes.

As we approach the colony, I smell campfires and see light through the trees. But I don't hear anything. I don't know what I was expecting. A carnival? People singing and yelling and smashing bottles? It sounds like sleep.

"Put your hands up where I can see them." We freeze. Our tromping through the underbrush masked the sound of a third person approaching.

The beam from a high-powered flashlight bounces over us. Ro has her hands in the air. I turn around first.

"Allen?"

The light shines on my face and then lowers to the ground. "What are you doing out here, Jenny?"

"What are *you* doing out here?" I can't hide the annoyance in my voice. But then I realize my mistake. I know why he's out here. He's looking for me. He just doesn't know it yet. Or maybe he does.

Ro drops her arms. "You are not a cop," she snarls. "It's illegal to pretend to be."

"All I did was tell you to put your hands up," Allen says. The two of them square off.

I have to do something before this goes bad. Before Allen decides to use that radio and call the real cops.

"We wanted to see the colony," I say, as if it's a perfectly reasonable thing to be doing in the middle of the night.

Allen's eyes bore into me, and his lips drop into a frown of disappointment—like maybe he thought I wasn't a silly, stupid girl, but now he knows better.

"I'll take you home." He holds out a hand to lead me away.

Allen helped me get information about Kara. He's still on my side. He doesn't know anything, right?

The lighter is in my pocket, but he wouldn't dare search me.

I grab on to Ro's sweatshirt and pull her with me as we get into the back of his car. When we get to the main road, I can see the Los Ranchitos.

"Please don't take us to the gate. I'll get in so much trouble." I try to use a tone that would belong to the disappointing girl who has no idea that he just saved her. Allen shakes his head.

"Please," I beg. "Drop us off at Henderson's. We'll sneak back in. My dad can't know I was out here. He'll get so mad at me." I rustle up a fake tear and bat my lashes.

Allen sighs and drives past the motel. He pulls into Henderson's parking lot. "Go straight across the street. No more sightseeing."

I nod. He glances at Ro. She nods too, but with a look

of bemusement on her face. I elbow her. She tries to feign contrition.

We get out and stand under the yellow lights of the parking lot until Allen drives away.

"He's crushing so hard on you," Ro sings.

Ruby is mopping the entrance to Henderson's. She looks surprised to see us. She waves. I wave back.

"Tonight was no fun. I'm going home," Ro says. Her tone is dark, like she's mad at me again.

"Okay." I look down at the asphalt. "I'll see you later?"

"Maybe," Ro says, then turns and marches off toward her aunt's house.

I roll my eyes. I have no idea what I did this time.

I go into Henderson's to wait until I'm sure Ro and Allen are really gone. Then I have to decide what to do next. Do I take another risk and go back into the trees?

If Allen is still out patrolling, he could find me again in the trees, twice in one night. That would be suspicious. He could use his police radio and get me busted before I get to the bottom of everything.

"You work the night shift, too?" I ask Ruby as I tiptoe across her freshly mopped floor.

"I pick up extra shifts whenever I can. It helps pay the bills."

I point to the rear of the store. "I came for ice cream." Ice cream. Sure. Why not?

I pick out a pint of mint chocolate chip and take it to the front. As Ruby rings me up, I motion at her neck. "Where's your pretty necklace? The family heirloom?"

She laughs and turns her head in a way that seems familiar to me, but I can't place it. "I don't wear it on the night shift. I never know who's going to come in." She hands me my bag. "You should go home."

I walk out into the night air clutching my ice cream. Trying again in the trees would be useless. With Allen out there, whoever has been following me won't risk a confrontation tonight.

They'd just watch as Allen took me down.

They'd watch me burn.

# 34

My alarm doesn't go off. I barely manage to shower and get into my uniform before Cam is pounding on the door. I glance in the mirror. My hair is wet. I don't have time for makeup. And I look like someone who was up all night. Great.

I open my door. Cam is in the truck now, yawning. Parked a few spaces over from him is Allen's car. I hear voices in the offices. My heart starts to pound. Why is he here? What is he telling Dad?

I press my ear against the office door, but I can't make out what they're saying. I shouldn't open it. I should get into Cam's truck and go to school. Allen could be on to me, but my jumpy heart won't let me walk away. I have to know what he's up to.

When I open the door, Allen seems happy to see me. He's drinking coffee out of a Breland Construction mug. Dad has a matching mug and is leaning up against the sink.

"Jenny, this is Allen."

"We've met."

Dad misses my lack of expression. His face lights up. I'm

sure that in Dad's head, Allen is perfect boyfriend material for me, the positive influence I need in my life.

"Allen came to check on us."

I examine Allen's face. It's cheerful. He smiles. His eyes sparkle. But it could go either way. He could be suspicious of me—or *acting* like he thinks I'm perfectly innocent.

"Why are you here?" I'm not a good actress today. There's no mistaking the irritation in my voice.

"With the all the fires . . . ," Allen pauses. His eyebrows rise slightly. "I wanted to stop by and see if there's anything I, or anyone on the force, can do to assist you."

"The force." I feel nothing but intense anger and hate toward Allen right now. I want to scream, *You are not a cop!* But I can't. Dad can't know that I was crawling around the cottonwoods in the middle of the night.

I fake smile and point over my shoulder. "I have to get to school."

"Have a nice day," Allen says. Dad beams at him. Great. I'm pretty sure Allen will be joining us for microwave surprise one of these nights.


After school, Ro is lying on her stomach on the bed, chewing a strip of red licorice. Her magazine is open to a spread of colorful sandals.

Her constantly being here hasn't really annoyed me before, but today, I can't stand it. I don't want her here. I need time by myself to come up with a new plan to trap the person following me.

I also need time by myself because my scar itches.

Ro puts the licorice down. "Hard day?" she asks.

"You could say that."

I dump my stuff on the floor. Ro's not going anywhere. She holds the licorice box out to me.

I don't take any.

"I know what will make you feel better," she announces.

"What?" I flop down onto the bed.

"You know those fires? The police know who did it."

I bolt up to sitting. "What?"

"Well, they don't know *exactly* who did it. But they have evidence now."

"Ro, what are you talking about?"

She points to the TV. "It was on the early news."

I fumble for the remote and flip on the TV. It's playing a commercial for erectile dysfunction. Ro giggles at every double entendre.

It takes twenty minutes of fluff news before they do the top-story recap. The Las Piedras fire chief comes on the screen. Microphones push their way into his face.

"We're getting closer to identifying and arresting the person responsible for the arson attacks in the bosque. We have a good piece of evidence left behind at the last fire scene."

The camera zooms in. I gasp. He holds up a photo of a round piece of black fabric lying on the ground. "We believe this is a piece of what the arsonist was wearing."

Ro turns and looks at me. "What?" she asks.

The fire chief keeps talking. "It is currently at the crime lab being tested. I've got a message for this guy." The camera zooms in until his face fills up the whole screen. "We're going to catch you."

I flip off the TV. Ro smiles. "That's good, right? You won't have to be scared anymore."

I nod and then grip my stomach. "I think I ate something bad. I'm going to puke."

Ro jumps up. "I don't want to see that. No offense or anything." She gallops toward the bathroom. "Hope you feel better," she calls, and dives out the window.

I wait a second to make sure she's gone. Then I rip open the bottom dresser drawer and retrieve my hat from where I hid it in the pocket of an old pair of sweatpants.

It only has one felt butterfly eye now.

How could I have not noticed that?

I bury the hat back into the drawer. I'm going to have to get rid of it. Destroy it.

There's a knock on the door. I jump out of my skin and run to the curtains. I peek out, which is stupid, because my eye is about a foot away from Allen standing on the sidewalk. He waves.

My heart can't beat any faster without me actually passing out. Is Allen here to turn me in? To present me to the investigators and play the hero?

I have to open the door. I can't run now. If I do, it'll erase any doubts he might have about me. It will make me look 100 percent guilty.

I take a deep breath and glance again at my closed dresser drawer.

I open the door.

"Hi!" I say with way too much fake enthusiasm. A smile erupts on Allen's face. I shuffle through the cracked door and close it behind me. My hand stays tight on the doorknob, holding it shut.

"I wanted to see how you were doing. Make sure you weren't going on any more late-night strolls through the bosque." He laughs, but his eyes are focused and unsmiling.

He has to be suspicious. It's right there in his eyes. In his words "late-night strolls"—plural—and "through the bosque."

"No. Doing my homework." I have to play along. He can't know that I've figured him out.

He looks down at his feet and rubs his hand along the back of his reddening neck. "I was wondering if you wanted to go out on Friday."

My stomach flips. I can't think of an excuse that won't sound fishy.

"Okay."

Allen looks surprised. "Really?"

I nod until it feels like my head's going to fall off. Friday is a project day. Fantastic. I will see my real boyfriend and then go on a date with this annoying—potentially dangerous—guy.

Allen smiles, showing me all his teeth. "I'll pick you up at seven?"

I try to show teeth too. "Great."

Now I really am going to be sick.

# 35

"I never guessed you were such a player." Ro smiles proudly at me.

"Shut up and help me find something to wear," I snap.

Ro giggles. "This is going to be so fun."

I had to tell someone about my date with Allen. The confession didn't make me feel better—and of course, I didn't tell her why I said yes.

"You're pacing again." She points at my feet and the line I've created in the carpet. I stop. "Two boys in one day." She shakes her head. Cam's truck pulls up. "I'll come back after school and find something for you to wear."

I'm so wired when I get into the truck that the smallest things make me want to jump out of my skin. I feel Cam's eyes examining me, but there's no way he could know about my date with Allen.

Next to the still-empty cup holder that once held his lighter, Cam's heavy collection of keys hangs from the ignition. I point to them. "You have a master key to the motel, right? One that opens all the doors?"

His eyes slide over to me again. "Why?"

"You leave your keys lying around a lot. Someone could take them."

"No one has taken them," he says, but his voice sounds unsure. He's remembering the key to the shed. The one some-one used to get the shovel that killed Suds. Anyone with a key could have gone into my room at any time. Anyone could have taken my hat and planted the eye to incriminate me. If they had been watching me, they would know I wear that hat when I sneak off at night.

I examine Cam. Ro said she lost him at the club the night Kara was killed. She couldn't find him again until closing time.

Where did he go?

When we pull up to the curb at Riverline Prep, I dive out of the truck like it might explode at any second. Then I watch it tool up the street until Cam has turned the corner and dis-appeared.

I'm being ridiculous. Cam doesn't have anything to do with this. He was only following me before because Monica is pay-ing him. He wouldn't have killed Suds, and definitely not Kara.

I want to figure out who else could have access to my room, but I can't think about it now. I have a more immediate problem.

Ben.

I have until this afternoon to figure out what I'm going to tell him about Allen. Maybe I could say I'm going out with Allen as a favor to Dad. I could even say that we need him for the Los Ranchitos.

Or I could tell Ben the truth. All of it.

I navigated the hallway of Riverline Prep without paying

any attention to the people around me. When I get to my locker, my mind is so worn out that it takes three tries to get my combination right.

My locker pops open. A heavy piece of paper falls out onto the floor and lands facedown. The back is embossed with the Henderson's logo. I pick it up and flip it over.

*You've got to be kidding me.*

It's a photo.

A photo of me.

I'm in Hailey's hat—still with two felt circles—crouched down in the thick brush under the cottonwoods.

Starting a fire.

My face is turned away from the camera, but it's clearly my hat. The police already have the missing felt eye with my DNA on it. If they have this picture, it's over for me.

*Who is doing this?*

There's a security guard by the door. Whoever's doing it has to be a student.

I shove the photo into my bag and whip my head from side to side. My adrenaline is off the charts. My heart feels like it's going to fly out of my chest, but no one is paying attention to me. No one is waiting to see my reaction.

I can't let whoever it is think they're getting to me. That's what they want. I put my books in my bag, as if nothing has happened. I take careful steps down the hallway so I don't look like I want to run. I stare at every face as I go by, seeking some sort of recognition from the person who wants to see my reaction.

All I get are blank looks in return. Since Kara died, I have no friends here. I'm invisible.

I sit at my desk in homeroom. Emma comes in. She doesn't like me.

Maybe Emma isn't as harmless as everyone thinks. I stare her down. She unconsciously checks her hair and rubs her nose. When I don't turn away, she whispers "Weirdo" under her breath.

All day I wait for someone to say something or do something suspicious, but it's the most normal of days.

When I go into the restroom to change out of my uniform and into my clinic clothes, something occurs to me: You don't have to be a student to get into the building. The guard never checks IDs. All you need is a uniform.

Anyone who's ever been a student here would have a uniform.

Cam went to school here. But Ben did too. My mind is so mixed up and confused that I can't see straight. The hallway is blurry when I come out of the restroom. I grip my bag with the photo inside next to my body. I should stand tall and show whoever is trying to get to me that it isn't working.

But it is working.


When I get to the clinic, I go straight to the kitchen and pull the peanut butter and bread off the shelves. I need to lose myself in a monotonous task.

A few minutes later, Ben comes up behind me. He wraps

his arms around my waist and puts his head on my shoulder. I will myself not to cry. Why does everything else have to be so awful, when things are so good with Ben?

He kisses my neck.

I turn around with the peanut butter knife still in my hand. Our lips meet. All the tension in my shoulders melts away. I let everything go. It's just the two of us kissing in a peanut butter cloud.

"I need everyone to leave the building in an orderly fashion," a loud voice says in the main room. Ben and I break apart. Fear like I have never seen before flashes over his face. He takes two steps back and jerks from side to side, like he's not sure if he should run or stay.

"What? What's happening?" I ask.

The kitchen door opens. A man in a blue windbreaker walks in. Over his heart is a yellow patch of a badge. "You need to leave the building, please." His eyes snap to the knife in my hand. That's when I see the gun strapped to his side. I drop the knife onto the counter.

The man steps forward and puts a hand on my shoulder to usher me out of the kitchen. He gives Ben a stern, fatherly look. "You too."

Ben is in some sort of trance. He can't move. I grab his hand and pull. He follows me out into the main room.

Half a dozen other people in dark blue windbreakers with "DEA" on the back in white block letters mill around or cajole others to leave. Doc stands in the middle of the room. One of the agents holds a piece of paper up to Doc's face. "We have a warrant to search the entire premises for evidence of illegal drug trafficking."

"You must be mistaken. This is a medical clinic," Doc says.

The hand on my shoulder becomes more insistent. I'm leaving whether I want to or not. Doc's eyes catch Ben's as we pass. Ben's are wide and terrified. Doc's are squinted and concerned.

Outside, three Las Piedras police cars are parked around the perimeter of the clinic. We get walked to the other side of them and released.

"Wait, I need my bag," I call after the agent. I take two running steps toward him. A police officer steps in front of me.

"Whoa," she says.

I point at the clinic. "I need my bag."

"You can get it later."

"But my homework . . ." She doesn't look sympathetic. I'm not going to win this argument. I step back.

Two agents walk Doc out to the porch and sit him in a folding chair. Every eye focuses on him, but he doesn't put up a fight. He looks tired. Defeated.

This is the final straw for the clinic, and he knows it. Ben knows it too. All the color leaves his face.

"It's a misunderstanding," I say to Ben, trying to put certainty in my voice that I don't feel. "It will all get worked out."

The news van—the sole news van that Las Piedras seems to have—pulls up. The same reporter jumps out, boobs bouncing in front of her. With the glee on her face, you would think someone just told her she was going to get to play with puppies.

She positions herself with her back to the clinic so the cameraman can get a clear shot of the DEA agents going in and out. She starts to talk into her mic. Her expression of concern is meant to portray that this is very, very serious.

The camera pans around the crowd. It stops on me. The cameraman gives a nod in my direction to the reporter. She looks over her shoulder at me and grins, showing her fangs.

I don't know what to do. I have to get my bag. I can't leave that photo in a place being searched by federal agents. But I can't be on the news. The reporter will find some way to spin this. Some way to connect me to drugs. After the report about Dad being a convicted felon, the Los Ranchitos can't take any more bad publicity.

We have to go. I grab Ben's hand, but he doesn't move. The look on his face is pure anguish. It's the same look he had after Kara died.

"Ben, we can't stay here."

The reporter is coming toward me, mic out and pointed at my face.

I'll have to leave without my bag. Inside it are my history book, a spiral notebook, pens, and a little pack of tissues. No drugs. No reason for the DEA to open the history book to the chapter about King George III and find the photo.

I pull on Ben's hand. "Please, come with me."

He's too caught up in the scene playing out in the clinic to respond. I don't have a choice. It feels like a betrayal, but I let go of his hand.

And I run.

I plunge through the crowd and don't stop until I get to the coffee shop. Jackie is at the counter. She looks up and smiles, then her face falls.

"What's wrong?"

"The clinic." I can't catch my breath. "The DEA is there. Ben . . ."

She fills up a glass of water and pushes it into my hand. I take a gulp.

"Ben is still there."

A customer comes in and stands in line behind me. I know Jackie wants to hear more, but she has to do her job.

I point to an open table. "I'm going to wait until he comes home."


After a couple of hours, Ben still hasn't shown up. I text him. And call. And text again.

His phone could be inside the clinic. Or he could be dodging my texts, trying to process this on his own.

He's already lost Kara. If he loses the clinic, too, I don't know how he'll keep it together. How he'll stay sober.

I have to help him, let him know that he's not alone.

I text the only other person I can think of.


When Cam pulls up, there's deep sadness in his eyes. I gave him a brief rundown in my text. The clinic was raided. Ben's not answering his phone.

We drive past the clinic. Everyone has gone. The lights are off.

Ben is nowhere.

"I know where we can look," Cam says.

We drive up and down streets. Some I've seen before, and others are in parts of town I've never been. Cam slows down and creeps past every alley we pass, looking. I don't think this is the first time he's done this.

Every time we see a figure in a doorway or huddled in a shadow, Cam's face fills with hope. Then it's dashed when the figure turns around and isn't Ben.

I'm hurting, but Cam is hurting worse. He seems so lost, so eager to do right by Ben. I reach out and put my hand on his shoulder.

"There's one more place," he says. "But you have to stay in the truck. For real. I'm serious."

"Okay."

We drive down a street that runs parallel to the cottonwood's access road. We pull off and go on four-wheel drive through the brush. There might have been a road here at one time, but now it's completely overgrown. I hold on to the doorframe as we thump up and down, and branches beat up the sides of the truck. Then the trees clear, and we stop in front of an abandoned warehouse. It's a shell with broken windows. One side is collapsed, leaving a pile of exposed wood. It looks older than the Los Ranchitos. Through the trees, I see the far end of the colony pressing up against it.

"Lock the doors," Cam says as he gets out. He puffs himself

up to look as big and mean as possible. As much as I want to follow him, that makes me change my mind. I've seen Cam look a lot of things, but never afraid like this.

What I thought was a quiet scene begins to move. There are people in the trees and in the warehouse. They look worse off than the patients in the clinic, worse than anyone I've seen trudging back and forth from the colony.

This place is for the hopeless. It's a place you go to die.

Cam stomps back to the truck. He gets in and starts the ignition before he clicks his seat belt. "He's not here."

I breathe a sigh of relief. We still don't know where Ben is, but the thought of him in that place breaks my heart.

"Did he used to come here before?"

Cam's eyes slide over to me and then flit back to the road. I take that as a yes.


When Cam drops me off at the Los Ranchitos, he doesn't get out. His shoulders are slumped, his jaw set. It's almost dark, but he's going to keep looking.

"Let me know if you hear anything," I say as he pulls away.

Before I can get my key, Ro pulls the curtain aside, and the door opens.

I push my way inside and collapse on the bed. The last few hours weigh on me like a bulldozer sitting on my chest. I have to fight for breath.

Ro bounces onto the bed next to me. "I saw the early news."

There's no concern in her voice. I sit up. She has an enormous smile on her face.

"Why are you happy?"

"You said that doctor was selling pills in the colony. He got what he deserved. Isn't that a good thing?"

Oh my God. Did I do this? I passed on Suds's story about Doc selling pills. Passed it on to Ro.

"Ro?" She doesn't look at me. I stand up and move around to look her in the eye. "Ro? Did you call the cops? Did you turn Doc in?"

"No!"

"Ro?"

She throws her hands up. "I didn't, I swear." But she wears a hint of a smile.

"I don't believe you."

She looks like I've slapped her. Her face changes. It grows dark. Her eyes narrow. I take a step back. "You're one to talk," she says. She lets it hang in the air. I don't know what she means, but my breathing speeds up. My heart pounds.

She saunters over to the dresser like someone who's in complete control. She opens the bottom drawer. I know what's about to happen, but I'm powerless to stop it.

She pulls out my hat, gingerly holding it between two fingers. She tosses it onto the bed.

*Shit.* I meant to get rid of it, but I got distracted. I thought I would have more time.

"Didn't it used to have two eyes?" Her tone is so cold that I wrap my arms around myself for protection.

I can't breathe. I suck in little gasps of air. But I have to fight. Fight for my life.

My lungs open, and I take one big, fortifying breath. "You tell me, Ro."

She flinches. "What?"

"You're always here, Ro. Every day when I come home from school, you're here. You sleep here. How easy would it have been for to you to take my hat like you take everything else?"

"We're best friends. I wouldn't do that to you." There's hurt on her face.

"You mooch my food. You act like this is your house. You spend my money on clothes to play dress-up with. That's not friendship. We're not friends."

Ro looks like I've slapped her. My own head snaps back in disbelief. I just said something that can't be unsaid. I didn't mean it. I'm just angry. Angry at her for finding the hat. Angry at myself for what I might have done to Doc and Ben.

Ro rallies. Her eyes sparkle, and her face twists into a smug smile. My lungs close up again. I've just released a monster.

"Where'd you go the night of the club? You were so sad. 'Oh, woe is me.'" She rubs her eyes mockingly. "'Kara is sleeping with the boy I like.' But then Kara died, and you got the boy."

My head beats in time with my heart. Black spots are filling my vision. I sit down before I pass out. "I didn't kill Kara."

"All I'm saying is that it worked out pretty well for you, huh?"

I point to the door. "Get out."

She plants her feet and crosses her arms. I jump up and use my fury to fly through the space between us. "GET. OUT."

She slowly drops her arms to the side and walks to the door. She opens it, but then turns around and smirks. "Don't forget about your date."

The door slams.

I run into the bathroom and kneel on the person-sized towel in front of the toilet. There's nothing in my stomach to throw up. I lean back against the tub. This has been the second-worst day of my life.

I crawl back into the bedroom and grope around for my phone. I have to call and cancel with Allen. I swipe my phone on. It's 6:50. Too late. He's already on his way—if he isn't already in the parking lot.

I'll have to pull myself together. There's a reason I'm going out with Allen. I can't let him get suspicious about *anything*.

Allen's name is at the top of my list of dangerous people. People who could send me to jail for a long, long time.

Now Ro's name is right under his.

I've never seen that look in her eyes before. Ro has become a wild card. If she called the cops on Doc, I don't know what she could do next.

But she was right about two things: the hat does prove I'm guilty of starting the fires, and, when the truth is twisted, it seems like I did have a motive to kill Kara.

But right now, I have to convince Allen that nothing would make me happier than being on a date with him.

I put on the first dress in the wardrobe and slap on some foundation and blush.

Allen knocks on the door. "Just a minute," I call. One last thing. I go into the bathroom and lock the window.


A white rose sits on the table in front of me. Allen presented it to me when I got into his car. I can't keep my eyes off it. Is it a message? Is this our final showdown? Does he think he's in some sort of superhero movie? That I'm the archvillain he's about to take out?

I've had so much adrenaline shot through my system today that I'm surprised my heart hasn't stopped beating. My whole body feels heavy. But I have to keep my guard up. I have to make it through this night.

"Did you grow up in Las Piedras?" I ask, to make neutral conversation.

"No. Santa Fe."

I give him a half smile. *Kara was from Santa Fe. Does he know about her mom and the baby?*

I've been holding the same tortilla chip for ten minutes. Allen scoops up a big dollop of salsa onto his and shoves the whole thing into his mouth. He's been talking and eating, while I've tried to smile and laugh in the appropriate spots. I don't let him see me looking for the emergency exits.

He suddenly leans forward and glances around the restaurant. "There have been some developments in your friend's murder," he whispers.

My heart takes off again. More adrenaline.

"Oh?" I break off a piece of my chip and try to lift it to my mouth, but it doesn't make it.

"They're looking into whether the fires and your friend's murder are related."

I start. "What?"

"Shhh . . ."

He glances around again. "You can't tell anyone. I overheard the detectives talking about it. They didn't know I was in the records room."

"Did they say why?" I whisper, and attempt to sound like a concerned friend and not like my heart is about to leap out of my throat.

"They got a tip. Usually those things are bogus, but they're taking this one seriously."

Ro.

I lean back and dip what remains of my chip in the salsa. "So what was the tip?"

He shrugs. "I don't know. But they've got us doing extra patrols out away from the colony. That's where they think the arsonist is."

"He's not in the colony?" The chip finally makes it to my mouth. I'm just a concerned—innocent—citizen.

Allen shrugs again. "I think he is. That's why I've been going out there at night."

I look away, but I breathe deeply. I might live to see another day.

"Oh, and the detectives mentioned that the feds gave them something too."

"Really? What?" My shaking hand dips another chip. Salsa splashes onto the table. Allen's eyes glance at it.

The waitress brings our food. A smothered carne adovada burrito for him. A chile relleno for me.

Allen picks up his fork and stabs the burrito. "All they said was that the feds were 'helping to connect the dots.'"

I look down like I'm admiring my food. But I can't let him see my face.

My bag and the photo inside it are in the hands of the feds.


I have two-thirds of a chile relleno in a Styrofoam takeout box. I told Allen it was too spicy. It wasn't, but after what he told me, I couldn't eat. He made me take it home anyway.

I tried to keep acting pleasant. Keep acting like there was no place on earth I would rather be than with him.

It seems to have worked. He's walked me to the door. I know the look on his face. He's going to kiss me now.

I see movement out of the corner of my eye in the still-blacked-out section of the motel. I focus on Allen. I'm even more confused than when this "date" started. Is he playing me? Or is he just cocky and overconfident, with some sort of hero complex?

I can't ruin this now. If he really doesn't know about me, I need him to keep feeding me details about the investigations.

His lips close the space between us.

But I can't. I can't do it.

I turn my head and receive a peck on the cheek. Confusion momentarily passes over his face, but then he puts his arms around me for a friendly hug. When he breaks away, he looks satisfied by the exchange.

He points over his shoulder toward the trees. "I'm going to go on another patrol."

I smile, hoping he can't sense my relief. I've done it. This night is over.

As he backs out of the parking space, I wave like I can't wait to see him again.

When he's through the gate, I turn to the blacked-out section.

To Ben running away into the shadows.

My scar sears across my arm.

# 36

Maybe Allen knows about me. Maybe he doesn't. But it's his arsonist-hunting, wannabe-cop fault that Ben ran away. That Ben is hurting even more.

Allen's getting a taste of his own medicine tonight. Right now he's learning what it feels like to have to run for your life.

The fire is coming to eat him.

I'm not trying to hurt anyone, not really. I know the firefighters will evacuate the colony. I just need Allen to know that I'm done playing games.

He might be dangerous. But so am I.

The wind is so strong, it's hard to stand upright. We're all assembled. Dad, Monica, Cam, and Mr. Vargas. Flames spin like tornadoes. Trees explode. Every fire truck in Las Piedras and three surrounding communities line the access road.

People from the colony trudge up the street, escorted out of danger by the flashing lights of a police car.

I have an old backpack of Dad's with my toothbrush and

a change of clothes slung over my shoulder. We're waiting to see if we have to leave.

I feel buzzed again, watching the flames. It's been a while since I felt anything other than a stomach-turning relief at watching them gobble up the trees. This time I feel empowered. This time I'm the hunter.

I was so very careful. No hat. No dark clothes. Just slow, silent movements and the uniform of an innocent jogger out for a late run.

Dad examines me and narrows his eyes. My hands are at my sides. This has been the longest day of my life. Exhaustion is starting to overtake me.

I pull out my phone for the thousandth time. No message from Ben. Everything good I felt when I pressed the lighter against the pile of kindling takes leave of me and is replaced by a horrible gnawing sensation in my abdomen.

"Have you heard from Ben?" I ask Cam, who also stares blankly at the inferno before us.

"No." His expression doesn't change. He still thinks Ben is just missing. He doesn't know that Ben saw me with Allen tonight.

Mr. Vargas leaps forward to meet the fire chief as he saunters toward us. "Looks like the wind is pushing it back," the chief says. "If it jumps the river, we'll have a mess, but they're no structures over there."

"So we're okay?" Mr. Vargas asks.

The chief nods. "For tonight? Yes. If this son of a bitch keeps at it?" He shrugs.

Dad puts a hand on my shoulder. "Let's go back to bed."

In my room, I open the drawer containing my magic sleeping pills. I could take one—I could take two and guarantee that the night and most of tomorrow slip away. That Allen and Ben slide right out of my mind.

I close the drawer. I don't deserve that. After what I did to Ben, I deserve to see, hear, and feel everything the night can throw at me.

I doze off. When I swallow, my throat, raw from the smoke, jerks me awake again. I look at the clock. It's two a.m.

There's a sound in the bathroom. A tapping on the window. I ignore it. I'm not letting her in. Not after she called the cops. Not after she accused me of killing Kara.

She can go sleep in a doorway somewhere, for all I care.

A few minutes later, the tapping is on my door. I roll over and pull the duvet over my head.

"Go away!" I snarl.

The tapping starts again.

I turn on the lamp and rip off the duvet. I open the door. "Go a—" Tears are streaming down Ro's face. Her clothes are covered in dirt and ash. My heart stops dead in my chest. She's holding her arm in front of her.

A fierce, angry burn slices across her wrist.

"He's coming for me," she whispers.

I grab her by the shoulder and pull her into the room. I shut the door, lock the dead bolt, and slide the chain into place.

I press my back into it, as if I can hold all the evils of the world out with my body.

Ro sits on the bed and whimpers.

"What happened?"

"I was in the bosque. The fire was coming so fast. I was trying to run away." She takes a deep breath. "A man came out of nowhere. He grabbed me, but I kicked until he let go. Then I ran. He was pushing me into the fire. I could feel it starting to burn."

My knees won't hold me anymore. I slide down to the floor.

"It was so hot I couldn't breathe. The flames were everywhere. I tripped. My arm"—she holds it out—"hit a burning tree."

My scar sends pain through my body in sympathy. I jump up and start riffling through drawers. I don't know what I'm looking for, but I have to find something. Something to fix this. I hurt someone. I hurt my friend.

"I'm so sorry I said those things to you." Ro starts to cry again, but quickly rubs her eyes. "I couldn't see his face, but he's the guy. The guy who killed Kara and started the fires. I know it." Her voice sinks down to a whisper. "He almost got me."

The tears I've been holding back all day spill down my face. I drop to my knees in front of Ro. "I'm sorry for earlier too." *I'm sorry you got burned.*

I take her arm. "We have to do something about this."

"Please let me stay here tonight. I'll go to Henderson's in the morning."

"This is bad. You need to go to the hospital."

"No!" She jerks her arm away from me. "They'll call my aunt. Or they'll send me to the group home." She stands up. "Never mind. Sorry to have bothered you."

"Ro, I'm not letting you go back out there. I'll do it. I know how to treat a burn. But first . . ." There's a voice that lives in the dark, hidden recesses of my mind. It's the voice that told me to lie about the matches when I was seven. It's the voice that watches out for me. Protects me. It's the one that speaks now. "Why were you out there, Ro?"

She shakes her head.

"Ro?"

She blinks tears out of her eyes. "I didn't have anywhere to go. You don't want me here. My aunt locked me out. I thought maybe I could find a spot in the colony. Somewhere I could sleep for tonight.

"Before I saw that man, I thought you were hiding something from me about the fires. I should have trusted you."

The knife of guilt twists deeper and deeper into my stomach.

"Did you call the cops on me? Leave an anonymous tip?"

She shakes her head frantically.

There's only one way to find out if the feds are on to me. If they have the photo that was in my bag, the one left in my locker of me starting the fire.

"I can't get what I need at Henderson's. We need real medical supplies. If I take you to the clinic, do you think you can get us inside?"


"That one." Ro points to the window above the sink in the kitchen. She works it back and forth until it pops open. She hoists herself up, wincing as her burned arm straightens to hold her weight. I glance over my shoulder. That guy is still out there somewhere.

I copy Ro and pull myself through the open window, but I fall into the sink and then roll onto the floor.

"Ow."

Ro laughs.

It was easy getting out of the Los Ranchitos. The security guard was down the street, watching the fire, and all the noise blocked the sound of the gate opening and closing. Dad always has a truck with the key stuck in a magnetic holder under the frame for anyone who needs to run a work-related errand. We were out and on our way in no time—much easier than all those times I sneaked out on foot.

I've never heard the clinic so quiet. Every squeak on the floor sounds like a cannon going off.

The place is a mess. The DEA didn't clean up after they searched it.

I walk a few paces behind Ro, scanning the hallway until I see it: My bag. Right where I left it.

I pick it up and throw it across my body. I'm not letting go of it until I can open my history book to the chapter on King George III.

Ro hops up onto the exam table, as if I'm a real doctor about to examine her. I dig through the cabinets until I find what I need.

It's hard to see in the dark, but I clean the area around her burn, put some ointment on it, and wrap it in gauze.

"Keep it dry. If it starts to look infected, you're going to have to go to the hospital."

"Okay. Where'd you get that?" She points at my bag. My hand slides over it protectively.

"I left it here." I look away from her. "We need to go. We can't get caught here."

I wait until Ro is asleep in the Los Ranchitos before I take my bag into the bathroom. I lock the door and sit on the edge of the tub. I don't know what I'll do if the photo is gone.

I open my history book. It's there, untouched. Ro was telling the truth. She didn't tip off the cops—not about me, at least.

I do what I should have done at school. I rip the photo into a hundred little pieces and watch them swirl down the toilet bowl.

# 37

Ro is still asleep in my bed when I wake up. I place a note that says *Do not leave* on the nightstand and step out into the cool, hazy air.

With Ro's burn, and the photo, I haven't had the thought-space to process that there's a murderer out here. He killed Kara and chased Ro. He knows about my secret. He could be anyone, anywhere. He could be watching me right now.

I want to duck back inside my room and bolt the door, but I can't. I have to find Ben. I have to apologize, beg, do anything to make him understand. I'll tell him everything. I'll accept my punishment.

When I get to the coffee shop, no one's seen him. He doesn't answer his door.

The walk home is long and miserable. But when I stop into Henderson's to buy snacks, I keep my head up and smile at Ruby, as if my whole world isn't crumbling around me.

Ro stays all weekend, so I know she has forgiven me for saying we aren't friends. We eat and camp out in front of the TV. I examine her burn over and over again and feed her ibuprofen. She doesn't seem too bothered by any pain. It seems to hurt me more than it hurts her.

I want to know more about the man who chased her, but I've been asked to relive the night I was burned too many times. I would never do that to her.

On Monday morning, she has to leave. I'm sad about that. It was nice not being alone this weekend—even considering the circumstances. And we're okay. Ro hasn't mentioned the fires again.

I dread going to school. It's a project day, and I don't have a project anymore.

Teresa meets me in the hallway. Her face is pinched. "Jenny," she says, but nothing else.

It must be hard for her to be the teacher that set up the project that got busted by the feds. I wonder if she got yelled at by the principal, or if she's worried that my dad is going to call and threaten to sue.

She starts to say something again, but I cut her off.

"I know," I say. "I was there."

"I'm so sorry. Obviously, you won't have any more project days. You did great work at the clinic. I'm giving you an A. You can spend your project time in the library until the end of the year."

"What's going to happen to Doc? Is he going to jail?"

Teresa shakes her head. "They released him. That's all I know."

I suddenly feel better than I have in days. Doc's not in trouble. He'll reopen the clinic. Ben will come back. I'll make a thousand peanut butter sandwiches. Do whatever it takes to get Ben's forgiveness for what he saw between Allen and me.

I don't go to the library. It's not like anyone is going to check, so I slip off campus during lunch.

I couldn't change first, so I'm in my bee uniform, walking down the street. I get leers and a couple of whistles, but they roll right off me. I've seen way too much to be intimidated by that now.

Some men I recognize as regulars are hanging out on the clinic's porch. The usually open and welcoming front door is shut. I walk up to it and knock.

"Doc won't let us in," one of the men says.

"But Doc's here? Is Ben with him?"

The man looks annoyed. "I don't know. Doc won't let us in."

I step off the porch and go around to the kitchen door. I try the handle. It pops open. "Hello?" I call inside. I hear the sweeping of a broom across the wood. My heart lifts up to the sky. Ben. I can explain what happened with Allen.

I bound into the front room. Doc turns around, startled. He stops sweeping and rests the broom against the wall. I look back and forth, scanning the front room, the exam room, the kitchen again.

Doc's alone.

"I don't know where he is," Doc says. "I wish I did."

He picks up the broom and starts sweeping again—pieces of paper, an empty bandage box, dirt tracked in by the agents.

This might all be my fault. But I can't—won't—live with that. Instead, I choose to believe Ro. She didn't call the cops on Doc. It was Suds and the story he spread around that caused this. The fault lies squarely with him.

He got what he deserved.

"What are you going to do?" I ask Doc.

He shrugs. "The news made this place sound like some sort of a crack house. No one's going to donate now. We'll have to close." My face must look horrified. He smiles sadly. "It'll be temporary. I'll find some way to raise more money. Restock. Reopen the doors."

"You should call Teresa," I say. He looks down. I see the shame on his face. "She cares a lot about this place. She'd want to help." I head back out, but in the doorway to the kitchen, I turn around. "If you see Ben, will you tell him I'm sorry?"

Doc doesn't ask what I'm sorry about. He nods. I step into the kitchen and pull the peanut butter and bread down. The men on the porch may not be allowed in, but at least they'll have something to eat.

This will be my first step at making amends with Ben.


The week is quiet. I don't get any surprises outside my door or in my locker. Ro's been in and out, but not as much as usual. It's the end of the semester. She said she has to catch up on all the schoolwork she hasn't done.

Three times I send Allen's calls to voice mail. I'm afraid to answer. I'm also afraid not to answer. I can't risk making him angry, but I won't go out with him again—especially since Ben is still missing after catching us together. The fourth time Allen calls, I tell him I have the flu.

The Los Ranchitos is almost finished. The formerly blacked-out section is now lit. Furniture is being moved in and construction equipment moved out. After the parking lot is repaved, the whole thing will be inspected and permitted, and that's it.

I try not to think about what that means. My room won't be my room anymore. It will be restored to its brand-new glory, and we will leave. I don't know where we're going.

Dad has Monica. I can't imagine us all living in a house with rooms that are connected. One where you can hear through the walls. One where Monica will watch me constantly.

Ben's still MIA. On Saturday afternoon, I try a final time. If Ben isn't home, if he keeps dodging my calls and texts, I'll have no choice but to declare us over. The thought spreads pain through my chest.

When I walk into the coffee shop, Jackie is at the counter alone. She gives me a sympathetic look and waves me over.

"Getting healthy is hard," she says. "Sometimes you feel on top of the world, and sometimes you feel like the world is on top of you. Don't take it personally. I know he cares about you. But when it gets bad, there are days when even love can't lighten that load."

I'm going to start to cry if I stand here and face her any longer. She knows it and turns to wipe a rag around the espresso machine.

In the stairwell, I rub my eyes. She's right. I'm being self-ish. All I think about is me. Why Ben won't talk to *me*. How explaining would make *me* feel better.

I haven't thought about him. About how he felt seeing Doc surrounded by federal agents and the clinic shutting down. About me betraying him with Allen.

I pause on the stairs. It all feels too big. Part of me thinks I should leave him alone. Let him heal without me ripping the scab off. I keep going up. This will be the last time. After today, I'll leave him in peace.

When I exit onto the second floor, I can tell something is wrong: his purple door is open. I run toward it.

"Ben?" I call, and push it open farther. I gasp. The apartment is trashed. The contents of the bookshelf are mixed in with the couch cushions on the floor. Glasses are broken in the kitchen. The sheets are in a heap at the end of the bed.

I pull my phone out to call the police, but then something catches my eye. I move forward and lift up one of the cushions. Under it is an empty vodka bottle.

No one did this to Ben. He's done it to himself.

# 38

Cam tells me to go home when I call him. He won't pick me up and let me ride around with him. I think it's because he wants to beat himself up over Ben without a witness.

I grip my phone in front of me as I stumble along the sidewalk. Tears run down my face. The people I pass jump when they see me. A woman asks if I need help. I ignore her and keep going.

When I get to my room, Ro isn't there. I didn't want to have to tell her about Ben, but at the same time, I wish someone were here to sit next to me. I don't want to be all alone.

I curl up into a ball on the bed. Flashes of Ben lying by the side of the road, cold and dead, keep playing through my mind. Is this my fault? If we had never met, if I had never gone to his apartment after Kara died, would he be okay? Would he be making cappuccinos and change at the coffee shop right now?

I wanted to be worthy of him—to turn my life around like he did. I tried, but not hard enough. I brought this on both of us. If only I were stronger. If only I could have stopped setting those fires. If only I didn't have to keep lying to everyone.

Maybe Ben and I were never meant to be together. Maybe I just have to accept that I will never be worthy of him.

It's getting dark. I don't turn on the lamp. I hide in the shadows. My arm burns as badly as it did when I was in that hospital bed with oxygen tubes in my nose ten years ago.

My phone dings. I jump up and paw for it in my pocket. I made Cam promise to text if he found out anything.

I swipe my phone on. The text isn't from Cam. It's from Ben. My heart starts to gallop. I open it.

It has one heartbreaking line: *I need you.*

A photo is attached. It's grainy and a little blurry, but I recognize it.

It's the old warehouse in the colony. The one where people go to die.

I run out of my room without grabbing a jacket or my purse, my shoes half on my feet. I only have my phone.

The extra truck is gone, but Monica's car is in the parking lot. The door is locked. I feel along the bottom edge of the door. No key.

The office and Dad's room are dark. I have no choice but to run. Into the cottonwoods and through the colony. Alone.

I go. Ben needs me. I have to get him out of there. Get him to Doc or someone who can fix this.

I dive into the trees. My ankle catches on something. I pitch forward and hit the dirt. I'm trying to go too fast. I know better than to run. I stand up and dust myself off. One slow step at a time, I pick my way through the under-brush.

The moon is almost full. The trees send ghostlike shadows

over me and the creatures dashing away. Too many creatures. I'm not alone.

I fight the urge to run again. If I fall, I'll lose seconds getting back up.

I don't look over my shoulder. I don't flinch at the crunching footsteps behind me.

I smell cooking food and woodsmoke. Raised voices and light come from the trees in front of me.

My next steps take me into the colony.

Five sets of eyes turn and look at me. They're bundled up around a fire pit. Some wear blankets; others, army surplus.

A few old structures are still half standing, but mostly tents dot the spaces between the trees. The trees themselves make up the back walls of plywood and cardboard shanties. A clothesline hangs above one, drying dingy T-shirts.

One of the men at the fire stands up. "You shouldn't be out here, darlin'."

I jump and instinctively curl in on myself when he steps in front of me. The other men stand. The first man holds out his hand. They sit back down.

"Please," I whisper. "I'm just passing through. I have to get to the warehouse."

One of the men at the fire whistles. Another crosses himself. The man in front of me laughs and points over his shoulder. "They think that place is haunted."

"I don't believe in ghosts." It's an automatic, stupid thing to say. Ghosts aren't my biggest problem right now.

The man laughs. The light from the fire catches his face.

I recognize him. He was on the clinic porch. I made him a sandwich.

"Please. Ben's there. I have to help him."

The man considers this. "Ben's a good guy." He motions over his shoulder. "That's a bad place. You're not going to like what you find there."

I step around him. He doesn't try to stop me. I feel all the eyes in the tents and lean-tos watch me as I make my way through.

When I step into the clearing where the warehouse stands, I suck in a lungful of fresh air, as if it's the last breath I will ever take.

My whole body shakes from adrenaline and cold. From fear.

A beam of light flashes in my peripheral vision. I run toward it and dive onto my knees in front of what used to be a large window. The flashlight beam sweeps in my direction. I duck. When I pull myself up to look again, a chunk of stone from around the window falls off in my hand. It's a decorative facade. The warehouse itself is made of dry, splintering wood.

"What the hell did you do?" a voice inside yells.

"I didn't do anything! Don't hurt me!" another voice answers.

It's a familiar voice that makes my blood turn to ice and freezes my limbs.

But I have to go inside. I have to help her.

"Get away from me!" Ro screams. I jump over the window ledge and run to where I hear a scuffle.

The light whips around, giving me flashes of what's happening. Ro is grappling with the man holding the light. He's much bigger than she is. She looks terrified.

I plan my attack. When his back is to me, I'm going to run and jump on him. Pull off his ears. Claw out his eyes. Whatever it takes to get him away from her.

I steady myself. I'm ready.

Ro bites his hand. He drops the light. It falls against something so that the beam is shining almost straight up. The man steps into it. He turns toward me. And I see him. Ro's attacker.

It's Cam.

# 39

Cam reacts to being bitten by shooting his hand out. His palm hits Ro's face, and she crashes down to the dirt floor of the warehouse.

"Stop!" I scream, and run toward them.

"Jenny? What are you doing here? I told you to go home."

"Get away from her, Cam." I sweep up the flashlight and put myself between them. He steps toward me. I shine the light in his eyes. "I mean it. I'm going to call the cops."

He puts his hands up. "I didn't mean to hit her. It was a reflex."

"Was Kara a 'reflex' too?"

"Kara?"

Ro cries behind me. I turn to look at her. Cam lunges for the flashlight. But I'm ready for him. I time my foot to kick him in the crotch.

He bends in half and stumbles backward. "I'm done!" he yells at a dark corner. "Do you hear me? I'm done." He limps out into the night.

I spin around to Ro. She gets up, holding her face. Tears shine on her cheeks. "Why did you do this, Jenny?"

"What? We need to go." I reach forward for her arm, but she jerks away and flattens herself against the wall like she can't get far enough away from me.

"You set me up. You left me that note on your bed telling me to come here after dark. Why, Jenny?" Her voice cracks, making my heart follow suit.

"Ro, I have no idea what you're talking about. I didn't leave you a note." I creep slowly toward her, holding out my hand. "Let's go back to the motel and call the police. Cam won't get away with this."

She slides along the wall away from me. "I don't believe you." She moves fast. One moment she's still in front of me; the next she's in the deep shadows of the warehouse.

I sweep the flashlight around. "Ro?"

A moan from the corner. I spin toward it. The light falls on a person huddled on the ground. He's surrounded by bottles. A syringe lies in the dirt by his right hand.

I fall to my knees next to him. "Ben?" I shake him. He moans again, but his eyes don't open. "Ben?"

Nothing.

I pull my phone out of my pocket. I don't have a signal.

Cam did this. All of it. He left Ro that note. He texted me from Ben's phone. Why? Why does he want us all together in this horrible place? To kill us? Like he did Kara?

"I'm going to get you help, okay?" I stand up and walk slowly to the window. Cam could be anywhere. I can't let him catch me off guard. The signal is better, but it's drifting in and out. It's not enough to make a call.

The cracking sound of a heavy foot in the debris makes me spin around again. "Ro?" I call out. There's no answer. The hairs on my arms stand up. My feet scream to run, but I can't move.

I smell smoke.

Suddenly, I'm seven years old again, standing in the bathroom doorway, watching the world turn into a burning hell in front of me. My scar pulses. My heart beats in terror. This fire is different from the ones in the trees. This is a fire I can't control.

Movement behind me. Ben's leg twitches. My feet unfreeze themselves. I have to get him out.

Smoke fills the warehouse and funnels out the window. I drop my flashlight and loop my hands under Ben's arms. His deadweight is too heavy for me with the smoke stealing my oxygen.

I pull my shirt over my mouth, but I still cough violently. My eyes sting, and tears stream down my face.

I drag Ben inch by inch. I don't have the time or the strength to be gentle. I flop him over the side of the window so his head is in the fresh air and then push him from behind until he hits the ground. I jump through the window after him and pull him as far as I can out of the path of the fire.

He doesn't move—not even a twitch. I fall to my knees. In the darkness, I can't tell if he's breathing.

"Stay with me, Ben." My phone has a signal now. I punch in 911.

"Jenny!" My heart stops. "Jenny!" Ro screams again. She's still inside.

The operator answers the phone. "Help! There's a fire!" I screech into the phone.

A cracking sound comes from the building. It's going to come down. Come down with Ro inside.

I drop the phone on top of Ben. The operator will trace the signal.

"I'll be back!" I yell to his unconscious figure, and run to the window to save Ro.

But when I reach it, my body stops. It refuses to go any farther. My eyes betray me. I see Hailey in front of me standing by the burning stove. I see Kara's body, limp and twisted outside that club. I hear the screams from that house while I'm curled up in the bathtub holding my ears.

If my feet don't move, Ro is going to die. She'll be another name on my list of ghosts.

One foot slides forward. Then the other. My adrenaline takes over, and I go headfirst through the window and into the smoke.

I scoop up the flashlight from where I dropped it trying to move Ben and sweep the beam through the warehouse. Smoke reflects the light back at me. I flap my arms, trying to clear a path.

"Ro!"

She doesn't answer. I drop down and crawl where the air is fresher. "Ro!"

"Jenny!" I hear the terror in her voice.

"Ro, come to me. This is the way out."

"Jenny, help me!"

"This way, Ro. Come to my voice."

"Jenny!"

She's not coming. I keep moving forward. Then I see them. The flames tearing through the roof and up the sides of the walls. The whole place is about to come down.

"Ro, you have to run. Run!"

"Jenny!"

She's ten feet away. I reach out my hand. "Come this way, Ro." She doesn't see me. Her eyes are looking up. She screams.

A beam crashes down in front of her. She screams again. A wall of flames rises between us.

"Ro!"

"Jenny, I'm sorry." Her voice is small and resigned. She knows she's going to die.

"No!"

A deafening crack. Another beam crashes and lands feet from me. I'm showered in sparks that bite at my skin and clothes.

"Ro!" I scream one last time, but she's gone quiet behind the wall of flames.

I fall down flat onto my stomach. I'm dizzy and light-headed. The inside of my nose burns. There's nothing I can do. She's gone. I couldn't save her.

It would be so easy to close my eyes, to join Ro and Kara and my sleepover friends.

I hear sirens outside. Ben could be dead. I could have killed him too.

Another piece of the roof crashes down. I've only got

seconds left to live. I don't want to fight anymore, but my body takes over. My survival instinct is stronger than my mind. My knees pull themselves underneath me and prop me up. They shuffle forward slowly, then quicker and quicker. My palms scrape along the hot wood and ash. The clean air of the window guides me forward, and I pull myself out.

On the ground, under the trees and the starry sky, my lungs fill over and over again.

# 40

Paramedics surround Ben's lifeless figure. I crawl toward them. They're too busy yelling out readings and cutting off Ben's shirt to notice me coming out of the darkness. Ben's still alive. Barely.

A stream of water shoots from a fire truck into the building. From the looks on the firefighters' faces in the glow of the flames, I know the water is an empty gesture. This fire is too dangerous to approach. It will have to burn itself out.

Will anything be left of Ro when it does?

A paramedic starts to pump Ben's chest. I want to throw myself at Ben's feet and beg his forgiveness. Beg him not to die.

But if I stay with Ben, the questions will start.

I've been through this before.

First the paramedics will check that I'm okay. They'll ask me what happened, but they won't push. It's not their job.

The police will come next. Their questions will start off routine: Why was I here? Did I see who started the fire? Who else was inside?

They'll give me a day or two to collect myself. Then a

detective will come knocking on my door. Someone will won-der why my stepfather was being investigated for tampering with evidence and falsifying information on an arson report. Someone will have decided that it's too coincidental for me to have been in two fatal fires in my short life.

The questions will get even harder.

There's nothing I can do for Ben, but I can save myself.

My phone was tossed aside by the paramedics and lies in a patch of weeds at the base of a tree. I scoop it up and crawl back into the darkness.

When I stumble into my room, my clothes are shreds. They reek of smoke. Of death. I take them off. I want to throw them out the bathroom window and make them go away for-ever, but I can't do that.

I pull the bag out of the trash can in my room. I stuff the clothes in the bottom of it and then replace the bag. I'll find a way to get rid of them later.

I stand under the shower until my hair and skin are no longer black with soot. When I step out and see myself in the mirror, I expect a monster to appear before me—one that lets people die. But I don't look any different.

My phone lies on the bathroom counter. There's only one thing I can do to try to redeem myself. To keep the monster hidden.

There were four of us in that warehouse. One is dead. One is hopefully still alive and at the hospital. One is dripping water on the floor of her stone bathroom.

That leaves the fourth.

And he has a key to my room.

Cam wanted us gone.

He didn't want to feel guilty about Ben anymore. He said it himself before he set the fire: *I'm done.*

I witnessed everything that happened with Suds. Suds was a threat to the project. Mike Vargas blamed Cam for that. So Cam got rid of Suds.

Ro and I both know how Cam felt about Kara, and that she didn't feel the same way. He disappeared from the club the night she was murdered.

Kara must have told him her story too. That's why he left her those things, so that it would look like someone from her past had found her and killed her.

Cam left the stuff for me so I wouldn't go to the police if I found out. Mutually assured destruction. If I told, so would he.

Well, *I'm done* too. It will destroy my life if Cam tells them about me, but I'm not thinking of myself anymore. I'm going to do the first truly selfless thing I've ever done. For Ro. For Kara.

I wipe the dirt and smeary fingerprints off my phone, and I call the police tip line.

It's a recording. After the beep, I tell the machine one simple thing: "Cam Vargas did it."

Then I claw open the drawer where my magic sleeping pills live.

I don't know how many I take.

•   •   •

My body reacts to the smell of smoke. It thrashes at the duvet covering my face. A figure stands over me. Her blond hair shines in the brilliant sunlight coming through the window. She holds up pieces of shredded cloth and tosses them in a black trash bag. She leans over me and glares.

Flashing police lights. Yelling outside my window. "We've been through this before. Either get a warrant and arrest my client or get off the property."

FaceTime ringing over and over and over again. Hailey's voice saying, "Don't cry, Jenny. Don't cry."

I hear the bathroom window slide open. I hear Ro bounce into the room. I feel her plop down on the bed. Then I open my eyes, and she's gone.

There's a knock on the door. My eyes unseal and blink in the dusky light. I pry open my mouth. It's sticky and dry and tastes like vomit.

The knock comes again. I sit up. My head spins. The room is foggy. I stand. My legs feel like Jell-O. They wobble me to the door. I open it a crack.

Dad smiles and holds out a bowl of broth. "Are you feeling better?"

I smack my lips, trying to remember how to make sound come out of them.

Dad's eyes narrow. "Should I take you to the doctor? Monica said you had a stomach bug. But you don't look so hot."

I reach out and take the soup. "I'm okay," I croak. "I just need some more rest."

"I'll let the school know you'll be out sick tomorrow."

"Thanks." I start to close the door, but Dad doesn't move. I ache to tell him what happened to Ro. To have him wrap me in his arms and tell me everything will be okay. But I can't. I don't want to place that burden on him. Two fatal fires. He'll know. And he'll have to conceal it from the police when they come around asking. He's already a felon. I won't be responsible for sending him back to jail.

"I need to lie down again. Is there something else?" I ask.

He glances over his shoulder at the empty parking lot. "Make sure you keep your door locked."

I take the bowl of soup to my bed. When I slurp a spoonful, it drags like barbed wire down my raw throat. I should see a doctor. Smoke inhalation is dangerous—even later, when you think you're fine.

I know I'm not fine. Ro is dead. Her screams still echo in my head. They won't let me rest.

I reach for my sleeping pills, but then put them back into the drawer. I can't take them forever. Even though I want to.

I flip on the TV and watch one mindless show after another until the late news comes on. It starts right away with a late-breaking news graphic. They've gone all out and created one for Las Piedras. It's magenta, with flames burning up the word "FIRE."

The reporter comes on the screen. She stands with her

back to the cottonwoods. Her boobs are covered. I know what that means. It makes my empty stomach churn; my heart pound; my sick lungs gasp for air.

She holds a piece of paper in front of her. "The police have released a statement about the body that was found in the remains of the building. It was burned beyond all recognition, but from a skeletal examination, they believe it was a woman. Those remains are now being sent to the lab to see if they can get an ID. We'll let you know more as soon as we find out."

I turn off the TV.

My first feeling is overwhelming relief. Ben isn't on the news. He must still be alive. Then the guilt comes back.

*Ro is dead.*

# 41

I spend my sick day pacing. And coughing. And trying to swallow. The curtains are shut. It's a dark, unidentifiable time of day in here.

I keep waiting for the police to show up. For them to walk me and Dad into the office and start the questions. I'm ready. I'm not even going to make them ask me a thousand things. I'm just going to confess—and then tell them absolutely everything I know about Cam.

The office door opens, and someone steps in front of my window.

"Here's the deal. My client admits to striking the young lady. He is willing to plead no contest to a simple battery charge. He'll pay a fine and do community service. Everybody wins." I creep forward and pull aside the curtains. The lawyer is on his cell phone. He rolls his tie up and down on his finger. He drops it.

"No, the girl in that abandoned warehouse. What are you talking about? What nightclub?"

The lawyer's eyes flit over to me. I drop the curtain.

There's a knock on my door. This is it. "Just a minute!" I yell, to give myself time for another couple of breaths.

The person on the other side doesn't wait. They have a key.

I glance up at the chain. It's hanging down. I never locked it.

The door pops open. I stand at attention, ready to dash into the bathroom and out the window if it's Cam.

"Feeling better?" Monica asks.

"I, ah—" The look on her face tells me that she doesn't care. I shut my mouth.

She closes the door and sits down on the bed. She points to the chair. "Sit." This is a different Monica. This isn't the one who made coffee in her underwear or cut off my wristband from the club. I sit.

"The police have been here asking questions about Cam."

"Oh?" I pick at a piece of lint stuck to the side of the chair. People who are guilty do things like that. I stop and look her in the eye.

"There are an awful lot of coincidences that all tie back to Cam. Suds, the girl at the club, this warehouse thing. They have some sort of evidence. An engraved lighter. It's at the forensics lab right now."

She gives me a second. I don't say anything.

"It got me thinking. All those things are tied to Cam. But they're also tied to you."

"What?"

"I love your father. Almost as much as I love this project." She stands up and steps forward until she looms over me.

She's accusing me of murder now? I should tell her everything. She deserves it. She can be the one who conceals it from the police to save her precious project.

She pulls a piece of paper from of her pocket. She unfolds it and smooths it out on the bed. "I found this outside your bathroom window."

It's a stick figure drawing of a girl with yellow hair surrounded by orange flames. On the top it says *Not so innocent* in red Sharpie.

I reach for it, but Monica whips it away. "I don't know what your deal is. I don't know if Daddy doesn't give you enough attention, or if you're mad at Mommy, but it stops now."

"I didn't kill anyone," I protest. "I didn't start that fire in the warehouse."

"Don't bullshit me, Jenny. I'm the queen of bullshitters. I can smell it a mile away. So here's the deal: Until this project is finished, you are going to go to school and come straight home. You aren't going to take any late-night walks or have any friends over. Once the ribbon is cut on the project, you are packing your bags and returning to your mother."

I shrink back at the force of her words. There's no way around it now. I've lost. I'm going back to Ohio. Everything that has happened here has been for nothing. People *died* because I came here. Overwhelming feelings of grief and guilt and horror wash over me. I slump down in the chair, wishing it would swallow me and end this hell.

"What if Brian won't let me come home?" My voice cracks, and not because of my sore throat.

"You better think of something to convince him, because

you know what I found stuffed in the bottom of the trash? The clothes you were wearing on Saturday, covered in ash and burn marks. I bet the police would love to send those to their forensics lab."

She walks to the door and turns the knob. "Do we have an understanding?"

"Yes," I croak.

I take a deep breath, pick up my phone, find the number I need, and press call. Mom answers on the second ring. "You scared your sister to death the other day. What were you thinking, talking to her with no adults around?"

"I'm sorry." I don't remember what I said to Hailey, but whatever it was, it's not going to help smooth things over with Brian. "I want to come home."

There's a sharp intake of breath on the other end. It's not the reaction I expected. She should be making soothing noises and getting her credit card out to buy a plane ticket.

"The project's almost complete. Dad's going to have to move. Please let me come home. I miss you guys and my friends and my old school."

"I don't know, Jenny." Mom doesn't sound mad anymore. She sounds tired, like this conversation is sucking out all her energy.

"Please, Mom." I give up pretending she doesn't know about the fire in the abandoned house in Ohio. "Tell Brian I'm better. I promise. It won't happen again."

A sigh. "Let me talk to your father about it."

. . .

The next day, I'm the best and most attentive student the world has ever seen. I sit up straight in my desk. I smile at incoming students. I don't have feelings. I'm a robot.

In homeroom, we're working on our final project reports. After what happened at the clinic, I don't have to turn one in, so I sit with my eyes stuck to the back of the head of the girl in front of me.

Teresa walks up and down the aisles. She stops at my desk, places a folded piece of paper in front of me, and keeps walking.

I slap the paper off my desk and slide it into my lap. I look around. Everyone is working.

Teresa is watching me. I don't understand the look on her face. I unfold the paper, cringing at every crackle it makes.

It's a note that says *From Doc: Ben's in the hospital. He would like to see you.*

I whip my eyes around the classroom, as if the message has been broadcast over the intercom. Teresa sits down at her desk. She nods at me.

I leave school at lunch. I'm taking a huge risk. Monica could be bluffing, or she might go straight to the police if she finds out I disobeyed her.

I walk out the back door and onto the street. At the corner with the traffic light, I pull out my phone and call what must be the only cab in all of Las Piedras.

It shows up a few minutes later. The driver looks me up and down like I'm one of his more interesting customers.

"You got money?" he asks.

I pull out my debit card and pray that Mom didn't cut me off after my FaceTime with Hailey.

"Okay," he says. "Where to?"

The hospital serves all the surrounding communities, so it isn't in Las Piedras. It sits in the middle of the desert off the interstate.

I swipe my card, which, thankfully, goes through, and ask the cab driver to pick me up in an hour. He shrugs and pulls out a newspaper. "I've got nowhere else to be."

I get Ben's room number and stand in front of the elevator. I don't know what I'm going to say to him. Apologize? Yell at him? Dissolve into a soppy mess on the floor? One thing I can't do is tell him about Cam. Not now while he's hurt in the hospital.

The elevator door opens, and Mike Vargas is standing in front of me. "Shit," I whisper under my breath. I might as well call the police on myself. As soon as he goes back and tells Monica I wasn't in school, it's all over for me.

I stagger back a step as he comes forward. He smiles. "He's in room 413. At the end of the hall."

"Okay. Thanks." He moves past me. "Mr. Vargas?" This is the only shot I have. "Could you not tell anyone that I came here?"

"Sure," he says, but then he straightens up. "Thank you for caring about my nephew." He buttons his suit jacket and marches away with his usual I-have-somewhere-important-to-be gait.

I find room 413, and I stick my head inside. It's a private room with a big window that looks out at distant mountains.

"Pretty nice digs for a junkie, huh?"

When I see him, I can't hold it together. I spin around and cover my face with my hands.

He says my name. There's no anger in his voice, just concern. It doesn't help me pull myself together.

"Please, Jenny."

I turn and rub my eyes. Ben's face is lined with pain and exhaustion. He has oxygen tubes in his nose. An IV line pokes into his arm. But he's still beautiful. Still Ben.

I move over to his bed. "I'm sorry. I'm sorry about everything."

"You saved my life."

I have to look away again.

"I don't remember much of what happened, but the firefighters said that someone pulled me out and a girl called 911. It had to be you. There's no one else who would do that for me."

"But it was my fault in the first place." I point to the tubes. "This is my fault." My fault for showing up in Las Piedras, my fault for falling for him, my fault for going on that stupid date with Allen.

"No." Ben takes my hand. "This is on me. All of it."

I have to change the subject before I start sobbing into his white hospital sheets. "I saw your uncle downstairs."

Ben's face shows a hint of a smile. "He came to see me." He points around the room with his free hand. "That's why I'm still here and haven't been kicked out onto the street."

"That's great." An awkward silence fills the space between us.

Ben breaks it. "I have to tell you something." His tone makes my heart stop. I swallow and my still-raw throat screams at me.

"What?"

"My uncle got me a bed in a rehab place near Taos. It's supposed to be the best in the state. I'm leaving tomorrow." He twists the sheet around and around his hand. "You know I care about you, Jenny, but—"

"But you need to get healthy," I finish for him. He needs to get healthy without me. I'm a reminder of this world that he doesn't want to live in.

"After the raid on the clinic, I felt like my whole world had been pulled out from under me. They're my *family*. When I saw the look on Doc's face, I knew the clinic wasn't going to survive. I couldn't think straight. So I did what was familiar, what I knew would take some of the hurt away. But this time, I didn't care if I died."

What he's not saying is that he came to me for help and saw me with Allen.

Ben narrows his eyes, like he's trying hard to remember something. "What happened at the warehouse?" he asks. "I remember Cam showing up and yelling at me. Then there was someone else. A woman, maybe? Cam thought she had given me the drugs. She didn't. It was me. My choice. Then I woke up in the hospital, and the doctor said I had been in a fire."

I nod. I can't tell him about Ro—even though it would make me feel better to tell someone. This isn't about me. It isn't his job to make me feel better this time. It never was, or at least it never should have been.

He sees that I'm not going to say anything. "Well, I'm glad you're okay." He looks down at the twisted sheet.

I stand up. "I'm going back to Ohio," I say, as if instead of ending our whole relationship, I've just canceled plans to go to the movies. The hurt shows on his face. But being a first-class bitch is the only way I know how to deal with my pain.

I lean over and wrap my arms around his neck. I kiss him on the forehead.

"Maybe someday . . . ," he says. I nod, but I know it's a lie. This is goodbye.

# 42

For another week, nothing happens. I become the robot again. Unfeeling, uncaring. I go to school. I come home. I do what Monica wants.

Dad knocks on my door on Wednesday. When I open it, a giant, fake smile is on his face. He steps inside.

"I spoke with your mother." The smile gets bigger, faker. "She thinks it would be best if you were to go back to Ohio." He shrugs. "You know I never could win an argument with her."

His smile turns into a cringe. He doesn't know how I'm going to react. "When?" I ask.

"The final inspection is tomorrow, and—"

"Tomorrow? I thought it wasn't for another week."

"Mike got it moved up. If everything goes well, the ribbon cutting will be Saturday morning."

"I want to leave Saturday afternoon."

Dad jumps at the force in my voice. If Mom and Brian will take me back, I have to get out of here as soon as possible. I'll find a way to deal with Ohio later. Right now I need to get away from Monica and Cam. Away from the swath of dry, crackly trees outside.

"But school isn't over until Memorial Day," he says.

"It's a couple of weeks. Call the principal and ask him why they sent your daughter to work in a crack house. I'm sure they'll be very accommodating." Just when I thought I couldn't possibly hate myself more, it turns out there's still some wiggle room.

Dad and I have never talked about what happened at the clinic, but I know he knows. Everyone does. His face falls.

"Okay," Dad says. He can't win an argument with me, either.


When I come home from my last day at Riverline Prep on Thursday, the office door is propped open. A bunch of people are gathered inside. Dad waves me over. He puts an empty champagne flute in my hand and pours the tiniest bit of bubbly in it. "We passed. The project is officially done and ready to open for business."

"That's great." I clink my glass around the room. When I get to Monica, she tips her head. I've fulfilled my part of the bargain. I already have my plane ticket for Saturday evening.

The lawyer appears in the doorway. His face is red and his slick suit rumpled. He looks through the crowd to Mike Vargas. "I held them off as long as I could."

A police car pulls into the freshly paved parking lot. I

don't see Cam hiding in the corner until Mike Vargas walks over to him and puts a hand on his shoulder. He leads Cam to the door. "Don't say a word without an attorney present."

One of the police officers steps forward. "Cameron Vargas, you are under arrest for the murder of Kara Johnston and the murder of an unidentified woman." The other officer steps around behind Cam and cuffs him as he's read his rights.

Mike Vargas and the lawyer jump into a car to follow them to the station. As Cam ducks his head to slide into the police car, his eyes catch mine. Fear and confusion twist his face. *That's right, Cam. You've been playing us this whole time, but you got caught.*

He may think his act now is convincing, but I know they've got the right guy.

He killed Kara and Ro.

I spend the night sorting through stuff. I'm only packing what I originally brought—minus the ultradown coat. As I put the new stuff into piles that are going to the charity shop or the clinic, I feel Ro all around me. The dagger of guilt, my scar, and the sadness won't leave me alone. I keep hoping that when I land in Ohio, it will disappear and I can erase the past five months from my mind.

I hold up the dress—minus the belt—that I wore to the club the night Kara died. I drop it in the donate pile.

Nothing will ever erase the past five months.

I jump at a sound outside. It's not the cops. But they could show up at any time—or not at all.

My hat and Ben's lighter are missing. I went through all my drawers ten times, but they aren't here. Cam must have them. I don't know what he'll do. Will he confess and take me down with him? Or will he plead innocence and save the info about me to use as a bargaining chip later?

I have to get out of here. If I can make it on to the plane to Ohio, I'll be fine. Are they really going to chase me across state lines? That sounds messy and expensive—two things that the people of Las Piedras aren't into.

Sometime in the early hours of the morning, I fall asleep in the donation pile. I'm startled awake by another sound. I look around. I'm still alone, but a strip of paper is sitting in my lap. I jump up. It wasn't there when I fell asleep. I glance over at the door. The dead bolt and the chain are locked.

With shaking fingers, I pick up the paper. It's torn off a bigger sheet so the bottom edge is ragged.

It says, in that same red Sharpie, *You almost fooled me.*

My whole body convulses in a shiver. Cam's in jail. It can't be him.

I rip it into a million pieces and race into the bathroom. I flush it.

The bathroom window is unlocked. I'd been keeping it open for Ro, as if the open window would bring her back to life.

I slam the lock shut. That's how he got in.

While I was sleeping.

I race around my room. There's nowhere to hide, but I search anyway. Under the bed. In the wardrobe. In between the donation bags.

Someone's still out there.

Watching me.

# 43

In the morning, I open my door a crack and look both ways. All the construction equipment has been moved out. The landscaping crew is fluffing bushes and planting flowers in the beds that separate the parking lot from the sidewalk. The ceremony is in twenty-four hours. Then I'll leave, and I'll be safe.

One of the landscapers holds a shovel. He looks up at me. I slam my door shut.

"Jenny, come have some lunch," Dad calls from outside.

I undo the chain, unlock the dead bolt, and slide back the chair I had propped up against the door. I stick my nose out. "I'm not hungry."

"Come on. Monica got us takeout from that fancy Italian place. This is one of our last meals together." Dad looks remorseful, as if he's actually sad about me leaving. I'm not sure why; I've barely seen him the whole time I've been here, but my heart can't take hurting anyone else.

I step out and make sure my door locks behind me.

As soon as I can, I go back to my room. I'm stuffed to the point that my stomach feels like it's going to explode. Monica was pleasant. Dad didn't notice the coldness in her eyes every time she looked at me. She made a point of telling me that the dumpster got emptied that morning. I guess that means that my trash bag of clothes was in it. She upheld her end of the deal.

I unlock my door and hold it open as I step inside. Everything is how I left it—except for the piece of paper in the middle of my bed.

I step back. The door closes in front of me. Dad exits the office and sees me in the middle of the sidewalk. "Did you lock yourself out?"

I shake my head. Part of me wants to tell him. Have him call the cops. Let me sleep on the floor of his room tonight. But I don't. I won't have an explanation for whatever that note says.

I rub my stomach. "I needed another breath of fresh air."

He laughs. "Best lasagna I've ever had." He walks away to inspect the flowers and chat with the landscapers.

I open my door and grope around the floor for something I can use as a weapon. The only thing I can reach is the black marker I was using to label things. I grip it like an ice pick.

I check under the bed and tiptoe to the wardrobe. I hold the marker over my head and scream as I rush forward into the bathroom.

No one's here.

I drop the marker, and it lands with a click on the marble

floor. I follow it down to my knees. The window is locked. It's someone with a key.

I crawl out to the bed and pick up the note between two fingers. This one is torn off at the top and the bottom, letting me know that I won't be done until there's a straight edge.

This note says *I thought you were afraid of fire, but I was wrong.*

Rip. Flush. Bye.

I'm not going to sleep tonight. I hold the marker and stare at the door. The chain and the dead bolt are locked. The chair is pushed in front of it. All the donation bags are piled on the chair. I sit between the bed and wardrobe with my suitcases making a nest around me and count the seconds until my plane leaves.


I jerk awake. My head was resting on my blue rolling suitcase, leaving behind a dark drool mark. I jump to my feet. The door, the chair, and the bags are all untouched. The bathroom window is locked. There's no new note on my bed.

I get dressed. I've seen *Psycho* one too many times to risk taking a shower. I'm wearing black jeans and a soft gray sweater. It's much too warm for the sunny spring day, but I was wearing it when I came from Ohio. I'm going back in it.

I smooth the duvet and put all the pillows on the bed. I arrange the donation bags against the wardrobe so that Dad can take them later. I pile my suitcases by the door. As soon as the ribbon has been cut and everyone's eaten cake, I'm out of here.

I step outside. A stage has been set up. A huge red ribbon stretches from one side to the other. In front of it, the parking lot is being filled with white folding chairs. A few people have already arrived. Mike Vargas shakes hands and slaps backs. Next to him, dressed in a suit, but unsmiling and looking like walking death, is Cam.

My heart speeds up. Why isn't he in jail? I stumble into the office. Monica, looking even more coiffed and well-dressed than usual, is leaning against the counter.

"Why is Cam here?" I demand.

"The police let him go. Too many coincidences, not enough real evidence."

"When?"

"When what?"

I start sucking in little gasps of air, trying to stay upright. "When did they let him go?"

"Sometime last night, I think." She examines me. "What's going on with you?"

Cam was still in jail when I got the notes. I take one big breath, and I try to keep the world in focus. "Nothing. I'm just excited to be going home."

And worrying about my sanity. *Are the notes even real?*

Monica raises an eyebrow. I leave before she can ask anything else.

# 44

My leg jiggles while I'm in the white folding chair. Mike's speech is going on forever. Monica, sitting on the stage, narrows her eyes at me. I put a hand on my leg to calm it.

Dad is sitting next to her, beaming. On the other side of him are assorted city officials. Cam is on the far end.

I hear the guests behind me shifting in their chairs. Coughing. We're all thinking the same thing: *Cut the damn ribbon already*. They're waiting for the elaborate cake to be rolled out, cut, and passed around. I'm waiting to throw my suitcases in the truck. I don't care if I have to wait four or five hours at the airport. I want to go now.

I glance around. My leg starts to jiggle again. The TV cameras are here. I keep expecting someone to stand up, point to me, and tell the world everything.

In what used to be the falling-down section—the section where I first met Ro—motion catches my attention.

The rooms are all unlocked to let the guests ooh and aah over each one. The outline of a person appears in the front window. The glare keeps me from seeing more than what looks like dark hair.

It disappears. Like a ghost. I'm starting to believe in them.

I keep my eyes on the window, but whoever—whatever—it was never comes back.

Finally, everyone on the stage lines up. Mike Vargas and a city councillor hold a pair of comically big scissors up for the camera. They snip the ribbon as a hundred flashes go off. The construction crew, hanging out in the back, cheers. The invited guests clap.

As everyone mills around waiting for the cake, I slip away. I'm going to load the truck now and sit in the cab until Dad is ready to drive me to the airport.

I open the door to my room and pop the handle of my big suitcase so I can roll it. I don't want to look at the bed.

I already know what's there.

And it's very real.

I only touch it because I can't have Dad or Monica or Mike Vargas finding the last piece when I'm gone.

The note says *You were afraid of you.*

It's not alone. Also on the bed is a phone. It has a sticky note on it that says *Watch me.*

With trembling fingers, I swipe it on. The video is already up on the screen. I recognize it. A figure wearing a pink hat with two black felt circles is crouched down between two cottonwoods. The video zooms in on the figure's hands. A silver lighter hovers over a stack of kindling. The lighter touches it. A small flame starts to burn. The figure tends to it until the surrounding brush catches.

Then the figure turns toward the camera, and the video freezes.

Every detail of my face is clear and sharp and unmistakable.

There's another video. I press play. The shaky camera walks up to a formation of rocks and lifts a tarp. Under it is Ben's silver lighter, Hailey's hat, the belt from my dress, and a shovel with the green Breland Construction logo on it.

A voice speaks dramatically. "You better run. The police are already on their way."

I rip open the curtains. The couple of police officers who were hanging around the ceremony in case of protestors are speaking into their radios. Another police car zooms by with its lights flashing.

I run.

Too much adrenaline flows through me to feel any pain when I go headfirst onto the ground outside the bathroom window. I dash around the edge of the property, sticking to the shadows until the cottonwoods come into view.

As I race through the brush and around the stumps of fallen trees, I don't trip. I know this route by heart. I've done it many times in the dark.

And I know exactly where the video of the hidden stuff was taken. It's in the one section that I made sure didn't burn. The trees are untouched. Their new green leaves tinkle in the warm spring breeze. I have to get the hat. I'm sure there's another copy of the video. Once the police see me in the hat and then find it with the murder weapons, it will be more than a coincidence. They'll have everything they need to convict me of all the crimes.

A laugh. I freeze in place. Someone takes a step. My head whips around, but I can't find them.

"Who are you?" I yell.

No response.

"Why are you doing this?"

The laugh again. I have to keep moving. I have to get to that stuff before the police find it—find me with it.

"You betrayed me." The voice stops me in my tracks. It's a voice I would know anywhere. One I've heard a thousand times.

I choke back tears.

"You were supposed to be different." The voice is getting closer. I spin around, examining every tree trunk and overgrown weed.

"Where are you?" I call.

I hear footsteps behind me. I turn around.

And collapse into the dirt.

# 45

"Ro," I whisper. Her hair is dyed dark now. The lightness in her step and eyes are gone. What I see are calculated movements and hate as she looks down at me. "But the warehouse—"

"That was good, huh? If you had gone around the back of that building, you would have seen that it didn't have one. I walked right out."

"But they found your body."

She chuckles. It makes my heart go cold. I don't know who this person is. "They found *a* body. Some sad tweaker. Don't worry. She didn't feel a thing."

I flinch away from her.

"And Kara? And Suds?" I try to make the ice in my tone match my frozen heart, but my voice shakes and makes me sound like a scared little girl.

Ro shrinks back in mock horror at my accusation, but then she smirks. "That bitch finally got what was coming to her. The pervert, well, that was a little messy. I don't recommend using a shovel." She shudders. "Kara was much cleaner. Easy. She almost begged me to do it."

"Why, Ro?"

"Ro's not my real name," she snaps. "And I already told you. You betrayed me. We were supposed to be friends. Best friends."

"I don't know what you're talking about. Is this about Ben? Because I was dating him?"

"Are you really that self-centered? You think I'm *jealous* of your little druggie boyfriend?"

"Then tell me why, Ro? How did I betray you?"

"You were just like Kara."

She steps forward until she's towering over me. I should get up and get ready to run, but my legs are still shaking and my body is too heavy.

"Everything was great. Momma and I have a house. Momma's happy. Once Kara was gone, *I* was happy. I had a friend." She looks away from me. "Then you betrayed me like she did."

Who is this version of Ro in front of me? I don't know what she's talking about. Her mom left her on a park bench in Santa Fe, and she only met Kara a couple of times. I never did anything to her.

"I don't understand. You live with your aunt. You barely knew Kara."

She shakes her head. "Momma would never leave me. You want to know why we had to sleep on that bench?" She pokes a finger at me. "It was because of that liar Kara. She ruined our lives."

The fuzziness and confusion begin to lift in my head. Kara got her housekeeper fired after the housekeeper accused her of stealing something.

The picture Kara posted before the club flashes through my head. She was wearing that necklace.

The one that wasn't found on her body.

The one that Ruby was wearing the next day.

It's like the earth shakes beneath me.

"Ruby at Henderson's is your mom. That's why you would never go inside."

Ro starts clapping, still mocking me.

I'm still not thinking straight. I can't put all the pieces together. "This is about a necklace?"

Ro's face burns red. "It's not about the necklace." She looks at me with a mixture of disappointment and disgust—like she thought I would be a more worthy opponent.

"Kara was my best friend. We did everything together. Then she met some girls at her fancy school. They didn't like my hair or my clothes or that my mom was a housekeeper. Kara ditched me for them.

"One of them dared Kara to take the necklace, but my mom caught her. Kara tried to save herself and got my mom fired for *killing a baby.*

"I knew Kara did it. I broke into her house while everyone was at the hospital. I found the bottle of lemon furniture polish hidden in her closet. Momma was a wreck. No one in Santa Fe would hire her. That's how we ended up on that park bench. Kara had to pay for it."

"What does this have to do with me? We didn't even meet until I came to the Los Ranchitos."

"In the beginning, I just needed your uniform. School was the only place I could get to Kara. But then you and Kara became friends." She smiles with delight. "You got me into her house."

A wave of nausea passes over me. I inadvertently helped Ro kill Kara.

"But what about the man who chased you in the fire? You have that burn on your arm."

She glances down at the still-visible mark on her wrist. "Curling iron. I had to get you to let me back in that night. You always set the fires away from people, like you didn't want to hurt anyone. I knew that if your fire hurt *me*, you would feel so bad that you'd do whatever I wanted." She chuckles again. "You should have seen the look on your face when you answered the door."

Now it feels like the whole world has dropped onto my back. I can't stand up. Tears form in my eyes. "What did Suds do to you?" I whisper.

She waves a hand at me like the question is unimportant. "I didn't want you to go home. That's when I still thought we were friends."

"We were friends, Ro."

She holds out her hand to stop me.

"At first I was just going to punish you. I left the article and the fire starter. I thought you'd make it up to me by telling me your secret. That's what best friends do. I gave you so many chances to tell me, but you didn't. You turned out to be just like Kara."

"I still don't understand." My voice shakes in fear.

"I took care of you, Jenny. I kept your secret. I let you play with my kitten, but you were like her—a stuck-up rich girl in your fancy room. You ditched me just like she did."

"I didn't."

"You said, 'We're not friends.' You used the exact same words as Kara."

"Please," I beg, "just let me go. I'll be in Ohio. You'll never have to see me again."

She shakes her head. "I let Kara get away. I should have taken care of her the day she decided we weren't friends anymore. If you had just told me your secret, Jenny, that would have been enough. Then I would have known that you couldn't hurt Momma or me without everyone knowing about the fires."

She crouches down so she can look me in the eye. Her voice is deceptively soft. "If I had gotten rid of Kara when she ditched me, none of the other stuff would have happened. I'm not making that mistake again."

Tears are streaming down my face. "I didn't mean what I said. You were my first friend here. Your friendship was everything to me. I would never hurt you or your mom."

Ro stands and examines me. I think maybe I have a chance; maybe she'll release me from her twisted version of friendship and let me leave forever.

Footsteps rustle in the distance. Ro shakes her head again, like she's clearing it. "No. You're too good a liar for me to believe you. You convinced everyone that you're afraid of fire so they wouldn't suspect you."

"I *am* afraid of fire," I whisper.

"You're afraid of what you'll do with it. That's why you got sent here, right? Your stepfather was afraid you were going to hurt your sister. Set her on fire."

"Stop!" I scream. "I would never harm Hailey!"

Ro looks unconvinced. "There you go, lying again." She points into the woods. "The cops are coming. You better get rid of that evidence before they find you."

"Why? So you can point them in my direction? Get me caught red-handed for *murder*? I'll tell them about you, Ro. I'll tell them everything you did."

"You don't even know my name. Besides, I'm dead, remember? And how long do you expect to hold out in a police interrogation? You're weak. You'll crack. Once they have you for the fires, it will be a hop, skip, and a jump to get you to confess to the murders."

My anger sends me up to my feet. I stand and come face to face with her. She looks like Ruby. I don't know how I didn't see it earlier.

"It wasn't me. I wasn't in my right mind. The sleeping pills made me start those fires." As soon as I hear myself say it, it sounds plausible. I could do it. I could play innocent and blame the pills. I could hold up in an interrogation.

Ro scoffs. "No, they didn't. You hardly ever took those things. When I followed you into the trees, it was all you, Jenny. You knew exactly what you were doing."

"In Ohio, after I took a pill, I woke up all wet from the rain. There was a fire in an abandoned house. My stepfather covered it up. The same thing happened again here. He'll testify to that." And I know he will. He'll take a hit at work, but we'll recover. Mom and Hailey will be protected. I'll be poor, sad Jenny who everyone feels sorry for. I won't be scary, dangerous Jenny locked away for the rest of her life.

Wait.

Ro's twisted this all around. She's made me into the evil one.

I'm not.

"I may have started the fires, but I didn't kill anybody."

Ro cocks her head to the side. "Except a whole house full of people."

"I didn't mean to. I was *seven*. I didn't know what I was doing." The words explode out of my mouth, and, for the first time in my life, I believe it. If I had known, I wouldn't have ever touched the matches. I did start that fire, but I didn't kill those people. They didn't have smoke detectors. They left those matches out where a child could reach them.

"Fine," I say. If Ro wants a worthy opponent, she's about to get one. "Tell everyone about the fires—all of them. I'll take responsibility and accept my punishment. It was worth it, having that kind of power in my hands." I step forward. "That control over life and death."

Ro takes a step back. I move forward until I'm in her face again. I have that control now. I feel the same rush as when a flame I've sparked dances to life.

"You can tell them whatever you want. . . ." I pause. "And I'll tell them about your mom."

Ro flinches. "You don't know anything about my mom."

"I don't have to. All I need to know is that she was Kara's housekeeper. Kara stole her necklace. Kara was killed, and your mom was wearing her necklace again. That sounds like a pretty good motive to me."

"You can't prove that. No one knew that Kara had the necklace. She hid it. My mom didn't even know Kara was living here."

"Henderson's has security cameras."

"What?"

"You're wrong. Your mom did know that Kara was here. Kara went into Henderson's. When your mom approached her, she took off running. Henderson's has security cameras. I bet they captured the look of horror on Kara's face before she ran—ran like she was terrified of your mom."

"That doesn't prove anything," Ro says. "Everyone knows kids go there to buy booze. Kara got caught. That's it."

"I don't have to prove anything. What did you say? 'A hop, skip, and a jump'? Doesn't your mom wonder why her missing necklace suddenly reappeared? She'll figure it out, Ro. And if she's as good a mom as you say, then . . . maybe they'll let you visit her in prison after she confesses to everything to save you."

Ro's face crumples into real fear. I step back in surprise. I think I won, but I don't have time to stop and enjoy it. I pull out the phone with the video and smash it against a rock. I take the pieces and toss them into the river.

"I'm going home now." I start walking in the direction of the Los Ranchitos.

Ro doesn't move behind me. The rustling in the bushes increases.

Allen charges through to where we're standing.

"Jenny? What are you doing here? I heard on the radio—" His eyes widen.

I smile at him. "I was saying goodbye to the bosque. I'm going back to Ohio today. What did you hear on the radio?" My heart is beating a million miles an hour, but I don't let it show. I'm fighting for my life, and I'm going to win. Again.

He glances back and forth between Ro and me. This is it. If she's going to turn me in, this is her chance. I feel her moving behind me. Her arm links through mine.

"I'll miss her." Her voice is light with a tinge of sadness.

I can see the debate raging in Allen's head. I know that I fit the description of who the police are looking for. He's trying to put the pieces together—or take them apart so that it isn't me.

I untangle myself from Ro and step up to him. I look coyly down at my feet. "I'm going to miss you, too." I raise my lips to his. "I'm sorry we didn't get more time together," I whisper before I kiss him.

Ro snorts behind me, but I take it for what it is. She's impressed.

"Bye," I say to Allen.

I don't turn around again.

• • •

I wave to Monica from the truck window. "See you at Christmas!" I yell. Her smile fades. Mike Vargas is too busy with lingering guests to see me wave to him.

Cam watches the truck go by with sad eyes. I don't know what comes next for him. Maybe he'll give up his dreams and work for Mike Vargas forever. Or maybe Mike Vargas will decide Cam is too much of a liability and cut him free.

Later, when I'm not still feeling the high of my escape, I might feel guilty about what happened to him. Or maybe not.

We pull out onto the street. The bosque shrinks in the rearview mirror. The police cars are still parked there.

Ro will destroy everything. She won't risk her mom getting in trouble. All those crimes will be more cold cases sitting in dusty files. Rumors for the town to collect and twist around and pass down through the generations.

We merge onto the interstate. It's not the sunset we're driving into, but it's the end of my story here.

Now I start over.

The sleeping pills are in my bag.

My scar still itches.

# ACKNOWLEDGMENTS

My biggest thanks to my editor, Kelsey Horton. I am so glad that the fates (and Beverly Horowitz) brought us together. Thank you for all the work you put into this book. I think you might be a little magic.

Thank you to my agent, Rachel Brooks, for taking the helm and steering the ship through some rough seas. (She's a little magic too.)

Thank you to everyone at Delacorte Press who works behind the scenes. You are the true heroes of publishing.

Thank you to Stacey Trombley for her insights; to Jamie Pacton, Jenny Ferguson, and Tracy Gold for being (amazing) early readers; and to Kelly Brocklehurst and Amber Byres-Richardson for their excitement and support.

A huge thank-you to Jeanette Alvstad, who I dragged along with me on this journey and who always listens with rapt attention (even when I'm whining). You are legitly awesome.

I couldn't have finished this book (or done much of anything) without the help and support of the 2017 Debuts and the PitchWars 2015 group.

And to Tara Goedjen—thanks for all the chats.

# ABOUT THE AUTHOR

Amanda Searcy is the author of *The Truth Beneath the Lies*. She earned a BA from New Mexico State University and an MA in human rights from the University of Essex in England. She works in collection development for a public library system and loves chocolate, cats, and curling up with a good book. She lives in New Mexico. Visit her online at amandasearcybooks.com or follow her on Twitter and Instagram at @Aesearcy.